D. B Cashman

The Life of Michael Davitt

With a History of the Rise and Development of the Irish National Land League

D. B Cashman

The Life of Michael Davitt
With a History of the Rise and Development of the Irish National Land League

ISBN/EAN: 9783744719636

Printed in Europe, USA, Canada, Australia, Japan

Cover: Foto ©Raphael Reischuk / pixelio.de

More available books at **www.hansebooks.com**

Sincerely yours
Michael Davitt

LIFE OF MICHAEL DAVITT.

WITH A HISTORY OF

THE RISE AND DEVELOPMENT OF THE IRISH NATIONAL LAND LEAGUE.

BY D. B. CASHMAN.

" The nations have fallen, and thou still art young,
Thy sun is but rising when others are set;
And, though slavery's cloud o'er thy morning hath hung,
The full noon of freedom shall beam round thee yet.
Erin! oh, Erin! though long in the shade,
Thy star will shine out when the proudest shall fade."
— MOORE.

BOSTON:
MURPHY & McCARTHY, PUBLISHERS,
548 WASHINGTON STREET.
1881.

Printed by Duffy, Cashman & Co.
603 Washington St., Boston.

CONTENTS.

CHAPTER VI.

CHAPTER VII.

CHAPTER VIII.

CHAPTER IX.

CHAPTER X.

CHAPTER XI.

CHAPTER XII.

CHAPTER XIII.

CHAPTER XIV.

INTRODUCTION.

A Brief History of British Tyranny in Ireland, from the Invasion in 1170 to the Act of Union in 1800, with an Account of the Penal Enactments in the Different Reigns.

"Who remember the past — the days gone by,
  Long wept in song and story;
When the hunted priest to a cave should fly,
  Or some mountain hollow hoary;
When your sires' blood was the gibbets' dye,
  And their shame their tyrants' glory?

"Who remember the past — the fearful past —
  Its deeds of blood and slaughter;
When the rush of the midnight's moaning blast
  And sob of the surging water
But echoed the dirge of your land downcast
  'Neath the wrongs the alien wrought her?"

—Merva.

"Who remember the past — the fearful past?" asks the poet! Who, being of Celtic birth or blood, or of any race, that having read the dark pages of Ireland's history — a history of blood and tears — a history born of a monster from a nation's travail — can ever *forget* the past, or fail to discern the clank of the slave-chain which binds it to the present? That sad history of oppression is still being continued, unrepented of by the oppressor, and borne by the oppressed; but not meekly borne — for the struggle for freedom by a brave people is vigorously continued; and, by brute force alone, coupled with state-craft and treachery, is England enabled to keep her knee upon Ireland's breast.

Let us glance down the centuries, and for a moment rest the eye of memory on a select few of the notable events in this history, since the landing of Robert Fitz-Stephen, Meyler Fitz-Henry, and others, on the coast of Wexford, and of Stiguel Strongbow at Waterford in 1170, and we shall build up an arch of iniquity through which we can picture the generations of Anglo-Norman robbers passing on to eternity, to reap the rewards in that life that such a monument of their erection in this, justly entitle them.

We shall take for the two corner-stones of this historic arch the following incidents from the sixteenth and seventeenth centuries. They are solid enough to bear the superstructure: In 1576, the English governor of the province of Connaught wrote as follows to her *virgin* majesty, Queen Elizabeth: "At Christmas I headed a military march through the country, and, finding that leniency was of no use, I resolved to destroy everything by fire and sword, sparing neither young nor old. I burnt their crops and houses, and put to the sword every human being that could be found: amongst others we have slain sixty of their most important leaders. Two of those leaders had asked me to spare, if not their own lives, at least those of the common people; but I easily saw that this was but a trick to gain time, and I immediately gave orders to burn or destroy men, cattle, houses, crops, and all. It was done in a storm of rain and hail, which is very convenient weather for such operations, as these people are then more easy to manage." That is one of our corner-stones; here is the other: The successor of Elizabeth, James the First — not Shamus *A'*——, for he did not come until after Charles the Second went to heaven in 1684. Well, James No. 1 continued the extirpating policy of his predecessor, and in 1607 the Lord-Lieutenant of Ireland wrote to the King as follows: "I have often said and written that famine is the best means of getting rid of the Irish; our swords could never operate with such speed as hunger. I have burned all the country about Lake Neagh; I have killed all the inhabitants, sparing neither sex nor age — not to mention the great number of women and children, horses and cattle, that were burned with the houses." That is our other corner-stone — solid also. And now we shall add on in the construction of our arch some of the other events so firmly embedded in Ireland's history.

Strongbow practised "wiles and treachery" to deceive and cheat the Irish; he took Pope Adrian's bull by the horns, and, with a pardon received from Henry II. in 1171, like a dutiful subject he carried the bull, the pardon, and fire and sword amongst the Irish chieftains. King John came next; he was a son of Henry's, and was *granted* Ireland by his father; he was "cruel and profligate." During the reigns of Henry III., Edwards I., II., and III., Richard II., Henrys IV., V., and VI., Edwards IV. and V., and Richard III., a succession of wars and spoliation occurred. Henry VII. came to the throne in 1475, and appointed Sir Edward Poynings Lord-Lieutenant, who had enacted the celebrated "Poynings' Act," which provided, that, prior to the holding of any Parliament in Ireland, the Lord-Lieutenant and Privy Council should first certify to the King the causes of assembling such Parliament, and specify such acts as they deemed requisite to pass.

We now come to the "Defender of the Faith," of blessed memory,—the man of eight wives. He set himself up as Protestant Pope, transferred the Abbey lands to laymen, and all the tithes to the Protestants, and placed on the Catholics the support of both churches. He died in 1537, after having sent thousands before him on short notice, who, no doubt, gave him a warm reception if he happened to arrive in their location. Edward VI. ravaged the churches and seized Irishmen's lands, which he gave to English adventurers. His sister, Mary Tudor, who succeeded him, extirpated the clans of Leix and Offalley; her troops massacred the inhabitants. Queen Elizabeth began her despotic sway in 1558. This infamous monster inherited all her father's brutality. She ordered the Catholic religion to be forcibly prohibited in Ireland, the rack to be employed, and directed her officers to torture the *suspected* Irish. Her Deputy of Munster,—Carew,—carried out the orders so, that, at the conclusion of his government, that province was nearly depopulated. She executed the clergy, slaughtered the people, and beggared the chiefs. James I. succeeded Elizabeth in 1603; his reign in Ireland was remarkable for the re-enactment of the penal laws, the plundering of Ulster chiefs in order to supplant the estates with English and Scotch adventurers. His tool, Sir William Parsons, roasted alive a man named Archer, on a gridiron, to make him swear to suit the Commission on Titles. Charles I. followed in his father's footsteps in bigoted hostility and treachery towards the Catholics. He took one hundred thousand pounds from the Catholic nobility, as a price for religious liberty, security of property, for the abolition of private prisons kept by the Protestant clergy, and free pardon for past political offences. He pocketed the money, but broke his word. His head was cut off January 30, 1649. And now came the "curse of Cromwell." This hero (Cromwell) butchered men, women, and children. He massacred the inhabitants of Drogheda in cold blood. The slaughter went on for three days; after which, in a despatch to the Parliament, he thanked God "for that great mercy." He next massacred three hundred women who had assembled around a cross in Wexford. He left the most ensanguined trail on Irish history.

Charles II. turned up in 1660. He confirmed the Cromwellians in the estates which they plundered from the Irish. An Act was passed in his reign to prevent the importation of Irish cattle into England. James II., of familiar fame, took the throne for a while after Charles died,—through, it was said, being poisoned. He offered the Irish Catholics civil and religious liberty, to aid him against William of Orange. They doubted him, but nevertheless took up arms in his cause. He was a coward, however, and ended his reign by flight.

William III. was the next king. He violated the treaty of Limerick, which guaranteed religious liberty to the Catholics. He passed a law disabling the Catholics from educating their children, or being guardians of their own or other persons' children; disarming all Catholics, and expelling all Catholic prelates and priests from the kingdom. He killed the Irish linen trade by enactments. By the 7th of William III., no Protestant in Ireland was allowed to instruct any "Papist," and no "Papist" was allowed to be sent out of Ireland to receive instructions. William died in 1701, and was succeeded by his cousin and sister-in-law, Anne Stuart. Queen Anne had the celebrated and abominable penal code passed, by which Catholics could not acquire landed property in fee, or by lease for longer than thirty-one years, and even then they could not possess an interest greater than one-third the amount of the rent. If a Catholic child became a Protestant, the parent could not sell his property, but would have to settle an annuity on the conforming child. Catholics could not inherit the estates of Protestant relations. A Catholic could not own a horse of greater value than five pounds. Forty pounds per annum were offered to Catholic priests who became Protestants. By the 8th of Anne no "Papist" was allowed to instruct any other "Papist." By the same Act, fifty pounds' reward was offered for all informers against Catholic archbishops and vicars-general. Anne was translated into Paradise A.D. 1714, and then came the first of the Georges. In the sixth year of George I.'s reign, a law was passed declaring that the English Parliament had full power and authority to make laws to bind the people of the kingdom of Ireland, and the Irish House of Lords was deprived of its final jurisdiction in cases of appeal. A law was attempted to be passed by the Irish Parliament inflicting a revoltingly indecent penalty on Catholic ecclesiastics; it was so abominable that Sir Robert Walpole, the English Prime Minister, secured its defeat.

George II. began his reign in 1727. A law was passed in the 29th year of George II. that barristers and attorneys were obliged to waive their privilege, and betray their clients, if "Papists," and that "Papists" residing in Ireland should make good to Protestants all losses sustained by the privateers of any Catholic king "ravaging the coasts of Ireland." Then came George III. in 1760. In 1778 the Irish volunteers sprang up, and in 1782 they blew away with their cannon *a portion* of the accursed laws which for nearly 700 years had enslaved the country.

The commercial and constitutional liberty gained for Ireland by the Protestant patriots of '82, and which was enjoyed for the following eighteen years, was to the nation what an oasis in the desert is to the weary traveller. From that year Ireland rose in wealth, in trade, and in manufactures, and in every branch of industry that could render her rich and prosperous. She had won her seat among the nations of the world, and advanced in prosperity and the happiness of her people, to an extent unparalleled in the annals of any other country within so short a period. But the jealous eye of her old persecutor was on her. England but waited an opportunity to destroy the rising greatness of the Irish nation. This opportunity she *made* in 1797-8, by brutally goading the people into premature insurrection. William Pitt sent into the country an immense army composed of British and hired German mercenary troops, who were aided by native Orange yeomanry. It is estimated that in those years, 137,000 soldiers were in Ireland. A persecution, accompanied with all the circumstances of ferocious cruelty, was begun; neither age, sex, nor acknowledged innocence could excite pity. The profession of the Catholic faith alone, was considered crime enough to justify the infliction of untold torture. Lord Moira, in a speech in the British House of Lords, Nov. 22, 1797, used these words: "I have known a man, in order to extort confession of a supposed crime, or of that of some neighbor, picketed till he actually fainted; picketed a second time till he fainted again; and when he came to himself picketed a third time, till he once more fainted, and all this upon mere suspicion." He also says that "men had been taken and hung up till they were half-dead, and afterwards threatened with a repetition of this treatment, unless they made a confession of their imputed guilt." He adds, "These were not particular acts of cruelty, *but formed part of the new system.* Twenty-eight men were brought out and deliberately murdered by the Orange yeomen and a party of the Antrim militia on May 25, 1798. Thirty-four men were shot without trial at Dunlavin. The tortures familiarly practised by the soldiery and yeomanry against the people were: Whipping, half-hanging, picketing.

The hair of some of the victims was cut in the form of a cross on the crowns of their heads, and the hollow thus formed strewn with gunpowder which was set fire to, and the process repeated till the sufferers fainted. There was also the torture of the pitch-cap, which consisted in applying a cap smeared with hot pitch to the shorn head of "a croppy," and dragging it forcibly off when the pitch hardened. The flesh was thus torn from the victim's head, and blinding was added to his other sufferings, as the melted pitch streamed down his forehead into his eyes. The cabins of the peasantry were burned, their sons tortured or murdered, and their daughters, in many instances, brutally violated by the armed demons.

The following incident will show what a relish the yeomanry had for the work of slaughter they were engaged in: Hunter Gowan, a yeomanry officer, marched into Gorey, at the head of his Orangemen, with a croppy finger on the point of his sword, and afterwards in a carousal he and his followers stirred their punch with it. Well, Pitt forced the country into rebellion in May, 1798, and on the 22d of the next January the union of the Parliaments of Great Britain and Ireland was proposed. Pitt, the British Minister, and Castlereagh, the Irish Chief Secretary, had now brought things to maturity; and the next move—the one all through aimed at, the destruction of the Irish Parliament—was forced through by bribery, fraud, and unparalleled rascality. The new law went into operation January 1, 1881, and with it departed from Ireland, happiness, trade, manufacture, and all that could give contentment to a nation. Was it zeal for the Protestant religion, or a hatred of Catholicism, that induced England to rob and torture the Irish people? We think not: Britain had her eye on the plunder to be obtained from the sister Isle, and religion was made a chief pretext to rob her. When the gorgon-face of British cupidity is turned in the direction of any land that she thinks she can with impunity despoil, little does she scruple the means used to attain her end.

In India England decorated the temples of the Hindoo gods, and provided the dancing girls, to engage the attention of the people while she pilfered their princes. Macaulay says: "She gilded and painted the images of the Hindoo Pantheon, and embellished the car under the wheels of which crazy devotees flung themselves, to be crushed to death, at every festival. She sent guards of honor to escort pilgrims to places of worship, and actually made oblations at the shrines of idols, in that country where human victims were offered to the Ganges, where the widow was laid on the pile with the corpse of her husband and burned alive by her own children." In Ireland she set a price on the priest's head, and hunted him like a wolf. She tore down and desecrated the temples of the living God, and tortured and murdered the people for practising the religion of Christ. She legislated the people into ignorance by destroying the schools and teaching. While she offered incense to Buddha, she sought to destroy the religion of the true God. We have now completed the monument of iniquity by these few fragments gathered from her myriad acts of infamy to the Irish race, and no doubt the reader will agree with us that it is a sufficient legacy of hate to nerve each succeeding generation of Irishmen in a continuous struggle to throw off the foul monster that pressed down on the vitality of the Irish nation, absorbing the blood and life of her people.

Here, then, are the sources in the past which, coupled with the injustice and oppression of British rule in Ireland to-day, call forth the undying patriotism of the Irish race the world over, towards their country, and make possible such splendid heroism and sacrifice as have been shown by Ireland's matchless son,—MICHAEL DAVITT.

LIFE OF MICHAEL DAVITT.

CHAPTER I.

THE GREAT LAND AGITATION.—MICHAEL DAVITT AGAIN IN A CONVICT'S GARB.—INNISFAIL.

> "Far dearer the grave or the prison,
> Illumed by one patriot name,
> Than the trophies of all who have risen
> On Liberty's ruins to fame."
> —MOORE.

IRELAND, to-day, is in the midst of a great struggle for constitutional freedom. She stands a central figure among the nations, bravely fighting against immense odds with a powerful, crafty, and merciless oppressor, for the right to give bread and security to her people,—to protect them against the extortion and eviction of a class who inherit by primogeniture from alien adventurers the plundered property of the Irish people. She has the sympathy and respect of the world,—because she deserves it. Her agitation is based on principles of right and justice, and her people are united and earnest in their demands for measures which the civilization of the century indorses, and which, had she the right of enacting in a legislature of her own, she would grant to the oppressed millions. How are these demands treated by Ireland's ruler? The Irish prisons yawn to receive the promoters and leaders of constitutional agitation, and they are being rapidly filled up. Thirty thousand troops, fourteen thousand military police, and a hireling magistracy are doing what they can to terrorize the people. Coercion Acts have been passed to destroy the right of individual freedom for two years. Arms Acts have been made additional pretext for imprisonment. In fine, England is straining every nerve in her strong body to break up this agitation and continue the chapter of the centuries sketched in our introductory remarks.

The Irish National Land League leads and directs the agitation. Its objects are to emancipate six hundred thousand Irish tenant farmers from landlord rapacity and cruelty, by abolishing the law of primogeniture and entail, and creating a peasant proprietary.

Thus far, the Land League has achieved undying renown. It averted the awful consequences attendant upon an Irish famine. It saved thousands of lives which inevitably would have been sacrificed but for its timely interference. It came between the landlords and the people when the former were flooding the country with ejectments the year after the famine, and cried, Stop! or we will Boycott you and your lands; and they did stop. Here is the proof: After the great famine of 1846–47, the landlords evicted three hundred thousand families, or one and a half millions of people. In the House of Commons, during the session of 1879, Gladstone, speaking on the Compensation for Disturbance Bill, which, amongst other things, was to restrict ejectments for two years until the effects caused by the famine would have disappeared, and which bill passed the Commons, but was killed in the House of Lords, said, that if the bill did not pass, fifteen thousand individuals would be ejected in 1880 from their homes, without remedy and without hope. Well, even this did not occur. The Land League was more powerful than the Gladstone Ministry. It brought the landlords to time, and saved the people.

From what did this great organization, that has the support of all sections of Irishmen—Extremists, Moderates, and even Orangemen—spring? We shall discuss that later on, and will here point to the central figure in the executive body, the indefatigable worker and great organizer, MICHAEL DAVITT, of whom James Redpath said, in one of his letters when in Ireland, and while Davitt was in the United States, "When Davitt is in Ireland, he and not Parnell is the real leader of the agitation." Mr. Parnell acknowledges the same. Where to-day is this great leader,—this man who was instrumental in saving the lives of thousands of his famine-stricken country-people, who has built up a constitutional agitation never surpassed in any country,—a man who gave mild advice, and calmed the passion and desire for revenge of an outraged people,—a man who accomplished what the British Cabinet failed in,—where? In the garb of an English convict, in the British convict prison of Portland!—in the prison where heretofore he was *tortured* for over seven weary years. Such is ever England's reward to Irishmen who try to raise up their fellow-countrymen. But Davitt is enshrined in the heart of every man, woman, and child of Irish extraction, and in that of liberty-loving people of other nationalities, who will remember his sufferings in his country's cause; and, if in the providence of God a day of reckoning for John Bull shall come, it will be added to the already heavy weight of iniquity to be atoned for. God send it soon and sudden!

In beginning a sketch of the life and labors, in Ireland's cause, of Michael Davitt, we cannot open in a more appropriate manner than by presenting to the reader a bold and fervid poem, written by Mr. Davitt while undergoing the horrors of Dartmoor convict prison, some years since, and never heretofore published. This emanation from his great heart is as *apropos* to-day as when the lines were written; for heroic Davitt is again "in England's felon garb clad, and by her vengeance bound." May the cry of love, loyalty, and daring, from the martyr's living tomb, breathed through these verses, fan into flame a fire of patriotism in the breasts of tens of thousands of Irish men and women, and be productive of as many sacrifices on the altar of Irish liberty:—

INNISFAIL.

In England's felon garb we're clad,
 And by her vengeance bound;
Her concentrated hate we've had—
 Her *justice*, never found.
Her laws, accurs'd, have done their worst;
 In vain they still assail
To crush the hearts that beat for thee,
 Our own loved Innisfail.

Nor can the dungeon's deepest gloom,
 But make us love thee more;
We'd brave the terrors of the tomb
 To keep the oath we swore:
In chains, or free, to live for thee,
 And never once to quail
Before the foe that wrought such woe
 To our loved Innisfail.

From Irish mothers' hearts has flowed
 This sacred love of thee;
And Erin's daughters' cheeks have glowed
 That love in deeds to see.
A coward-born fair lips will scorn,
 Whilst joyously they hail
The hearts that beat for love of thee,
 Our own loved Innisfail.

Then let our jailors scowl and roar
 When cheerful looks we wear;
The Patriot's God that we adore
 Will shield us from despair.
Fair bosoms rise with love-drawn sighs
 By mountain, stream, and vale,
And day and night in prayers unite
 For us and Innisfail.

Here, chained beneath the tyrant's hand,
By martyr's blood, we swear
To Freedom and to Fatherland
We still allegiance bear.
Nor felon's fate, nor England's hate,
Nor hellish-fashioned jail
Shall stay this hand to wield a brand
One day for Innisfail.

CHAPTER II.

MICHAEL DAVITT.—HIS EARLY LIFE.—EVICTION FROM HIS FARM HOME IN MAYO.—EMIGRATION.

"Like the bright lamp that shone in Kildare's holy fane,
And burned through long ages of darkness and storm,
Is the heart that sorrows have frowned on in vain,
Whose spirit outlives them, unfading and warm.
Erin! oh Erin! thus bright, through the tears
Of a long night of bondage, thy spirit appears."
—MOORE.

THE story of the life of Michael Davitt is one of unostentatious devotion to the cause of his country and his fellow men, and is withal a life of sacrifice and purity. He was born in 1846, of respected parents of the farming class, residing near Straide, County Mayo. The year was one of trial and intense suffering to the Irish people; but, as the adage says, "Out of evil cometh good," so, out of that black famine year of evil, came good to the people in the birth of a strong champion and fearless advocate of the same class that was then dying of hunger on the roads' side, who was destined to overturn the sytem that produced the famine horrors which surrounded his birth. While he was yet young, the little home in which he first saw the light was torn down over his head, by that ruthless institution which has played so prominent a part in Ireland's history,—the Crowbar Brigade, the executive of the landlord's will; and he, with his parents and family, were thrown upon the road-side to live or die, as they might for all the reigning power cared. But they didn't die, unluckily for Irish landlordism; and the evicted child lived to return to the site of his desecrated home, and, in the presence of fifteen thousand persons at one of the great land meetings, denounce the law and blasphemy that allowed such deeds to be perpetrated. The recollection of this crime has had its effect upon Davitt's life; for on the occasion referred to, February 1, 1880, standing upon a platform erected over the ruins of his family's homestead, he said:—

"Does not the scene of domestic devastation now spread before this vast meeting bear testimony to the crimes with which landlordism stands charged before God and man to-day? Can a more eloquent denunciation of an accursed land-code be found than what is witnessed here in this depopulated district? In the memory of many now listening to my words, that peaceful little stream which meanders by the outskirts of this multitude sang back the merry voices of happy children, and wended its way through a once populous and prosperous village. Now, however, the merry sounds are gone, the busy hum of hamlet life is hushed in sad desolation; for the hands of the house destroyers have been here and performed their hellish work, leaving Straide but a name to mark the place where happy homesteads once stood, and whence an inoffensive people were driven to the four corners of the earth by the ruthless decree of Irish landlordism. How often in a strange land has my boyhood's ear drunk in the tale of outrage and wrong and infamy perpetrated here in the name of law and in the interest of territorial greed! in listening to the accounts of famine and sorrow, of deaths by landlords, or coffinless graves, of scenes—

"'On highway side, where oft was seen
The wild dog and the vulture keen
Tug for the limbs and gnaw the face
Of some starved child of our Irish race.'

"What wonder that such laws should become hateful, and, when felt by personal experience of the tyranny and injustice, that a life of irreconcilable enmity to them should follow, and that, *standing here on the spot where I first drew breath*, in sight of a levelled home, with memories of privation and tortures crowding upon my mind, I should swear to devote the remainder of that life to the destruction of what has blasted my early years, pursued me with its vengeance through manhood, and leaves my family in exile to-day, far from that Ireland which is itself wronged, robbed, and humiliated through the agency of the same accursed system! It is no little consolation to know, however, that we are here to-day doing battle against a doomed monopoly; and that the power which has so long domineered over Ireland and its people is brought to its knees at last, and on the point of being crushed forever; and, if I am standing to-day upon a platform erected over the ruins of my levelled home, I may yet have the satisfaction of trampling on the ruins of Irish landlordism."

After the eviction, the Davitt family left Ireland, a portion coming to America, but the parents going to England. In the factory town of Haslingden, near Manchester, in Lancashire, young Davitt grew up, and, like most children of such surroundings, he was early serving a master in one of the factories. Here he learned the sufferings of the factory slave, and suffered a mishap which caused the loss of his right arm; that limb having been caught in the machinery and crushed, it had to be amputated at the shoulder. For five years afterwards, he attended the Wesleyan school in Haslingden, and when 15 years old, got employment as assistant letter-carrier, and book-keeper, in the printing-office attached to the post-office there. In 1868 he became a commercial traveller, dealing extensively in fire-arms. This brought him into contact with a gunsmith named John Wilson, from Birmingham, with whom he was afterwards tried.

During the time of the Murphy anti-Catholic

riots, when that firebrand worked up the English fanatics to attack Catholic churches in Lancashire, Davitt showed the temper of the metal that was in him. He organized a band of young men of Irish parentage to protect the churches that were to be attacked. On one occasion, he and another young man, with revolvers in their hands, routed a large party of those fanatics, who were about attacking a Catholic church in Rochdale, by firing over their heads. The mob thought that Davitt and his companion were but the advance-guard of a large party, and fled for their lives; by the intrepid stand of these two young Irishmen—for there were only the two defenders present—the church was saved.

Whenever it became known that any of the Catholic churches in Rochdale, Bacup, Haslingden, or in any of the adjoining Lancashire towns, were to be attacked by the fanatical mobs, there Michael Davitt and his faithful and gallant band were to be found, ready to prevent the desecration of the House of God, or die in the attempt. He rendered great service, and prevented the destruction of many a temple erected by the religious fervor of Irish Catholics in England. A strange event occurred some years afterwards in this, at that time, hot-bed of bigotry. When Davitt was released from prison, in 1877, after having suffered seven years and seven months of untold agony, he visited those very towns in Lancashire, and was everywhere received by the same people with a perfect ovation. They turned out without regard to creed or party to receive him, and by public manifestations recognized and approved the great patriotism and sacrifices rendered to his country by their once-uncompromising foe.

The English atmosphere which surrounded him, —owing to his patriotic parents and his association with the Irish exiles, who form a large portion of the north of England population,—the victims, like himself, of landlordism,—did not affect his love for his native land, and we find him at the inception of the Fenian movement an active, but, as ever, an unpretending apostle of the new hope for Ireland. He soon gathered round him some of the staunchest stuff which that organization brought out, and made the north of England the very bulwark of the Irish cause. Davitt went into the movement with all the sincerity of a man who felt that a great wrong had been, and was being, done his country, and that it was his duty to do all that he could to overthrow that wrong; and it was not due to such men as Michael Davitt that more in that direction was not accomplished. When the call came from Ireland for men in '65, Davitt was one of the first to respond, and was not the least disheartened at the failure, as was shown by his willingness to obey a second call in leading a detachment of the 2,000 North of England men who had gathered to attack Chester Castle. When those above him countermanded their orders, Davitt led his men back to their homes, disposing of his personal valuables to aid his less fortunate comrades.

CHAPTER III.

Davitt as a Literary Man.—His Arrest, Trial, and Prison Sufferings.

"O God! why should so brave a man
His noble life thus yield?
A patriot would rather die
Upon the battle-field.
But England's judges doomed the man,—
Alas! that it should be;
Let others emulate him still,
And Ireland will be free."

As a literary man, Michael Davitt stands high. He is a man of educated thought, and wide and varied reading. Among his many accomplishments is a thorough knowledge of the Irish, French, and Italian languages, whilst the purest English is to be found in his public utterances.

In the re-organization of the Irish movement, which followed the attempt on Chester Castle, and while the British Government were doing to death the martyrs,—Allen, Larkin, and O'Brien,—Davitt threw into the movement his whole heart and soul, and worked with grim energy to repair the breaches made in the Irish national ranks, selecting the most dangerous work of arming the people. While thus engaged, he was arrested in London on May 14, 1870, with a gunsmith named John Wilson, from Birmingham; the latter being in no way associated with the revolutionary movement, and not being supposed to know the uses intended for the arms which he sold. The following particulars of his trial at Newgate are gleaned from the London Central Criminal Court Petty Sessions papers:—

He was indicted for feloniously conspiring to depose the Queen, and to levy war against her. The Attorney-General, the Solicitor-General, Mr. Cole, Mr. Poland, and Mr. Archibald conducted the prosecution. The first witness, Detective Seal, of Birmingham, deposed to the despatch (under Wilson's supervision, from Birmingham) to Leeds of a box containing nineteen muzzle-loading rifles, nineteen bayonets, and a Snider breech-loader; also, a cask addressed to Glasgow, which contained thirty-six large-chamber revolvers, with packages of cartridges. A few days later, Detective Seal swore, he saw Wilson and Davitt together, and watched them despatch three boxes to Newcastle-on-Tyne. These boxes were ultimately opened, and were found to contain revolvers and ammunition. The case occupied a considerable time, as it was necessary in each instance to prove that the consignment of arms had been sent either by Davitt or by Wilson; to prove its despatch, its delivery, and its contents; that there was no genuine business invoice, and no genuine consignee in any way connected with it; and to prove from a variety of small circumstances that Wilson and Davitt were acting in concert. An important witness after Detective Seal was John Bodley, head constable of the Irish Constabulary, who gave evidence as to the opening of a case containing ten rifles, six revolvers, five sword bayonets, three bayonets, and three turnscrews. The arms were all fit for use, but were not finished as they would have been had they been intended for sale. Superintendent Dixon, of the Newcastle police, proved that he impounded three cases, each containing twenty-five revolvers. Detective Henderson, of Manchester, gave evidence as to a box which contained 11,000 rounds of revolver cartridges and 400 rounds for Snider rifles; that the weapons were not in a finished state, and could not have been intended for sale, as no gunmaker would have shown them in his window; that they were despatched in fictitious names, and were addressed to fictitious consignees; in each case they were ultimately traced back to the possession of Wilson and Davitt.

The principal event in the course of the trial was the examination of the infamous informer, John Joseph Corydon. "I was at one time," he swore, "an officer in the Federal Army in America. I left it in 1856. I became a member of the Fenian Confederation in 1862. I remained so till 1865. An organization of the Fenian conspiracy existed in New York, and in several parts of America. Meetings were held at which I was present. The object of the conspiracy was to overthrow her Majesty's Government in Ireland, and establish an Irish Republic. An oath was administered to the members. I took it. It was to be faithful to the Fenian organization, and to take up arms when required for the establishment of the Republic in Ireland. The organization was very extensive in America. The headquarters were in New York, and there were branches at different cities throughout the United States, with State centres at the head of them. I was sent to Ireland in 1865 by John O'Mahony. He was then the head of the Fenian organization in America. The Fenian organization existed at that time in Ireland. The head-centre of all—Stephens—was in Dublin. The organization was ready to fight at any time if he gave the word. We had frequent meetings at Liverpool. Money was collected at these to buy arms. Arms were procured at Leeds, Birmingham, and all the manufacturing towns in England. I know Colonel Burke. It was his function to buy arms. A great quantity were bought. In February, 1867, an attempt was made to seize the arms in Chester Castle. The mail train from London to Holyhead was to be seized as it was passing Chester. The telegraph wires were to be torn down. The rails were to be taken up. The arms taken at Chester Castle were to be put in the train and taken to Holyhead, where the mail boat was to be seized and taken to some port in Ireland. That port was not Dublin. I gave information, and the enterprise was disconcerted. It was arranged that as many as 1,200 or 1,400 Fenians were to surprise Chester Castle. I did not myself go to Chester. I only went as far as Birkenhead. I saw as many as 600 going from the Liverpool district. After the attempt on Chester Castle, Fenian meetings were held every day in Mullan's house. These meetings consisted entirely of Fenians. M'Afferty and Flood were there. Captain Deasy and several others were present. They were mostly American officers. The subject of discussion at these meetings was the loss of not having taken Chester Castle, and the making of arrangements for the rising of the 5th of March in Ireland. Davitt was there the whole time."

Corydon's evidence regarding meeting Davitt before was as false as his dark heart was vile. Michael Davitt solemnly declared that he never saw the wretch until the latter came to the prison to identify him, whilst awaiting trial. On that occasion, the following contemptible dodge was resorted to, by the prison officials, in order that the informer might be enabled to identity, and swear away the liberty of the prisoner. Corydon and others being in the prison corridor, Davitt was ordered to come out of his cell, and go into another. Of course the informer saw him when doing so, and was told it was Davitt. He then came to the cell, and identified the prisoner. When Davitt saw Corydon, he at once recognized an informer, and said to him: "So you are one of the reptiles that had to fly from Ireland to save your life." Corydon replied, with a devilish leer, "You will find that I will live long enough to settle you." And so he did; for it was mainly on the evidence of the perjured rascal that Davitt was found guilty and sentenced to fifteen years' penal servitude.

During the trial, the following evidence of Davitt's nobleness of nature showed itself: He made a feeling appeal to the Judge in behalf of Wilson, who was a man with a wife and family. He said Wilson was totally unconnected in any manner with the Irish movement; "that he was entirely innocent of the charge on which he was indicted; and that he (Davitt) would willingly take the sentence intended for the Englishman, in addition to his own." For this generous act, he was complimented by the Court, and was told that the matter would be considered. Wilson was subsequently sentenced to the lighter term of seven years' and Davitt to fifteen years' penal servitude;

seven years and seven months of which he served in different British bastiles.

The terrible sufferings endured in those weary years were afterwards told by Michael Davitt, in a pamphlet which he published soon after his release on ticket-of-leave, December 19, 1877. The record is a heart-breaking one, and proves what an overmastering devotion Mr. Davitt must have had to his native land, when even the recollection of his frightful sufferings, and the possibility—which has since happened—of his being re-arrested and sent back to the horrors of a convict prison, by the cancellation of his ticket-of-leave, never prevented him for one moment from laboring for the emancipation of those of his fellow-countrymen who are victims to a cruel, unjust system of land tenure. We shall let him in his own words give the heart-rending recital. He says:—

"When arrested in London on the 14th of May, 1870, I was taken to the Paddington Police Station, and underwent the customary questioning, searching, and other preliminaries to a 'lodgings in a lock-up.' From Saturday night until Monday morning, I was confined in an almost darkened cell, in which was a water-closet with its inseparable offensiveness. I was allowed neither bed nor bedding, and had consequently no sleep during the time I remained in the station, from Saturday till Monday. I was allowed but a little light, only when eating my meals. On my arrival in Clerkenwell

House of Detention, after the examination before the Marylebone Police Court magistrate, I was immediately stripped naked, and compelled to undergo the indignity of being searched in a manner almost too disgusting to describe. Each article of dress was minutely examined by one warder; while another was employed in watching, lest I should resent the insult to which I was subjected in being made to stand naked in presence of the two warders; one of whom was coolly satisfying himself that I had nothing concealed upon my person. After each of the five or six examinations I underwent before the magistrates, previous to being committed for trial, I had to submit to the same searching, in the state of nudity I have described, on arriving in the House of Detention.

"The first time the Governor visited me in my cell, he inquired what I was arrested for; and on my answering that I was taken on suspicion of being a Fenian, he replied, 'I don't care what you are; you must clean those traps [pointing to water-closet taps and other utensils in the cell] while you remain here;' and during my confinement there, I was compelled to do so, as also to clean my cell floor and windows. I was only allowed one hour each day for exercise, and, of course, not permitted to speak to anyone. There were none but religious books allowed me during my stay in that prison. The bedding was the worst and scantiest I have seen during my whole imprisonment, being nothing but a dirty blanket and rug, and a bare, unmattressed hammock. Having paid for my own keep while awaiting my trial, I cannot speak as to the quantity or quality of the food supplied to prisoners in Clerkenwell.

"When the informer Corydon was brought to identify me, I was taken from the cell in which I was located, and marched along the ward in sight of the informer and detectives who accompanied him, and placed in a cell for identification. The informer was then supposed to look through the inspection hole of each cell in the ward to find me; and after being permitted to see me taken out of one cell and put into another, it was not a very brilliant achievement, even for John Joseph Corydon, to find me in the cell he saw me enter. In addition to this, I may be pardoned for detailing another incident that occurred; and which I believe contributed not a little to my conviction. A few days previous to being committed for trial, I drew up instructions for my solicitor as to the mode of my defence; and this I had done in exact accordance with the rules suspended in my cell, which rules also specified that such instructions could be handed by prisoners to their legal advisers, without previous inspection by the Governor or other prison officials. When my solicitor's clerk visited me for the purpose of receiving those instructions, I handed him the envelope containing them, in the presence of the warder who presided at the interview, and who had brought me from my cell to the visitors' or solicitors' room. Two days afterwards, I was again visited by my solicitor's clerk, and astounded to hear that the Governor had demanded my letter after the previous visit, as the officer had reported that he saw me draw a plan of the prison upon a piece of paper and give the same to the clerk! When I saw the Governor on the following morning, I demanded an explanation of this strange proceeding, and had to remain satisfied with being told that it was the officer's fault, and that if I had no objection to his (the Governor's) reading my letter, it would be given to my solicitor. I replied that I had not the least objection, owing to what the officer had reported; but that I protested against the whole proceeding as unfair, and directly opposed to the rules hung up in my cell. Now mark what transpired within those two days. A sensational paragraph had appeared in one of the London dailies, announcing that another plot had been discovered to blow up the House of Detention, and that on this occasion it would be attempted from within the prison. It is unnecessary to say what effect this would have upon the public mind, and how small the chance would be of my obtaining an unprejudiced jury and an impartial trial in London after this. Two great points had, by this heartless canard, been made against me; the plan of my defense had been discovered, and the public feeling directed adversely towards me, owing to the report that I had intended to effect another explosion."

Mr. Davitt was then removed to Newgate, where his treatment was not so severe, he says, as it had been in Clerkenwell. His first experience of the horrors of penal servitude he thus describes:—

"My trial commenced on the 5th of July, and at six o'clock in the evening of the 18th I was sentenced to fifteen years' penal servitude, and poor Wilson to seven. Immediately after sentence, I was deprived of my clothes and put in convict uniform; my hair and beard being cut close at the same time. I remained in Newgate but eleven days after receiving my sentence, and in that short period I was being initiated into the reality of penal servitude.

"My work, however, was not very heavy, nor otherwise disagreeable; but the classification with thieves had already commenced, and the prospect of spending perhaps fifteen years in such company made Newgate then appear—what in comparison with other prisons it is not—a veritable Inferno.

"On the 29th of July I was removed to Millbank, and saw Wilson for the last time on that day. If my prayers could have spared him the sufferings he has since undergone, I would have left Newgate with a much lighter heart. Chains were fastened round my ankles in such a manner that I could only stride some twelve or fifteen inches when walking; and, to insure my offering no resistance, I was compelled to hold the end of the chain with which my feet were bound. Thus dressed and manacled, and guarded by a couple of warders, I was driven from Newgate, along the Thames Embankment, to Millbank penitentiary. Not quite three months had yet elapsed since I had walked that promenade free and unfettered, without any foreboding of what fate had in store for me; and now I was only allowed, by the necessity of my removal from one prison to another, to look upon that scene for a few moments, and imprint upon my memory the liberty it portrayed, and the life from which I was to be debarred for years. To leave the broad and cheerful light of day, and be immurred in a solitary cell,—to exchange the social amenities of life, home, country, and friends, for an existence undreamt of by those who know not what a world of suffering is comprised in the meaning of the words 'solitary confinement,'—is a feeling impossible to be expressed in words. John Mitchel has attempted to record his own sensations when, after sentence for treason-felony, he found himself in 'solitary' for the first time:—

"'It came at last; my door was shut, and for the first time I was quite alone. And now I do confess that I flung myself upon my bed and broke into a raging passion of tears,—tears bitter and salt, but not of base lamentation for my own fate. The thoughts and feelings that have so shaken me for this once, language was never made to describe.'

"This is the testimony of one whose proud soul had never acknowledged its susceptibility to the common weakness of humanity; but solitary confinement wrung tears from Mitchel. The vagrant sunbeam that finds its way to the lonely occupant of a prison cell, but speaks of the liberty which others enjoy, of the happiness that falls to the lot of those whom misfortune has not dragged from the pleasures of life. The cries, the noise, and uproar of London which penetrate the silent corridors, and re-echo in the cheerless cells of Millbank, are so many mocking voices that come to laugh at the misery their walls enclose, and arouse the recollection of happier days to probe the wounds of present sorrow. And if, despite all this, a prisoner should try to raise himself above those depressing influences, and cheat despair of its prey, he will then experience how far man can go in his inhumanity to man, by finding himself denied the only consolation left him in his utter loneliness,—the solace of solacing himself. He will find men who will watch for a smile, or some other sign of a happy obliviousness, and then, by some of the many arts practised for the purpose, end the momentary forgetfulness of imprisonment by an exercise of the almost uncontrolled power they wield over their unfortunate charges."

Speaking of his life in Millbank, Mr. Davitt says:—

"To relate every incident of my ten months' incarceration in Millbank penitentiary would only be a tedious repetition of each day's experience, so uniform is the system of punishment in that prison.

"A description of the cells, together with an account of the daily routine and work that had to be done, will suffice to form some idea of what punishment has to be borne in what is termed 'probation class.' The cells are some nine or ten feet long, by about eight wide. Stone floor, bare, whitewashed walls, with neither table nor stool, and of course with no fire to warm, by its cheerful glow, the oppressing chillness of such a place. My bedstead was made of three planks, laid parallel to each other at the end of the cell, and raised from the stone floor but three inches at the foot, and six at the head, of this truly low couch. The only seat allowed me was a bucket, which contained the water supplied me for washing purposes,—this bucket having a cover so as to answer the double purpose of water-holder and stool. The height of this sole article of furniture allowed me was fourteen inches exactly, including the lid, and on this 'repentance stool' I was compelled to sit at work ten hours at least, each day, for ten months.

"The punishment this entails upon a tall man can be easily conceived. The recumbent posture and bent chest necessary while picking oakum, with nothing to lean one's back against to obtain a momentary relief, is distressing in the extreme. The effect upon me, in addition to inducing a weakness in my chest, was singular, but not surprising.

"On entering Milbank, my height was exactly six feet, as measured by the prison standard for that purpose; but on my departure for Dartmoor, ten months after, I had illustrated the saying that some people can grow downwards, for I then measured but five feet ten and a half inches.

"The bedding supplied was miserably insufficient during the winter months; and owing to this, and the sitting posture during the day, with feet resting upon cold flags, with no fire, and with a prohibition against walking in the cell, many prisoners have lost the use of their limbs from the effects of a Millbank winter. But one hour's exercise in the prison yard was allowed each day, and that was forfeited if the weather proved unfavorable. Owing to my health beginning to break down, I was permitted an extra half-hour's exercise, after I had been eight months in the prison. This was granted by the doctor's order.

"I had to rise at six each morning, fold up my bed very neatly, and afterwards wash and scrub my cell floor quite clean with brush and stone used for that purpose. This washing and scrubbing was, I need scarcely remark, very distressing upon me, owing to my physical infirmity; but I was compelled to do it, nevertheless, once each day during the whole term of my imprisonment. After cells were cleaned in the manner I have described, work was then commenced, and continued until a quarter to nine at night; allowing, of course, for meals, exercise, and prayers in chapel each morning.

"The work I was put to in this prison was coir and oakum picking. I was not tasked; but I had to sit working all day, and pick a reasonable share of my coir or oakum, as the case might be. When I inquired, on being first ordered to this sort of work, how I could possibly do it with but a limited number of fingers at my diposal, I was told by the warder that he had known several 'blokes' with but one hand who had managed to pick oakum very well with their teeth. As I declined to use my teeth to tear old ropes to pieces, I had to do the work as best I could.

"During the whole of my stay in Millbank, my conversation with prisoners,—at the risk of being punished, of course,—as also with warders and chaplains, would not occupy me twenty minutes to repeat, could I collect all the scattered words spoken by me in the whole of that ten months.

"I recollect many weeks going by without my exchanging a word with a single human being.

"The food allowed me for daily rations was as follows: Breakfast, eight ounces of bread, and three-quarters of a pint of cocoa. Dinner, four ounces of meat (including bone), four days a week, with six ounces of bread and a pound of potatoes; one day in the week I was allowed a pint of shin-of-beef soup in lieu of meat, and on another one pound of suet pudding, ditto. Dinner on Sunday was twelve ounces of bread, four ounces of cheese, and a pint of water. And for supper each night I received six ounces of bread, and a pint of 'skilly,' containing—or rather supposed to contain—two ounces of oatmeal.

"This was the ordinary prison allowance.

"After subsisting for three months on this diet, I applied to the doctor for a little more food, on the ground that I was losing weight, owing to the insufficiency of the quantity allowed; but my application was of no avail.

"The books supplied me while in Millbank were almost exclusively religious, and but one library book was allowed to each prisoner in a fortnight.

"I asked to have mine changed once a week, but was promptly told I could not be favored beyond other prisoners. The class of books supplied to the Catholic prisoners was such as would be suitable to children, or people ignorant of the truths of the Catholic faith.

"I had often no book to read but one that might answer the requirements of a child; such as the history of 'Naughty Fanny,' or 'Grandmother Betty,' and like productions, which, though doubtless good in their way, were not what could lessen the dreary monotony of such an existence.

"A circumstance in connection with the situation of Millbank may (taken with what I have already said on that prison) give some faint idea of what confinement there really means. Westminster Tower clock is not far distant from the penitentiary, so that its every stroke is as distinctly heard in each cell as if it were situated in one of the prison yards. At each quarter of an hour, day and night, it chimes a bar of the 'Old Hundredth,' and those solemn tones strike on the ears of the lonely listeners like the voice of some monster singing the funeral dirge of time.

"Oft in the lonely watches of the night has it reminded me of the number of strokes I was doomed to listen to, and of how slowly those minutes were creeping along! The weird chant of Westminster clock will ever haunt my memory, and recall that period of my imprisonment when I first had to implore Divine Providence to preserve my reason and save me from the madness which seemed inevitable, through mental and corporal tortures combined.

"That human reason should give way under such adverse influences is not, I think, to be wondered at; and many a still living wreck of manhood can refer to the silent system of Millbank and its pernicious surroundings as the cause of his debilitated mind.

"It was here that Edward Duffy died, and where Rickard Burke and Martin Hanly Carey were for a time oblivious of their sufferings from temporary insanity, and where Daniel Reddin was paralyzed. It was here where Thomas Ahern first showed symptoms of madness, and was put in dark cells and strait-jacket for a 'test' as to the reality of these symptoms. Ten years have passed their long and silent courses since then; but that same Thomas Ahern is still a prisoner, and his mind is still tottering on the brink of insanity. I have anxiously watched him drifting towards this fate for the past six years, unable to render him any assistance, and I can predict that if he is not soon liberated he will exchange Dartmoor for Broadmoor Lunatic Prison, like so many other victims of penal servitude."

CHAPTER IV.

FROM MILLBANK TO DARTMOOR.—SIX YEARS AND SIX MONTHS OF AGONY.

"O men who have passed through the furnace,
Assayed like the gold, and as pure!
By your strength can the weakest gain firmness,
The strongest may learn to endure;
When once they have chosen their part,
Though the sword may drive home to each heart."
—ANON.

"IF the whole United Kingdom was searched through for the purpose of discovering a place whereon to erect a prison, with the view of utilizing the rigors of a severe climate, damp fogs, more than average rainfall, and a lengthened winter season, with all that was desolate and uninviting in the aspect of nature to assist in the punishment of prisoners, no more suitable place than Dartmoor could be found if a Procrustean spirit guided the search. Buried in the midst of barren and bowlder-strewn Devonshire moors, it is peculiarly adapted for an abode of misery. It was here where the French and American prisoners of war were incarcerated during the wars with the first Napoleon and rebel America, and many a gallant foe of England's there sank beneath the hardships of the climate and the treatment he received.

"The chivalrous Lord Dundonald denounced the Government of the day, in the strongest terms, for confining brave and honorable enemies in such a place; 'enveloped,' as he declared, from observation 'in almost perpetual fog.' Well, governments were no more indifferent in those days to the inhuman treatment of their fallen foes than in more modern, and I shall say more humane (?) times; but now, as then, there are a few generous-hearted Englishmen to be found courageous enough to say they do not glory in this, the shame of England; and that, whether cannons are charged with foes in India, enemies tied to trees and fired at for practice in Jamaica, or the youth of Ireland done to death by penal servitude in England's prisons, it is a disgrace to any country boasting of its civilization, and repugnant to the generous instincts of humanity.

"It would be impossible for me, in the limited time at my disposal, to detail every circumstance connected with my six years and six months confinement in Dartmoor: I can, therefore, only dwell upon the most prominent incidents connected with my treatment during that period, by a simple statement of facts as to what that treatment was.

"For the first week after my arrival from Millbank I was located in the penal cells, and had to make application for removal from same into some other part of the prison. The penal cells, or rather some of them, are much preferable to the ordinary or iron cells, being somewhat larger and much better ventilated; but owing to their being constructed and set apart for incorrigible prisoners,—men who are taught obedience by means of starvation, and consequently maddened by hunger and cold,—it is almost impossible to obtain any sleep in such a place. I will have more to say anent these cells by and by, as I was confined in them from August, '76, until November, '77. The iron or ordinary cell I was next located in, and remained an inmate of for close on five years, I will now describe. So much attention having been directed to these veritable iron cages by the exposure of poor M'Carthy's treatment, and his confinement in such cells, I purpose giving an accurate description of them, and removing any doubts, if such exist, as to the account already given of their size, construction, and ventilation. The dimensions of one of them will answer for that of the whole, as they are uniform in almost every respect. Length, seven feet exactly; width, four feet; and height, seven feet one or two inches. The sides (or frames) of all are of corrugated iron, and the floor is a slate one. These cells are ranged in tiers or wards in the centre of a hall, the tiers being one above another, to the height of four wards; the floors of the three upper tiers of cells forming the ceilings or tops of those immediately beneath them. Each ward or tier contains in length forty-two cells, giving a total of one hundred and sixty-eight for one hall. The sole provision made for ventilating these cells is an opening of two and a half or three inches left at the bottom of each door. There is no opening into the external air from any of those cells in Dartmoor; and the air admitted into the hall has to traverse the width of the same to enter the hole under the cell doors. In the cells on the first three tiers, or wards, there are about a dozen small perforations in the corner of each, for the escape of vitiated air; but in those on the top or fourth ward—or, speaking more confidently, in those on that ward in which I was located a portion of my time—there were no such perforations,—no possible way of escape for foul air except where most of it entered as 'pure,'—under the cell door. In the heat of summer it was almost impossible to breathe in these top cells; so close and foul would the air become from the improper ventilation of the cells below, allowing the breathed air in each cell to mix with that in the hall, and thus ascend to the top.

"I, on one occasion, begged the Governor of Dartmoor to remove me from such a situation, for the additional reason to those I have given that I had not sufficient light to read in the cell I was in; but I begged in vain. I was, however, soon after removed to a lower tier, after foul eruptions began to break out upon my body through the impure air I had been breathing. It has been since denied by Chatham prison officials that Charles McCarthy ever slept with his bed across the inside of his cell door, in order to catch sufficient air to breathe. From my own experience I can fully believe the necessity of his doing so, as it was quite common in Dartmoor for prisoners to sleep with their heads towards the door for a similar reason; and I have often, in the summer season, done this myself, and had, repeatedly, to go on my knees and put my mouth to the bottom of the door for a little air.

"The light admitted to those ordinary iron cells is scarcely sufficient to read by in the daytime; and, should a fog prevail, it would be impossible to read in half of them. The cells are fitted with a couple of plates of thick, intransparent glass, about eighteen inches long by six inches wide each, and the light is transmitted through this 'window' from the hall, and not from the extern of the prison. I have often laid the length of my body on the cell floor, and placed my book under the door to catch sufficient light to read it.

"The food in Dartmoor prison I found to be the very worst in quality and the filthiest in cooking of any of the other places I had been in. The quantity of daily rations was the same as in Millbank, with the difference of four ounces of bread more each day and one of meat less in the week. The quality, as I have already remarked, is inferior to that of any other prison: but from about November till May it is simply execrable; the potatoes being often unfit to eat, and rotten cow-carrots occasionally substituted for other food. To find black beetles in soup, 'skilly,' bread, and tea, was quite a common occurrence; and some idea can be formed of how hunger will reconcile a man to look without disgust upon the most filthy objects in nature, when I state as a fact that I have often discovered beetles in my food and have eaten it after throwing them aside, without experiencing much revulsion of feeling at the sight of such loathsome animals in my victuals. Still I have often come in from work weak with fatigue and hunger, and found it impossible to eat the putrid meat or stinking soup supplied me for dinner, and had to return to labor again after 'dining' on six ounces of bad bread.

"It was quite a common occurrence in Dartmoor for men to be reported and punished for eating candles, boot oil, and other repulsive articles; and, notwithstanding that a highly offensive smell is purposely given to prison candles to prevent their being eaten instead of burned, men are driven by a system of half-starvation into an animal-like voracity, and anything that a dog would eat is nowise repugnant to their taste. I have seen men eat old poultices found buried in heaps of rubbish I was assisting in carting away, and have seen bits of candle pulled out of the prison cess-pool and eaten after the human soil was wiped off them!

"The labor I was first put to was stone-breaking, that being considered suitable work for non-able-bodied prisoners. I was put to this employment in a large shed, along with some eighty or ninety more prisoners; but, my hand becoming blistered by the action of the hammer after I had broken stones for a week, I was unable to continue at that work, and was consequently put to what is termed 'cart labor.' This sort of work is very general in Dartmoor, and I may as well give some description of it.

"Eight men constitute a 'cart party,' and have an officer over them, armed with a staff, if working within the prison walls, and with a rifle and accompanied by an armed guard, if employed outside. Each man in the cart party is supplied with a collar, which is put over the head and passes from the right or left shoulder under the opposite arm, and is then hooked to the chain by means of which the cart is drawn about. The cart party to which I was attached was employed in carting stones, coals, manure, and rubbish of all descriptions. In drawing the cart along, each prisoner has to bend forward and pull with all his strength, or the warder who is driving will threaten to 'run him in,' or report him for idleness. It was our work to supply all parts of the prison — workshops, officers' mess-room, cook-house, etc.— with coals; and I was often drawing these about in rain and sleet, with no fire to warm or dry myself after a wetting. I was only a few months at this sort of work, as I met with a slight accident by a collar hurting the remnant of my right arm, and was in consequence of this excused from cart labor by the doctor's order. I was again set to breaking granite, and remained at that job during the winter of 1870–71.

"I may remark that in June, when I was first put to stone-breaking, I was employed in a shed; but during the winter I was compelled to work outside, in the cold and damp, foggy weather. I was left at this work until spring, and was then removed to a task from the effects of which I believe I will never completely recover. My health on entering prison was excellent, never having had any sickness at any previous period of my life. The close confinement and insufficient food in Millbank had told, of course, on my constitution, though not to any very alarming extent; but the task I was now put to laid the germs of the heart and lung disease I have since been suffering from. This task was putrid bone-breaking.

"On the brink of the prison cesspool, in which all the soil of the whole establishment is accumulated for manure, stands a small building, some twenty feet long by about ten broad, known as the 'bone-shed.' The floor of this shed is sunk some three feet lower than the ground outside, and is on a level with the pool which laves the wall of the building. All the bones accruing from the meat supply of the prison were pounded into dust in this shed, and during the summer of 1872 (excepting five weeks spent in Portsmouth prison) this was my employment. These bones have often lain putrifying for weeks in the broiling heat of the summer sun, ere they were brought in to be broken.

The stench arising from their decomposition, together with the noxious exhalations from the action of the sun's rays on the cesspool outside, no words could adequately express: it was a veritable charnel-house. It will be noted that I was at work outside the previous winter, and when the bright days and summer season came on I was put in a low shed to break putrifying bones! The number of prisoners at this work varied from thirty to six, and I may remark that the majority of these were what are termed 'doctor's men,' or prisoners unable to perform the ordinary prison labor. When all the bones would be pounded, we would then be employed in and around the cesspool, mixing and carting manure, and at various other similar occupations.

"I made application to both Governor and doctor for removal from this bone-breaking to some more congenial task, but I would not be transferred to any other labor. After completing a term of my imprisonment which entitled me to a pint of tea in lieu of 'skilly' for breakfast, I was then removed to a hard-labor party, as, owing to my being an invalid, or 'doctor's man,' I could not claim the privilege of this slight change in diet without becoming attached to some hard-labor party,—invalids, or 'light labor men,' not being allowed tea at any stage of their imprisonment. I very willingly consented to a heavier task, in order to be removed from the abominable bone-shed, in which I had worked and sickened during the summer.

"My employment after this was various: drawing carts, bogies laden with stone, slates, etc., delving and shifting sand, at which work I was in the habit of using a pick and shovel (though not, I must fairly admit, *compelled* to do so), as the extreme cold made it necessary in order to keep myself from being congealed. I was next employed in winding up stones at an iron crank, during the building of an additional wing to the prison; and this was, beyond doubt, the heaviest work to which they could have put me. A crank party consisted of four men, and my being one of the four compelled me to perform as much work as either of the others, as the task would fall heavier upon them otherwise. This employment was occasionally diversified with 'spells' at mortar-making, water-carrying for same, sand-shifting, cement-making, and various other jobs, among which carrying slates to the roof of the new prison was one — not, of course, up a ladder, but by a steep incline.

"I may remark in passing, that three prisoners lost their lives while this building was going on, and, in my opinion, those accidents were attributable to the ignorance of scaffolding arrangements shown by the warders appointed to superintend them. Inquests were held, of course, *inside* the prison; but I never learned that any intelligent prisoner was called upon to give evidence, nor what verdicts were given by what the prisoners in Dartmoor called 'the standing jury.' I may add also that my friend, Mr. Chambers, fell from a scaffolding at the same building, and, on the principle that 'a man who falls deserves to be kicked for falling,' he was taken to the punishment cells instead of the infirmary, and turned out to work again the following day. When my services as a mason's laborer were no longer required, I was once more put to the old job of stone-breaking, and remained thereat from about the latter part of 1873 until August, 1876.

"During the long winters of those years I was thus employed in a part of the prison yard known to be the coldest place within the walls, where the north-east wind—so prevalent during Dartmoor winters—blew in my face, without my having the slightest shelter from its cutting blast, or any means of keeping my freezing blood in circulation except by plying of my stone-breaking hammer. When snow had fallen during the night, I would have to clear it away from the heap of stones in the morning and smash away as usual. So excessively cold and long are the Dartmoor winters that during the past few years the prisoners have had to be supplied with small bags made of the same material as their clothing, by which to shield their hands from the frost-bite and chilblains. Without some such provision to protect them from the effects of the severe, cold, little or no outside work could be done by the prisoners.

"I made application to the Governor for some inside labor in winter time; but all requests of mine for change of task were invariably refused, and I had to await unforeseen circumstances to effect what would not otherwise be granted me. An event of this nature saved me from a fourth winter's campaign amidst granite and snow; but as a 'compensation' for this relief it entailed very much heavier work, and caused me to be placed under special surveillance and located in penal cells for the remainder of my imprisonment. This event was what has been called 'the unconstitutional amnesty' of Western Australia.

"After this I was not considered sufficiently safe, as I could have been seen at my stone-breaking in the prison yard by any mischievous people who might hold anti-ticket-of-leave notions on my account. I was therefore removed to the prison wash-house,—a place securely situated in the very centre of the prison, and free from all apprehensions of a 'surprise.' A wash-house is a place where it might be thought I could not earn my 'skilly;' but without boasting of having distinguished myself in the capacity of a 'washerwoman,' or built a reputation in the art of bleaching, I can say, without fear of contradiction from the prison officials, that my work there was the heaviest of any prisoner employed in the wash-house. Another prisoner and myself were told off to the wringing machine, in which linen, etc., for a thousand men, and washings for officers' mess and rooms, etc., had to be wrung each week, with flannels and sheets for same number once a fortnight and month respectively, in addition. My assistant on this machine was changed every week, as men—able-bodied men—had been reported for refusing to remain constantly at such heavy labor; but, as I was physically unable to wash the linen, I was compelled to turn the machine as my principal occupation. The machine being made with a couple of handles, I had to turn as much as my assistant, and very often more, if he proved an idle one. I was considerably reduced in weight while at this employment (which lasted until my release on the 19th of December), from the amount of sweating it entailed, especially during the summer months, and the heavy nature of the work.

"My weight a week after my liberation was but nine stone four pounds, including my clothes, or some eight stone ten pounds without—not, I think, the proper weight for a man six feet high, and at the age of thirty-one. In addition to turning the wringer, I had to sort my share of the dirty linen each Monday morning; and singularly enough the infirmary portion was part of my share, and I had consequently to handle the articles worn by prisoners suffering from all manner of skin diseases and other disgusting afflictions. This will finish the necessarily brief account of my various employments in Dartmoor, and, with a description of the daily searchings I was subject to, will conclude my narrative of ordinary treatment while a prisoner.

"I will now briefly relate my exceptional punishment as a political prisoner, and adduce proofs that this treatment was more severe than that of ordinary malefactors, unmerited by my conduct as a prisoner, and therefore contrary to the prison rules I was compelled to observe to the very letter. Each prisoner is searched four times each day—Sunday excepted—by the officers under whom he is employed, and liable, in addition to this, to be stripped naked, and subjected to a minute and disgusting examination, or, as it is more properly termed in prison slang, 'turned over,' whenever an officer wishes to do so. I was searched four times each day in common with other prisoners, and had in winter and summer alike to open my jacket and vest, take off my cap, hold out my hand at arm's length, and stand in this manner in the open air, and allow a warder to run his hands from my neck downwards over my body to satisfy himself I had nothing concealed upon my person.

"I was also at regulated intervals taken with other prisoners into a part of the prison where we had all to strip in presence of each other and be minutely searched, but not compelled to strip beyond the shirt. This often occurred in the depth of winter, and I had to stand in this plight while an officer was carefully examining every article of my dress, after having rubbed his hands over my body, and made me open my mouth to assure himself I had nothing contraband upon me. I was never exempt from any of these searchings during the whole of my imprisonment.

"The charge has often been made against the Government that the Irish political prisoners were treated with greater severity, and subjected to more indignities, than ordinary malefactors, and both Ministers and Government organs have as often denied the truth of these allegations. I will allow facts to substantiate the charge so far as my own treatment is concerned, and leave the public to draw the inference in the case of those who are still in prison.

"From my arrival in Millbank, in 1870, until my discharge from Dartmoor, I was classed and associated with the ordinary prisoners, placed on the same footing with regard to diet and work, and had in every particular to perform the daily task of penal servitude as laid down by the prison rules.

"A strict compliance with the requirements of these rules entitles a convict to certain privileges at stated intervals during his imprisonment, as regulated by the Penal Servitude Act, which came into force in July, 1864; and such privileges are accordingly allowed to prisoners who strictly observe the conditions imposed upon them. There was no provision made in that act for the treatment of prisoners convicted for treason-felony, or other offences arising out of insurrectionary movements, and consequently there is no clause in the prison rules specifying the punishment to be awarded to political prisoners, or the granting or curtailing of privileges in such cases. A political prisoner, therefore, who is compelled to observe these rules in every particular like other prisoners, and to undergo the same penal discipline, is as clearly entitled to all the privileges allowed by those rules as men who are convicted for non-political offences, such as murder, theft, forgery, bigamy, etc. Such, however, has not been the case in regard to myself, and I adduce proofs to confirm this statement. One of the most coveted rewards of good conduct in prison is the privilege of receiving visits from friends, at intervals of three, four, and six months, according to the class and time served. A prisoner who has not forfeited his claim to such a privilege by any breach of discipline is as justly entitled to it as to his daily rations of food. Well, during my seven years and seven months' imprisonment, I have been, by the admission of prison officials, a 'good conduct' prisoner, and had consequently a right to a visit whenever I demanded one in accordance with the rules; but from the day after my sentence until the day of my discharge, I was not allowed to see a friend or receive a visit from any one.

"I made another effort while in Millbank to see some friend, and thinking that no possible objection could be raised against my seeing a lady, I tendered the name of one whom I was anxious to see, as she was a correspondent of my family and a most intimate friend of my own. This application was also refused by an order purporting to come from the then Home Secretary, Mr. Bruce (now Lord Aberdare), to the effect that a visit from the lady I had named would not be granted. I was now convinced that I would not be allowed an interview with any of my friends under any conditions, and made no further application for the next few years. I complied with the prison rules in the mean time, notwithstanding my deprivation of the privileges such compliance entitled me to. Several of my friends had also made efforts to obtain leave to see me, but to no purpose. I renewed my application again in August or September, 1874, and was again refused, and no explanation of such refusal given. On the 24th of November, I once more endeavored to see a friend, but the order for the visit was not forwarded, and I left prison on the 19th of December, without being permitted to see a friendly face during the whole term of my imprisonment.

"I may remark that one of my objects in seeking an interview with some of my friends was to have attention drawn to the case of John Wilson, who had been sentenced with me. Perhaps this was one reason why no visit would be granted.

"Another proof of exceptional treatment. Ordinary convicts, when located according to class, were allowed to select a companion from the same ward to exercise with on Sunday. Mr. Chambers and myself were never allowed this privilege. We could select 'companions' from among thieves and murderers, but would not be permitted to even speak to each other at any time, Sundays or other occasions. We made repeated applications to Governors and Directors to have this small boon allowed us, as it was allowed to others; but to no avail. No explanation would be given us why we were thus deprived of what others enjoyed.

"Another instance of unjust treatment is one which

I have already touched upon in the particulars of my various employments. Applications for transfer from party to party are of every-day occurrence in prison, and are invariably granted by the Governor, as prisoners are entitled to change of labor when their employments may be either too heavy or injurious to their health, or when they can show themselves more capable of performing one class of work than another. Every application made by me for more suitable employment was refused, and I was invariably put either to labor that would throw as much work upon me as if I were able-bodied, or to some task—such as bone-breaking in a low shed by the prison cesspool in summer, or stone-breaking in the open air during the rigors of winter—which would insure punishment the most injurious to my health being inflicted upon me. No other conclusion than this is possible from the singularly harsh manner in which I was treated, while complying with the rules in every particular.

"I have before remarked that in the labor of washing and scrubbing my cell, polishing utensils, etc., there was no allowance made for my being deprived of an arm; but I must admit that other prisoners similarly afflicted were treated in that respect in a like manner. This cell work, in addition to my ordinary labor, would tell more upon me than upon an able-bodied prisoner; and, as it also subtracted considerably from the short time at the disposal of prisoners for repose from labor, reading, etc., it would necessarily take more time from me, owing to the difficulties I had to contend with. In order to squeeze the floor-cloth, with which I washed my cell twice a-day, I would have to sit on my stool, place my feet upon the rim of my bucket, then put the cloth round the bucket-handle, and twist it until the water was wrung out of it. As a general rule, I had only a few minutes to spare for reading, so much of my time being necessary to the keeping of my cell as clean as others.

"In June, 1872, I was sent to Portsmouth Prison, along with twenty-nine other prisoners from Dartmoor. In cases of transfer from prison to prison, convicts are handcuffed, by one hand only, to a chain that runs the whole length of the number of prisoners, and passes through a ring in each man's handcuff. By this means, each convict has one hand at liberty to eat his food, attend to calls of nature, etc., if he is fortunate enough to be possessed of two; and, if not, it is customary to substitute a body-belt for a handcuff, in order to give him the use of one hand also. No such consideration was shown to me. I was purposely placed between two of the filthiest of the twenty-nine convicts, and had my wrist handcuffed back to back with one of them. I appealed against this ere I left Dartmoor, and requested a belt in lieu of a handcuff, or at least to be put at the end of the chain; but neither would be granted. One of the two between whom I was chained was afflicted with mephitis, or stinking breath, and the other, I think, with scrofula. During the journey to Portsmouth, this latter one, to whose hand mine was linked, had an attack of diarrhœa, and I had to submit to the horrors of such a situation, as my hand would not be unlocked from his. All this, however, may have been through the petty malice of the chief turnkey in Dartmoor, and may not have been ordered by the then governor of that prison.

"In Portsmouth prison I was placed on reduced

diet, because I was incapable of performing heavy labor, such as barrow-wheeling and the like. Yet, at the task I was put to—"skintling bricks"—I did as much work as those who had two hands to labor with. I explained this to the medical officer, as a plea in favor of being allowed the ordinary prison rations, but I was told that the Secretary of State had ordered that ordinary diet should not be given to men employed at light labor, and that an exception could not be made in favor of me.

"I am bound to remark, however, that the quality of the food in Portsmouth was far superior to that of Dartmoor, and that I suffered very little from the reduction in diet during my five weeks' stay in the former prison. While there, I was once reported for falling out of the ranks to see the doctor, through an attack of quinsy. I was not punished with bread and water, but I had to work for a couple of days without any food whatever, being unable to swallow anything, and receiving neither treatment nor remedy for my indisposition.

"I was ordered back to Dartmoor again on the 16th of July, 1872, and on this return journey I was accompanied by a madman, or, as he would be termed in prison slang, a "barmy bloke." I was handcuffed to him, of course, and, while waiting for a train at Exeter, he managed to divest himself of most of his clothing, because he would not be allowed to ask people for tobacco. My journey back was not much pleasanter than the one coming away. I have made this digression from my exceptionally harsh treatment in Dartmoor, in order to show that in whatever prison I might be incarcerated the fact of my being a political prisoner exposed me to, rather than saved me from, the most inconsiderate treatment at the hands of the prison officials.

"But to return to proofs of my exceptional punishment in Dartmoor.

"On one occasion (I believe it was in the latter part of 1871) I was ordered by a warder to assist another prisoner in carrying a tub that answered the purpose of a closet for eighty or ninety men, and, on my refusing to do so, I was taken to the punishment cells and kept there — though not on bread and water — for three days, until the doctor had inspected the tub and found that it was too heavy for me to carry. It was on that occasion I was told by the Governor that I was just like another prisoner, and that he could not 'make fish of one and flesh of another.'

"During the whole of Easter week, 1876, I was confined to punishment cells, and underwent four days' bread and water, with deprivation of privileges of writing and class for two months, for simply refusing to substitute "sir" for "here" when answering my name to the assistant-warder in charge of the party to which I belonged. He had no other object in insisting upon this than to satisfy his vanity, unless prompted by some of his superiors to involve me in punishment in this manner. I had always been respectful in my language towards this fellow, though his ruffianly conduct, ignorance, and dirty habits were by-words among both officers and prisoners alike; and, on the occasion of his reporting me, my conduct had not changed towards him in the least from what it had previously been. The prison rules require prisoners to be respectful at all times, but do not lay down specific terms to be used in addressing warders. Hence my punishment was nothing more than a gratuitous piece of petty tyranny.

"It is a rule in prison that a convict's punishment, over and above the ordinary penal discipline, is determined by his conduct as a prisoner, and not by the nature of his offence. This rule is, generally speaking, followed by the Governor, if not by his subordinate officers, in dealing with convicts. Both governors and subordinates have reversed this rule in my case, I think, as I have already shown. Several instances more can be given. In addition to the same punishment I underwent with the other prisoners, I was subject to closer watching and numberless other annoyances, neither authorized by the rules nor merited by my conduct. During the first winter I spent in Dartmoor, I used to find my cell rummaged and bed-clothes strewn about the damp floor several times a week, and generally upon wet days. I have often come into my seven-foot-by-four cell, dripping wet, after drawing a cart about like a beast of burden in the winter's rain or snow, and with saturated clothes upon my back had to gather up my bed and bedding and put to right what had been disarranged for no other motive than to give me work to do during my dinner hour, and thus deprive me of whatever little pleasure I might otherwise enjoy.

CHAPTER V.

Released on Ticket-of-Leave.—Grand Reception in Dublin.—Sergeant McCarthy's Death.—Davitt visits Mayo.—His first Lecture in England.

"And now with shouts and clapping, and noise of weeping loud,
He enters through the river-gate, borne by the joyous crowd."
—Macaulay.

On Wednesday morning, December 19, 1877, at 10.30 o'clock, as Davitt was turning the handle of the wringing-machine in Dartmoor Prison wash-house, a warder entered the room, and said, "Davitt, put on your jacket, and come this way." Mr. Davitt says: "At this time I was very busy, sweating, in fact, at my work, and I thought Mr. Ryan had come to visit me. I was taken to the Governor's office. He said to me, 'Davitt, on several occasions I have spoken to you about how good conduct in prison is rewarded, and I am very happy to say that the Secretary of State has taken your case into consideration, and I have now the pleasure of telling you that your good conduct has met with its reward. I have received a communication from the Secretary of State to the effect that you are to be discharged on a ticket-of-leave for the remaining portion of your sentence.'"

It need hardly be said that the prisoner was

rejoiced by this news. The Governor next turned to the warders present, and said, "Let him be photographed, and send him off at once." This was done promptly. The prisoner had a suit of clothes given him, £3 put in his pocket, as well as the ticket-of-leave. He was taken to the railway station and sent off to London. "These," says Mr. Davitt, "were the circumstances attending my release. I cannot pretend now to tell how high-spirited I felt at regaining my liberty. I rejoiced even in the muddy streets of London. I had spent seven years and seven months in jail. They had done their best during all these years to injure my health and to break my spirit, but I left prison as good an Irishman as I entered it."

On coming to London he was met by his friends, including the members of the Political Prisoners' Visiting Committee. The Chairman, Mr. O'Shaughnessy, M.P., heartily congratulated Mr. Davitt on his release, and expressed the hope that the other prisoners would soon be free. Mr. Davitt thanked his friends and the committee for the cordial reception given him, and the sympathy so earnestly expressed by them at his regaining his liberty. These were the first sincerely kind words that had reached his ear for nearly seven and a half dreary years; they acted as a healing balm, poured on his weary spirit. He again breathed the pure air of freedom, and was surrounded by sympathetic friends, the warmth of whose welcome brought blushes to his attenuated cheeks.

Davitt spent the Christmas in London; and, in a few days afterwards, on Saturday, January 5, 1878, he was joined by Color-Sergeant McCarthy and Private John P. O'Brien, both of whom were sentenced in 1866 to penal servitude for life, and were liberated on the day named. Corporal Thomas Chambers, who was undergoing a like sentence with McCarthy and O'Brien, was also released the week following. The four released prisoners set out at once to visit the land they loved so well, and for which they had suffered so much, and arrived in the city of Dublin, via the Holyhead steamer, on Saturday night, January 12. A magnificent ovation awaited them at the Westland Row Station of the Dublin and Kingstown Railway.

The following account of the reception of the patriots in Kingstown and Dublin is taken from the *Freeman's Journal*:—

"The reception given by the patriotic citizens of Dublin to the released prisoners was in every way creditable to the Capital of Ireland. Such a scene as that which was witnessed on the night of their arrival literally defies description. From five o'clock, expectant crowds had begun to gather on the Kingstown Pier, and, as the time of the arrival neared, the masses of people began to solidify, until from one end of the Carlisle Pier to the other there was a dense crowd, which must have been composed of several thousands of people.

"The following distinguished Irishmen were present from the Reception Committee: Messrs. C. S. Parnell, M.P.; Major O'Gorman, M.P.; John O'Connor Power, M.P.; Richard Power, M.P., and John Ferguson, of Glasgow.

"Shortly before six, the lights of the steamer were seen close to the pier; and immediately the cheering, which was continuous for several minutes, and deafening in its heartiness and intensity, commenced, and was caught up from one to another, until it was sent almost to the railway terminus. A bonfire flashed out on Howth, and a little later the signal was caught at Bray Head and Dalkey Hill, and blazes on those heights acted as beacons of rejoicing to the country round. On the Club-House Pier, green lime-lights were shown, torches were lit on the Carlisle Pier, rockets were let off, and, amid these illuminations, waving of hats, cheering, and the crashing of bands, the steamer came alongside. A rush was made on board and a comparative silence followed, broken again by cheers, which told that the four released men had been found. In a few seconds later they came ashore, and an enthusiastic hand-shaking followed.

"First came Sergeant McCarthy, a pale, worn-looking old man, evidently in delicate health. He was most warmly received, Major O'Gorman and several others kissing his hand as they shook it. Then Michael Davitt, a comparatively young-looking man, with a heavy black moustache, followed. He had lost his right arm. After he had been greeted a delay occurred, and then O'Brien and Chambers quietly joined their companions, and to the four men then assembled Mr. Brennan read the following address, frequently interrupted by hearty applause:—

"'ADDRESS OF THE PEOPLE OF DUBLIN

"'*To Messrs. Charles McCarthy, Thomas Chambers, John Patrick O'Brien, and Michael Davitt, on their Release from Imprisonment, suffered for Ireland:*

"'FELLOW-COUNTRYMEN,—We approach you, on your release from the sufferings which you have for many years so cheerfully and heroically borne for our country in the prisons of England, to offer you our warmest congratulations, to bid you, with all the fervor and affection of our hearts, welcome home to Ireland, and to thank you for your courageous and uncompromising devotion to the National Cause.

"'Roman history reveres the tradition which tells of the heroic self-sacrifice of the patriot Marcus Curtius, who saved the city by casting himself into the yawning abyss opened in the forum. With a self-denying patriotism equal to his you have made an offering of life, fortune, and liberty, on the altar of your country; and if by such sacrifices as yours her freedom has not been achieved, her honor has been saved, the manhood of her sons vindicated, and a fund of public virtue created amongst us which will yet redeem and regenerate the land.

"'Mindful of this, and of all the horrors of penal servitude through which you have been condemned to pass, the capital of your country rejoices in your liberation to-day, and stretches forth its hand to receive you with delight and gratitude.

"'The pleasure which we feel, however, is diminished by the recollection that some of your brave companions are still held in captivity; and we cannot conclude without expressing the hope that they, too, may soon be restored to liberty.

"'Wishing you every blessing and prosperity in the future, and assuring you of the gratitude of all your countrymen, we again say to you from our inmost hearts, *Cead Mille Failthe.*

"'Signed on behalf of Reception Committee—Charles S. Parnell, M.P.; J. G. Biggar, M.P.; John O'Sullivan, John Dillon, J. Taafe, Patrick Egan, Treasurer, James Carey; Hon. Secretary, Thomas Brennan; John Burns, Robert Woodward, R. J. Donnelly, Daniel Curley, Edmund Hayes, J. Brady.'

"The four released prisoners having got into arailway carriage with some of their friends, Mr. Davitt read a reply on behalf of himself and fellow-prisoners.

"The demonstration of welcome was one of extraordinary magnitude and enthusiasm. For a full hour before the express was due in Westland Row, the elements of a vast torchlight procession were gathering from all the ends of the city in the surrounding streets. Bands of music, with flags flying, and trades' bodies marshalled behind, passed and repassed until they were lost in one great living mass, which overspread Westland Row and stretched out into Merrion Square and beyond. The evening being fine, the crowd of ordinary promenaders was increased tenfold; and by half-past six there was not an unoccupied square foot of space in Westland Row. More remarkable even than their numbers was the orderliness and good-humor of the people. The rough element that is apt to obtrude itself into popular assemblages after nightfall was almost entirely absent. Women and young children passed through the thick of the crowd without annoyance; and, even where men were packed together in thousands within a space that should not have contained hundreds, there was nothing but cheerful words and a pleasant bantering during their long wait.

"A tremendous burst of cheering arose when the prisoners were recognized, and it travelled outside, until the street rang with cheers and welcoming music. A United States flag was waved over the carriage, and the enthusiasm of those who were nearest was positively dangerous to the prisoners themselves, who are all of them in delicate health, and several of them marked with signs of prolonged and terrible suffering. So furious was the eagerness of the crowd to clasp hands with them that it was found hopeless to attempt a passage to the street on this side of the platform, and the expedient was adopted of releasing the travellers by the opposite door of their compartment, and smuggling them across the rails to the Ladies' Waiting Room, where they took refuge for nearly half-an-hour. It is said that Sergeant-Major McCarthy fainted from excitement; and it is certain that during the whole ordeal, the poor fellow showed signs of having passed through years of dreadful suffering. It was seven o'clock before a way could at last be cleared to the entrance-door, and then the rush was something terrific.

"How the released men themselves managed to reach the carriage in the street outside without being crushed or trampled in the whirl, is amazing. It was nobody's fault, for everybody did his best to make way and keep order; but the crowd was so densely packed that it was impossible for it to open or to move without crush or confusion. The enthusiasm was very great. Mr. Parnell, M. P., was recognized within the station, and was heartily cheered. A stout body-guard of young men managed at last, by almost superhuman efforts, to cleave a passage through the crowd by using their long wands horizontally as a kind of battering-rams, and in this way the released men were brought to a wagonette and mounted amidst a scene of terrific enthusiasm. The procession lay, all this time, in irregular segments in all the surrounding district, with hundreds of flambeaux flaming at their heads, and bands playing the national battle-music. Any enumeration of the component parts of the line was out of the question in the darkness, and with the density of the crowd that surged around the processionists. Some eighteen brass and reed bands were crashing away in the line.

"The trades' bodies mustered in great strength, and the general body of processionists was of vast extent; while every street they passed through was thronged with thousands, who were literally innumerable. By the time the demonstration had taken full shape, one huge mass of human beings covered above a mile of streets. Several thousand torches blazed in knots of about a hundred here and there; and what with the movement of those enormous crowds, the deafening sounds of cheers and martial music, and the glare of all the torches, the scene was one of extraordinary impressiveness. At College Green the processionists cheered as they passed the Grattan statue, and the prisoners, as they went by in the wagonette, pointed silently to the old Parliament House. At Cork Hill another vast section of processionists from the Thomas Street district joined the line, and at this time the entire of Dame Street, Parliament Street, and Capel Street were covered over with people, illuminated by thousands of torchlights. The procession took three hours in its progress by Dame Street, Parliament Street, the southern quays, Carlisle Bridge, Sackville Street, Henry Street, Mary Street, and so by Capel Street to the European Hotel, Bolton Street. The entire roadway in front of the hotel was densely packed. In all the windows and elevated positions around crowds assembled, and the enthusiasm and excitement that prevailed were such as have seldom been witnessed in Dublin. A perfect storm of acclamation rent the air when it was known that the procession was near, and when the carriage containing the released prisoners crept through the narrow portion of the street leading to the open carriage-way facing the European, the impatience of the crowd made it almost a physical impossibility that a passage could be made for the procession, the first portion of which arrived shortly before nine o'clock. In one of the large rooms Dr. Grattan, a well-known advocate for national independence, was entertaining some friends at dinner, and a motion was at once made to lift the released prisoners from the street into his apartment. O'Brien was lifted up first. The scene inside the hotel was of a most exciting character; the wringing of hands, the congratulations, and the cheers of welcome of which the prisoners were the objects surpassed description; and when McCarthy was lifted from the street to the window, the excitement of the moment, and the exhaustion of the day seemed to tell upon him very much. He was placed on a couch, in a fainting condition, and was quite unable to give utterance to his acknowledgments. The other released prisoner was also raised on the shoulders of the crowd, and passed through the windows. Davitt was brought in by the chief entrance to the hotel.

"Mr. Leahy, a local Nationalist, addressed the people from the windows, and was followed by some other gentlemen. Loud cries were given for 'a speech from the prisoners,' and ultimately Mr. O'Brien came forward, and addressed a few words to the multitude. Several members of Parliament called on the released patriots during the evening. The immense crowd remained outside the hotel for some hours, and dispersed in the most peaceable and orderly manner, little thinking that in a couple of days one of the men, in whose honor they had made such an imposing demonstration, would be alike beyond the thanks and congratulations of the Irish people, and the torments of the British Government."

A sad event, which threw a gloom over the joy felt by the Irish people at the prisoners' release, and their arrival amongst them in Dublin, occurred two days afterwards. The four ex-prisoners had been invited by Mr. Charles Stewart Parnell to breakfast with him in Morrisson's Hotel. On arriving at the hotel they proceeded upstairs; and, after a few minutes' conversation, McCarthy was observed to grow deadly pale and totter across the room. Davitt was the first to notice him and rushed to his assistance;

poor McCarthy was laid on a sofa, where Chambers and O'Brien supported his head. Davitt, with admirable presence of mind, did all he could to revive the sinking patriot, while Mr. Parnell, Mr. John Dillon, and some other gentlemen stood around, sad spectators, unable to give relief to the dying man. All efforts proved unavailing; in a few moments the noble spirit of the martyred soldier passed away beyond the reach of the British tyrant who, for twelve weary years, had tortured it by all the means that hate or devilish ingenuity could devise, in an English convict prison. Poor McCarthy was no more! Worn out by physical starvation and mental agony, the sense of freedom was too strong for him, and he succumbed. The scene around the remains was one of intense sadness. O'Brien raved in his grief; while Chambers, whose nervous system had been shattered during his twelve years' imprisonment, had to be taken away ill. Davitt, who felt the blow as keenly as the others, never lost his strength of mind, which came to the aid of all; he assumed the management of affairs connected with the mournful event until the termination of the obsequies.

On January 16, an inquest was held on the body of Sergeant McCarthy, and his fellow-prisoners were examined as witnesses. They testified that he had been most severely treated for years in Chatham Prison. He had complained of his heart, and stated that if he died in prison the Governor would be his murderer. The jury gave a verdict of death from heart disease, accelerated by the treatment he received in prison. The announcement of the verdict was received with loud manifestations of concurrence by those who were present.

On Sunday, January 20th, 1878, the funeral of Charles McCarthy took place in Dublin. He was buried in Glasnevin, and it is estimated that sixty thousand persons followed the remains to the cemetery in procession, while two hundred thousand were in the streets to express a common sorrow. There were forty bands in the procession, the largest seen since the burial of Daniel O'Connell. The other released prisoners were among the principal mourners. It was a wonderful popular demonstration.

Davitt remained for nine or ten days in Dublin, to rest after the fatigue and excitement through which he had just passed, and then went down to Mayo to visit the scenes of his childhood's home. When it became known that he was in the county, turf bonfires blazed on the hills, to welcome him back to the grass-grown spot where once stood the happy home from which landlord tyranny had driven him and his family, to seek a living among strangers, in a strange land. Bonfires blazed, processional torches were lit, and music floated through the air to welcome back a man who had done a patriot's work for his country, and who had suffered for having done it.

Little was it then thought that shortly afterwards, on those same Mayo hills, Michael Davitt was to kindle a blaze in the breasts of his countrymen, which was destined to destroy forever the landlord power that had torn him, and thousands like him, from peaceful homes in the land of their love and hope,—the land which God had given them, but of which man had robbed them.

Enthusiastic receptions were given the patriot in Castlebar, Balla, Westport, and Ballina. Torchlight processions illumined the streets, and the entire people gave a grand and unanimous verdict *slightly* at variance with that given nearly eight years previously by the English "Twelve" and the British Government. The verdict of the former was that Michael Davitt was a patriot, a martyr, a hero; of the latter, that he was a conspirator, a traitor, and a felon. Well, we suppose Davitt was satisfied with the verdict of his countrymen, and cared little for the opinions of Ireland's enemies. His welcome from the warm-hearted people of the West was such that the "Irish Government" in Dublin Castle took note of the event; and when the fuel-famine visited that section, a year later, on Chief Secretary "Jimmy" Lowther being appealed to for aid, he replied that,—"They could find plenty of turf not long since to give bonfire receptions to a released convict." After a brief stay in Mayo, Mr. Davitt returned to Dublin, and from thence went to London, accompanied by Chambers and O'Brien. The three released prisoners were cordially received, and shown over the House of Parliament by Messrs. Parnell, Biggar, O'Connor Power, Redmond, and Chevalier O'Clery. It was a novel sight to see men who so recently wore the broad arrow on their party-colored convict-jackets received as honored visitors in the House of Commons. The evidence given by Davitt and his companions, at the inquest held on Sergeant McCarthy's remains, as to the cruel treatment to which he and the other political prisoners had been subjected in prison, awakened intense sympathy for the released men and for those who were still enduring its rigors, and great indignation was expressed against the inhuman system, and the government that permitted it. Davitt was not slow to take advantage of the opportunity presented, to turn the feeling in favor of the release of the men still held in prison. O'Connor Power conducted the ex-prisoners to a private room in the Parliament House, where they wrote out statements giving the details of sufferings endured and the treatment to which they had been for years subjected; and showing that such had broken down McCarthy's health and caused his death. This was the record of prison horrors so well told by Michael Davitt in a previous chapter, and which was mainly instrumental in procuring the release of Robert Kelly, O'Meara Condon, and the other three men some time afterwards. O'Connor Power presented the statements made by Davitt and his companions to the Home Secretary, and asked to have them printed. This was of course refused, as the Government did not want to place on record against itself such a terrible indictment. He and Davitt, therefore, had them printed in pamphlet form and circulated.

During his long imprisonment, Davitt made a careful study of the present condition of Ireland, and her dreary past history, and in his solitary hours of thinking he discovered the root of the disease that was eating away the life of the nation for hundreds of years, and the cure that should be applied. The land question was the ulcer, and the remedy is being adopted to-day by the Irish National Land League.

After this, Mr. Davitt, accompanied by Corporal Chambers delivered lectures in the north of England, in Scotland, and Ireland, on the treatment of Irish Political Prisoners. He devoted himself to the task of working for the release of the men in prison, and was unremitting in his exertions in their behalf. He enlisted the sympathies of the English and Scotch people, and worked hard until his efforts were crowned with success. His first lecture was delivered in St. James's Hall, Piccadilly. It being the first public appearance on the lecture platform of a man who has since become famous we give the announcement entire:

> IRISHMEN!!!
>
> A MEETING WILL BE HELD IN ST. JAMES'S HALL,
>
> PICCADILLY,
>
> *On SATURDAY, the 9th MARCH next,*
>
> For the purpose of directing PUBLIC OPINION to the subject of the treatment of the
>
> IRISH POLITICAL PRISONERS.
>
> Mr. MICHAEL DAVITT, one of the lately released prisoners, will give
>
> AN ADDRESS.
>
> ---
>
> JOHN O'CONNOR POWER, Esq., M.P., will take the Chair, and the following M.P.'s have promised to attend:
>
> Lord Francis Conyngham, Mitchell Henry, C. S. Parnell, J. G. Biggar, T. Earp, D. Davies, John Barron, J. W. Pease, A. M. Sullivan, Dr. Ward, J. D. Hutchinson, E. Dwyer Gray, G. H. Kirk, Keyes O'Clery, Joseph Cowen, Major O'Gorman, Sir Joseph N. McKenna, Bart.; also Messrs. Chambers and O'Brien, late Political Prisoners.
>
> ---
>
> The Chair will be taken at 7.30 o'Clock.

Robert Kelly was released in the following August, in a dying condition. On Saturday morning, August 3d, at about eleven o'clock,

Captain Barlow, the Governor, Mr. Hackett, and Chief Warder Murphy, went to Kelly's bedside in the prison "hospital," Mountjoy prison, Dublin. Captain Barlow acted as spokesman, and said: "Kelly, I have come to you with news that will not be altogether unpleasant, and I hope you will hear it without allowing your excitement to get the better of you. I have brought you the free pardon of His Grace, the Duke of Marlborough, on the usual conditions of a ticket-of-leave." The news came like a thunderbolt upon the prisoner, who, after recovering himself, said that he would not accept a pardon on such conditions. He added, that, from what prisoners told him of a ticket-of-leave, he would always feel as though he dragged a long chain about with him through life, which any policeman might trample on at pleasure, to drag him back again to penal servitude.

He was right! It has proved so in Davitt's case; *he* has been dragged back by the chain that bound the ticket-of-leave to the convict prison. The *Freeman's Journal* commenting on the condition of Kelly on his release, and examination by Dr. Kenny, said:—

"The plain fact is, these revelations cannot be any longer tolerated. No nation could maintain legitimate prestige which systematically repressed crime by crime. It matters not to what class of politicians a man may belong; politics do not make us savage; and we believe no one will read the story of this wretched man without feeling that England is shamed and disgraced before the world by permitting men to be done to death by a cold-blooded and relentless discipline."

A notable event happened during the month of August, which we cannot pass over without mentioning. It was the death, in raving madness, of a miserable renegade—a wretch, the events in whose political career are a blotch on his country's history, who was hated and despised by all honest Irishmen—the infamous Judge Keogh, one of the surviving worthies of "*the Pope's Brass Band*." He was staying near Brussels for his health, and went mad; he made an attempt on the life of his valet with a razor, dangerously cutting him in several places. He died raving; and when the news of the tragic event reached Ireland, his obituary was chanted in curses by his outraged countrymen. He who had sent so many into British dungeons, with a string of vituperation tacked on to their sentences—for a *crime* (!) to which he himself had sworn allegiance; but, like Iscariot, perjured himself, on receiving the "thirty pieces of silver" as the price of the betrayal of his country—met the reward he deserved, by a miserable death in a strange land. He went down

"To the vile dust from whence he sprang,
Unwept, unhonored, and un—" *hung!*

as he deserved to be.

CHAPTER VI.

DAVITT'S FIRST VISIT TO AMERICA.—SEED OF THE LAND LEAGUE SOWN BY ADVANCED NATIONALISTS.—THE NEW DOCTRINE EXPOUNDED BY DAVITT.—A NATIONAL PLATFORM PROPOSED.

"O lovely isle beyond the waves,
Ireland, our home!
Where shamrocks deck our fathers' graves,
Our childhood's home!
In far, far climes we kneel in prayer,
To Him who rules earth, sea, and air,
To end thy bondage and despair,
Ireland, our native home!"
—R. D. JOYCE.

ABOUT the beginning of August, 1878, Michael Davitt made his first visit to the United States, his object being to bring back to Ireland his mother and sisters, then living in Manayunk, Pa. After his arrival, he wrote as follows to England, to his friend, Thomas Chambers:—

"MANAYUNK, PHILADELPHIA, August 15, 1878.

"*My Dear Tom,*—You will be glad to hear that I found my mother in much better health than I expected, after her long years of trouble and anxiety. She appears twenty years younger since I promised to take her back to Ireland. My voyage was a very pleasant one; and so far I like the country and the people I met very much. Philadelphia is the handsomest city I ever saw. I only stayed a few hours in New

York, as John [Devoy] and myself were invited to a picnic at a distance. . . . I am to lecture in Philadelphia on the 16th of September; subject, 'The Ireland of the present.' About the 20th, I am to give a 'prison' lecture in New York, and I am to devote the proceeds to the relief of Daniel Reddin and John Wilson,—he who was tried with me. Health capital. Fear I won't get back as early as I expected, as I am requested to go out West, as far as San Francisco, and lecture. . . . Ever sincerely yours,

"MICHAEL."

Invitations to lecture now came pouring in on Mr. Davitt. The Irish-Americans everywhere were anxious to see and hear him, so that he was kept busy on the lecture platform.

Meanwhile Mr. Parnell, and the intrepid half-dozen Irish members who acted with him, had attracted much attention, and the admiration of their countrymen, by the obstructive tactics so successfully practised in the House of Commons. They were only a few; but they demonstrated to the Irish people what even a few determined men could do, by clogging the wheels of legislation, and—as the champion of universal liberty, Wendell Phillips, says—"forcing John Bull to listen." The Home Rule organization, after years of unsuccessful agitation was languishing. Isaac Butt, the leader, and his immediate followers having on various questions supported the Ministry, much dissatisfaction was caused, and people were beginning to tire of the frequent defeats in Parliament of the party, and to give up all hope of obtaining their demands through agitation. Parnell and his fellow-workers, however, struck a chord that reverberated pleasingly on the Irish ear; he threw vigor and spirit into the fight, and infused a new soul into the dying Home Rule organization. He, and not Butt, was henceforth the leader. *Parnell* was the people's choice. The young Hercules, calm, determined, wise, and energetic, revolutionized the old petitioning — begging — method, and began to attack the enemy's weak point. He first compelled Parliament to listen, then *demanded*, and now *dictates* the measures that Ireland will accept as final, or otherwise.

On October 21, 1878, a Convention of Home Rulers met in the Rotundo, Dublin, and continued their sitting for three days. Mr. Parnell presided. A large number of delegates from England and Scotland attended. In the course of his speech Mr. Parnell said: —

"I want the country to know its own mind above all things, and when the country knows its own mind I want it to be united in carrying out that mind, whatever it is. Upon the question of policy and conduct, let Ireland make up her mind upon what she is going to do; and when she has made up her mind, let her show her mind, and it must be obeyed; but if she hesitates about her attitude, then I say you are lost, at all events for some years. I don't believe in any country, or in any cause, much less Ireland and Ireland's cause, being lost for any long time; but you will lose it for some time — for some years. Anything that has been gained, has been got by good luck rather than by good management. I said when I was last on this platform, that I would not promise anything by parliamentary action, nor any particular line of policy; but I said we could help you to punish the English, and I predicted that the English would very soon get afraid of the policy of punishment. Well, they did not stand that process of punishment very long last session — they stood it for about four months. They tried every plan and every method to get over us, and we beat them. They gave us the last two months of the session all to ourselves, for Ireland. That was a thing they never did before, but I venture to predict that they will do it again."

He asked that help be sent the active party in Parliament, as otherwise nothing could be got from that body, and said, that if such did not result, he and his friends would retire into private life as "that would be the only course open to an honorable man." An active policy was agreed on; sixteen Irish members gave in their adhesion to the new programme, and it was agreed to contest all the seats occupied by Home Rulers who opposed obstruction, and to make an open issue with Isaac Butt before the people.

While this change of front was taking place in Ireland, new seed was being prepared in America to cast into the field of Irish politics, which was destined to take deep root in a soil ready to receive it; to spring into life and spread its roots and branches all through the land; to blossom into THE IRISH NATIONAL LAND LEAGUE, and render the fruit of PEASANT PROPRIETORSHIP.

Michael Davitt's busy brain was at work. He was in frequent consultation with one of Ireland's noblest and most daring sons, John Devoy; with one of her most successful revolutionary chiefs, John J. Breslin — the man who accomplished the two great actions, of liberating James Stephens from his Dublin prison, and the military prisoners from the convict prison of Fremantle, in Western Australia — and with others of ability and keen foresight. The result was, that about the end of October, immediately after the Home Rule Conference had closed its session, the leaders of the advanced Irish Nationalists in America cabled from New York "to Mr. Parnell and his political friends," the following proposal of co-operation on the conditions mentioned. The despatch, however, was to be submitted to a number of representative Nationalists in Dublin for their approval, before being presented to Mr. Parnell. It was as follows:—

"The Nationalists here will support you on the following conditions:—

'*First*, Abandonment of the federal demand, and

substitution of a general declaration in favor of self-government.

'*Second*, Vigorous agitation of the land question on the basis of a peasantry proprietary, while accepting concessions tending to abolish arbitrary eviction.

'*Third*, Exclusion of all sectarian issues from the platform.

'*Fourth*, Irish members to vote together on all imperial and home questions, adopt an aggressive policy, and energetically resist coercive legislation.

'*Fifth*, Advocacy of all struggling nationalities in the British Empire and elsewhere.'"

The seed was sown by electricity; we see to-day the blossom; the fruit is ripening.

A new Irish national movement that could embrace on a common platform all organized bodies and the whole Irish race — was born; it has since grown to immense proportions, and has the support of all classes of Nationalists. It has not yet, however, grown to its full proportions, but it is rapidly developing, and is to-day strong enough to withstand the shock of British coercion without being badly damaged by the encounter.

Davitt now began in earnest the task of spreading the seed in America of the new Irish national movement. His lectures opened new ideas to the minds of the thousands who came to hear him. His language was clear, liberal, and bold. He reconciled the extremists everywhere he spoke to the new policy, and laid the foundation of the great American organization. The following masterly address on the "Future Policy of Irish Nationalists," which he delivered in Mechanic's Hall, Boston, on December 8, 1878, before his departure for Ireland, being his first great effort in oratory, and a clear exposition of the reasons for unity of action amongst all classes of Irishmen, we give in full:—

"It would be difficult to conceive a position more unenviable than that in which an Irish Nationalist places himself when he attempts to review the past of his party in order to point out what he believes to have been rash or impolitic in its career. A criticism of the wisdom of an action that has failed or a line of conduct which has been injudicious, is at once construed into disloyalty to the principles or party which may have prompted such action by a sincere but imprudent resolve. But when he expresses himself dissatisfied with the narrow sphere of a policy which tends to exclude from National labor every one but a pronounced Separatist, and adds his belief that a change of tactics would turn the exertions of sincere Irishmen, though now pronounced Separatists, into the National cause, he is at once assumed to have 'forfeited his principles,' and to be on the high road to West-Britonism.

"In consequence of this proneness of the Irish mind to hasty and uncharitable deductions, men (who *think* while working in Ireland's cause) are deterred from condemning what they know to be injudicious, lest they should find themselves ostracized from its ranks for their anxiety to see it directed the surest way to success. In my humble opinion, a want of moral courage belittles a man far more than a deficiency in the physical article, and that real cowardice consists in dreading the sentimental consequences of an upright, honest action. It has ever been the practice to pander to the popular prejudices of our country, by hyperbolical eulogies on everything Irish, and we have thus become the spoiled children of struggling nationalities, and, as a necessary consequence, backward in our political education as a people, as well as behind the progressive march of the age. Holding these opinions, I will endeavor to-night to show you how we ourselves are to blame for past failures, and how essential it is, that the causes which led to such failures be guarded against in the future. The indestructibility of Irish nationality is no more its distinguishing characteristic, than is its past inapplicability to the working out of its own success, or the winning of an advanced social and political position for the people who profess it. We can boast that hundreds of years of the worst rule that ever cursed a country has failed to crush it; but can we say that Ireland is to-day in a condition commensurate with the struggles and sacrifices of her sons on her behalf during the past seven centuries? I think not; and the "why and wherefore" of this fact is what should focus upon it the thought and studies of practical Nationalists of the present. That there has been an unmethodical application of energies, or rather, a reckless waste of national strength in this long contest, is but too patent from a comparison between the position, social and political, of our country to-day, and that of other peoples who have struggled successfully against the same enemy. The very strength of our purpose and determination of our resolves were the means which invited defeat. We grasped at liberty in the intoxication of sincerity, and blindly discarded every other practical consideration. We "resolved," and "swore," and "determined" to *avenge Ireland's wrongs!* but took no essential method to win her liberty. We were actuated as much by *revenge* as by patriotism, and received the penalty which follows the obeying of a passion instead of the dictates of a virtue. While recognizing that it was a war of races, Saxon against Celtic, we refused to shelter ourselves behind the ramparts of expediency or employ any of the many justifiable means by which a weak people might utilize their strength; and we therefore marched into the open plain inviting destruction. Instead of watching our enemy from behind the Torres Vedras of Ireland's imperishable national principles, and determining our action by his weakness or strength according to the powers arrayed against him, we left our position exposed in order to challenge him to single combat, and we never marched to the Paris of the British Empire to see him relinquish his spoils or surrender his conquests.

"No greater mistake could be made by Fenianism than the drawing of but a single line of distinction between a West Briton and the Irishman who accepted its programme of action as the safe, certain, and only means of winning independence. The assumption that all Irish Nationalists were included in the Fenian organization was a piece of disastrous folly, as it engendered a bitter hostility to earnest Irishmen who only refused to follow a leader whom they did not know in a movement which confined itself to a single class of their countrymen. Thus, a host of enemies were created where the reserve force of a real national movement should find strength and support.

"Now, a fault-finder or critic has no claim to a fair hearing, unless he has something reasonable to substitute for or amend in what he condemns. I will, therefore, with your indulgence, attempt to point out what, in my opinion, would place our national cause upon a stronger footing, and multiply its chances of success in the near future.

"As I have freely censured the past policy of my own party, it may have created a suspicion in your minds that it was the *party* itself or its *principles*, which I attacked under cover of a review of its past history. I trust it will not need my assurance to convince you of my belief in and adherence to the doctrine of physical force, and that whatever other agencies, expedient, moral, or diplomatic, which I may desire to see added to the factors at work in the national cause, I am convinced, that it is only the manhood strength of Ireland which can give the *coup-de-grace* to her enemy's rule over her. This belief does not exclude the employment of any of the other means I have just alluded to as an auxiliary to the final *dernier ressort* as being unjustifiable or antagonistic to the principles involved in the contest; and it is on this ground I rest a claim for the utilizing of every safe and justifiable expedient in the working out of our country's social and political redemption. It is well, therefore, to look outside the National party in Ireland, to reconnoitre our friends or enemies, and see how far the one can be counted upon and how much the other is to be dreaded.

"The Ireland of the present may be divided into four distinct sections of political strife, presumably in her interest: the Nationalist or party of action, 'National' Constitutional, West British, and neutral, or rather non-participant, Irishmen.

"Take the first of these parties, which, on account of its being the custodian of Ireland's non-forfeited right to independence, should necessarily be the most powerful in numbers and influence; yet we must admit that it is not so, when it is looked at either in the light of its recent past endeavors or from its present hold on the public mind of Ireland. But let it be disassociated from the consequences of sincere but injudicious or premature action, and pitted against anti-national feeling in Ireland, and it possesses at once the unquestioned representative sentiment of the Irish people, and outnumbers in its adherents all the other parties combined. The position which we occupy in the political world is, therefore, a singularly anomalous one; for while our people are unquestionably national in their inward convictions, they exhibit in their external or public aspect a contradiction to that very fact. Hence the world either misunderstands or discredits our political aspirations. Now how is it that the Nationalist party is numerically the strongest in sentiment and sympathy, while not so in action? And why does external opinion remain sceptical as to Ireland's real desire for separation?

"To answer the first question, I will crave permission to place myself in the position of a tiller of the soil in Ireland,—say one of Patten Bridge's victims, on the barren slopes of the Galtees. I will assume I have just reached the level of my mud-walled cabin, on the mountain side, after carrying a load of manure on my back from the plains below. I have seen the short-horns, and black-faced sheep, from England and Scotland, grazing upon the rich land at the foot of the mountains,—the land which formerly belonged to my ancestors, and the produce of which is now fattening brute beasts while my six children are starving with hunger. I might be supposed to say,—'How is it that I, who have done no wrong to God, my country, or society, should be doomed to a penal existence like this? Who are they that stand by and see the beasts of the field preferred before me and my family? I am powerless to do anything but provide for the cravings of those whom God has sent to my care, and to relax my labor for a day might be a day's starvation to my little ones. If I go down to the castle and avenge my wrongs on the head of Patten Bridge, I am but injuring him, and not the system which enables him to plunder me. I must therefore refrain from an act which would see *me* die on the scaffold, and *my children* in the workhouse. If no one else will assist me, I am condemned to this miserable existence for the remainder of my life. Who are they that have time and energy to take part in the political strife of the day, and say they are working for Ireland and me? The Nationalist party tells me that when independence is won, I will no longer be at the mercy of an English landlord. That is like feeding my children with a mind's-eye-view of the dinner that will be served in Galtee Castle to-day. Yellow meal porridge is a more substantial meal than visionary plenty, and if the

Nationalists want me to believe in, and labor a little for, independence, they must first show themselves desirous and strong enough *to stand between me and the power which a single Englishman wields over me.* If they show they can *do that*, and thereby better my condition, they will convince me of their strength in Ireland, and earnestness in my behalf; and it is not in Irish nature to refuse a helping hand to those who assist another. Let them show that the social well-being of our people is the motive of their actions, and aim of their endeavors, while striving for the grand object ahead, and then the farming classes in Ireland will rally round them to assist in reaching that object. They look upon a man's existence in an abstract light, and think he should be moved in their cause without consulting that selfishness which is invariably the main-spring of human actions. God only knows how much I would like to fight for Ireland to-morrow if I could only see a chance of success, or had my wife and children in a similar position to that in which I am told the farmers of France and Belgium have theirs; but every former attempt at success has failed, me and mine are still at the mercy of the landlord, and therefore I can only give the Nationalists my sympathy and well-wishes, for my labor, time, and life, is necessary to the feeding of little Nora and the other children. The Parliamentarians promise to do more for me than any other party, but they break their promises in Westminster, and show as great an interest in Turkey as in Ireland. They are also at war with the Nationalists, and consequently the government and the West Britons have it all their own way over the vast majority of the Irish people. Me and the likes of me are told we have friends in all parties; but we never are made to feel anything but the power and influence of our enemies,—the landlords. I must bring up another creel of dung from the bottom of the mountain before mid-day, and then share my bowl of stirabout with my little ones. God's will be done, but it is a hard life to lead in the Nineteenth century!'

"This is no exaggeration of the thoughts or attitude of the people who are compelled to stand aloof from political strife in Ireland; and this vast class, recruited alike from the one instanced as well as from all those whose avocations and actions have their root in the *virtue of the honest, selfish cares of social life*, are within reach of the party of action, if the necessary steps are taken to enlist their assistance and co-operation.

"Turning to the political aspect of Irish nationality as it is viewed from abroad, it is easy to show how we have been, and are still, discredited with practical earnestness in our opposition to English rule. We have flattered ourselves too long with the belief that we were assured of French and American sympathy in our contest with the enemy of our race, and that these and other countries would accept of our spasmodic struggles against a dominant power as proving the disaffection and determined opposition of a whole people, while 'representatives,' municipalities, religious and other bodies, public men and public writers, were convincing them to the direct contrary. 'Tis true that periodical attempts at insurrection have shown that though our country is subjugated it is not reconciled to alien government, willing to forfeit its national birthright; but, convincing as all this may be to *Irishmen*, others will look upon our repeated risings in the light of past events, and speak of them in proportion to their importance as looked at from an external point of view, while weighing us in the political balance of nationalities in exact accordance with the public spirit and political tendencies of our people of the present. The collective opinions of foreign nations, in sympathy with or indifference towards the Irish question, will be formed from its present phases, and not, as *we* would desire, from past occurrences; and therefore the less our national aspirations and convincing opposition to alien rule are manifested to the world by the public tone and attitude of our people, the less interest there will be taken and sympathy felt by the world in our cause. Our connection with the past of Ireland — the inspiration we draw from its history, and the events therein recorded— must influence, of course, our line of action in the working out of the political destiny of our fatherland; but our glorious past will not win for us one iota of sympathy from outside the Irish race beyond what is demanded by the consistency of such actions with the object aimed at, and the practical manner in which the national desire for the attainment of that object is manifested.

"When we appeal to mankind for the justice of our cause, we must assume the attitude of a *united*, because an earnest, people, and show reason why we refuse to accept of our political annihilation. We can only do this by the thoroughness of purpose which should actuate, and the systematic exertions which alone can justify, us in claiming the recognition due to a country which has never once acquiesced in its subjugation, nor abandoned its resolve to be free. Viewing that country then, as she presents herself to-day, the problem of her redemption may be put in this formla: Given the present social and political condition of Ireland, with the spirit, national tendencies, physical and moral forces of her people — together with the power, influence, and policy arrayed against them — to indicate what should be the plans pursued, and action adopted, whereby the condition of our people could be materially improved, in efforts tending to raise them to their rightful position as a Nation.

"I confess to the difficulty of solving such a problem, but not so much as to the putting it into practice if theoretically demonstrated; but

"'Right endeavor's not in vain—
Its reward is in the doing;
And the rapture of pursuing,
Is the prize the vanquished gain.'

"Let us see if we can discover a key to the difficulty of the Irish question. I will assume that there are certain matters or contingencies important to or affecting the Irish race which are of equal interest to its people (irrespective of what differences of opinion there may be amongst them on various other concerns),— such as the preservation of the distinctive individuality of the race itself among peoples; the earning for it that respect and prestige to which it is by right and inheritance entitled, by striving for its improvement, physically and morally, and its intellectual and social advancement, revival of its ancient language, etc; and that there are past occurrences and sectional animosities which all classes must reasonably desire to prevent in future, for the honor and welfare of themselves and country,— such as religious feuds and provincial antipathies. I will also assume that the raising of our peasant population from the depths of social misery to which it has been sunk by an unjust land system, would meet with the approval of most classes in Ireland, and receive the moral co-operation of Irishmen abroad, as would also the improvement of the dwellings of our agricultural population; which project, I also assume, would be accepted and supported by all parties in Irish political life. Without particularizing any further measures for the common good of our people, for which political parties cannot refuse to mutually co-operate, if consistent with their *raison d'etre* as striving for their country's welfare, I think it will be granted that Nationalists (pronounced or quiescent), Obstructionists, Home Rulers, Repealers, and others, could unite in obtaining the reforms already enumerated by concerted action on and by whatever means the present existing state of affairs in Ireland can place within their reach. Such concerted action for the general good would necessitate a centripetal platform, as representing that central principle or motive which constitutes the hold and supplies the influence that a country's government has upon the people governed.

"A race of people, to preserve itself from destruction by an hostile race, or by partisan spirit and factious strife internally, or absorption by a people among which it may be scattered, absolutely requires some central idea, principle, or platform of motives of action, by which to exercise its national, or race-individuality, strength, with a view to its improvement and preservation. A people's own established government supplies this need, of course, but where, as in Ireland, there is no government of or by the people, and the dominant power is but a strong executive faction, the national strength is wasted,—1. By the *divide et impera* policy of that dominant English faction; 2. By desperate attempts to overthrow that power; and 3. By hitherto fruitless agitation to win a just rule, or force remedial legislation from an alien assembly by means repugnant to the pride of the largest portion of our people; while here, in this great shelter-land of peoples, the Irish race itself is fast disappearing in the composite American. If, therefore, a platform be put forth embodying resistance to every hostile element pitted, or adverse influence at work, against the individuality of Ireland and its people, and a programme of national labor for the general welfare of our country be adopted, resting upon those wants and desires which have a first claim upon the consideration of Irishmen,—such a platform, if put forth, not to suit a particular party, but to embrace all that is earnest and desirous among our people for labor in the vineyard of Ireland's common good, a great national desire would be gratified, and an immense stride be taken towards the goal of each Irishman's hopes.

"Such a centre-composite platform would not necessarily require any control over the organization of its respective party-adherents, nor need the resources of the party of action except when the final appeal for self-government should be made. All that it would demand from its individual elements would be such support as should make it superior in influence over the public life of Ireland to that which the *English faction* wields to our disgrace and disadvantage to-day.

Apart from the material good which would assuredly follow from such a platform being adopted, how inestimable would be the collateral advantages that would accrue from Irishmen *acting together at last* for some tangible common benefit to be conferred upon themselves and their country! The gradual but certain sweeping away of West-British ideas before the advance of a united national Irish sentiment; the harmonizing of the hitherto conflicting elements in political parties; the developing of our people's political education; the creation of a healthy and vigorous public spirit which would at once attract and challenge the attention of foreign opinion, and concentrate upon Ireland an international interest in a *renaissant* people, who can exert a powerful influence over the destiny of a declining empire, the prestige and power of which are obnoxious to rival nations. Then the immense impetus which would be given to the national cause by the moral support of a sympathetic participation in it by the vast Irish and Irish-American element in this country, by far the greater part of which has heretofore stood aloof from Ireland's struggles, in consequence of having no feasible plan laid before it, whereby its assistance and influence could be profitably employed in the same.

"The difficulties in the way of such an united Irish public movement are to be found in the unreasonable prejudice and suicidal antagonism which exists between the two parties who each assume to be Ireland's benefactor,—the Nationalist and the Irish-Constitutional bodies. This mutual opposition has weakened both, diffused bad blood among the community, increased the number of non-participants in the political life of the country, and strengthened the position of the coercive faction. Condemnation of Nationalist action by Irish Constitutionals is permissible only within the limits of a censure upon desperate, untimely resolves on insurrection, as their opposition is unjustifiable upon any other ground.

"The Nationalist party is the guardian of their country's inalienable right to be mistress of her own destinies; its records are those which tell of a nation's fight against the extermination of its people; its martyrology is that of Ireland; and all of which we can justly be most proud of in her history—her seven centuries' struggle against overwhelming odds for the highest ambition of a nation (independence)—is the platform of the party of action. Its very defeats have won victories for the Constitutionalists; and the intensity of its earnestness has compelled remedial measures to be conceded to Ireland. As the Irishman who believes that his country could not govern herself if politically isolated is too contemptible to be noticed, the objection against the Nationalist party by its Constitutional opponent is belief in the improbability of final success,—and not antagonism to the object aimed at.

"On the other side, the prejudice existing among Nationalists against Constitutional action is in proportion to the anti-National complexion which it assumes; hence, Home Rule, from its being so much more un-Irish in essence and scope, is looked upon with greater antipathy than Repeal. Giving the Constitutionals credit, as in charity bound, for the best intentions, we must assume that they are actuated by the following reasons and motives:—Believing in the impossibility of separation, they rely upon moral force as a means of advancing the interests of the country, and that they employ this means in the conviction that it is the safest and most efficient plan by which an improvement of the people can be effected, and their country benefited. When the acts of Constitutionals belie these motives, they become reprehensible; but in their honesty of conduct within the lines of their good intents, they are deserving of, and entitled to, recognition and tolerance as laborers in behalf of Ireland and its people. They are as prominent in the political arena as the Nationalists,—more so, in fact, as they have a public policy to catch the public ear and eye. They have a following in Ireland which is at once powerful and influential, and cannot, therefore, be ignored. They have enlisted the support of the Catholic clergy, and count the middle class of the country as belonging to their party. Since the passing of the ballot-bill they can appeal with more force to Irish voters, who no longer run the risk of eviction for opposing landlord nominees. This freedom from restraint in the exercise of the franchise among a remedy-seeking people must logically impel them to look for redress, and men to champion their cause, in the safest, and, to them, most effectual means within their reach.

"To these facts must be added still stronger ones, namely, that, whether we Nationalists like it or not, Irish voters, as well as non-electors, will participate in elections, and interest themselves in their results. So long as the infamous Act of Union lasts, men will be sent to Westminster to represent or betray their country, in exact proportions to the interest or indifference with which the whole Irish people look upon Parliamentarianism. An indication of a national resolve to minimize the disgrace of a traitor-representation in an hostile assembly would curb the self-seeking place-hunters in the auction of their 'patriotism,' and themselves in St. Stephen's political mart. Hostility towards, or complete isolation from, parliamentary action by the Nationalist, will engender and encourage West-Britonism in Irish representation, and the world, which persists in looking at the Irish question through the medium of the House of Commons, will form its opinions on the wants and political tendencies of Ireland from the conduct and utterances of her 'representatives.' The amount of national sentiment and hostility to alien rule exhibited in Westminster by Irish members of Parliament will be to Russia, France, and America the gauge of the same sentiment and hostility in Ireland, where such members are elected. With the public ear in Ireland, and the eye and attention of the world in the world's most conspicuous assembly, *how are the Constitutionalists handicapped in a contest for party influence with the Nationalists, who have neither?* Suppose the positions and advantages reversed in the last respect, at least, would the Nationalists be weaker and the cause of Ireland worse situated? I think not.

"Having defined the relative positions and strength of the two great parties in Irish politics, no other conclusion can be come to but this: that until an understanding, base of public union, or common public platform, is established between them, the Executive faction, *alias* Castle government, will influence, direct, and domineer the official and public life of Ireland,

and her people 'may whistle to the winds for self-government, or escape from the Saxon's control.'

"Now let us put prejudices one side and honestly look at facts, and we will find that parliamentary action during the past few years has been trying to clothe itself in the garb of honesty, notwithstanding numerous instances of betrayal of trust. Mr. Isaac Butt, in giving a Federal complexion to Ireland's constitutional holiday garment for Westminster parade, was endeavoring to make Imperial broadcloth out of Irish frieze, and he has become politically bankrupt, in consequence of failure. Abstract this disagreeable feature, together with the un-Irish conduct and treachery of some of Mr. Butt's supporters, from the action of Irish members in the House of Commons during the past few years, and we will find a more national and determined stand taken for Ireland and against the government than at any former period in that assembly. Seeing this, finding large classes of our people boasting of it, and recognizing the fact that the centre figure of this stubborn attitude in an hostile assembly, has, in the small space of four years, become the most popular and most trusted of Irishmen, is there not something good can come out of Nazareth, after all? If so, let us see how it can be increased.

"For the present good of Ireland, and as a policy of expediency, I, as a Nationalist, could support the following programme consistently with my own principles and Ireland's present wants:—

"'1st. The first and indispensable requisite in a representative of Ireland in the Parliament of England to be a public profession of his belief in the inalienable right of the Irish people to self-government, and recognition of the fact that want of self-government is the chief want of Ireland.

"'2d. An exclusive Irish representation, with the view of exhibiting Ireland to the world in the light of her people's opinions and national aspirations, together with an uncompromising opposition to the government upon every prejudiced or coercive policy.

"'3d. A demand for the immediate improvement of the land system by such a thorough change as would prevent the peasantry of Ireland from being its victims in the future. This change to form the preamble of a system of small proprietorships similar to what at present obtains in France, Belgium, and Prussia. Such land to be purchased or held directly from the State. To ground this demand upon the reasonable fact that, as the land of Ireland formerly belonged to the people (being but nominally held in trust for them by chiefs or heads of clans elected for that among other purposes), it is the duty of the government to give compensation to the landlords for taking back that which was bestowed upon their progenitors after being stolen from the people, in order that the State can again become the custodian of the land for the people-owners.

"'4th. Legislation for the encouragement of Irish industries, development of Ireland's natural resources; substitution, as much as practicable, of cultivation for grazing; reclamation of waste lands; protection of Irish fisheries, and improvement of peasant dwellings.

"'5th. Assimilation of the county to the borough franchise, and reform of the grand jury laws, as also those affecting convention in Ireland.

"'6th. A national solicitude on the question of education by vigorous efforts for improving and advancing the same, together with every precaution to be taken against it being made an anti-national one.

"'7th. The right of the Irish people to carry arms.'

"It will be objected by some, that to meddle in parliamentary action, no matter how honest, is contrary to Nationalist principles, and therefore censurable. No man likes to put his hands in pitch; but if he is tarred and feathered for no fault of his own, and against his will, he must clean himself as best he can. The pitch of English rule on Ireland will not be removed by kid-gloved indifference and straight-laced, lofty patriotic consistency; it is better to commence scrubbing it off wherever more can be otherwise added. It will be again objected that if a strong National party were sent to Parliament, and it succeeded in obtaining some remedial measures, the people of Ireland would be contented with what they would thus obtain, and cease to strive for separation. Granted that a portion of our people would 'rest and be thankful' for a better condition of affairs than they live under at present; but would the Nationalist party be so? If it would, it is not the real representative of Ireland's past; if it would not, there is no earthly justification for an abstention from endeavoring to benefit even those that would accept the situation, when side by side with their social and political advancement would be that of those who would not take it as a final settlement of the question.

"It is showing a strange want of knowledge of England's hatred and jealousy of Ireland to suppose that a government formed from any of the English parties would ever concede *all* that could satisfy the desires of the Irish people; and to ground an apprehension upon such an improbable contingency is a mistake.

"Again, the supposition that the spirit of Irish nationality, which has combated against destruction for seven centuries, only awaits a few concessions from its baffled enemy to be snuffed out thereby, does not speak highly for those who hold that opinion of its frailty. In my opinion, we may expect to hear no more of 'the cause' when the genius of Tipperary shall carve the Rock of Cashel into a statue of Judge Keogh, and Croagh Patrick shall walk to London to render homage to the Duke of Connaught. Every chapter of our history, every ensanguined field upon which our forefathers died in defence of that cause, every name in the martyrology of Ireland, from Fitzgerald to Charles McCarthy, proclaim the truth of Meagher's impassioned words: 'From the Irish mind the inspiring thought that there once was an Irish Nation self-chartered and self-ruled can never be effaced; the burning hope that there will be one again can never be extinguished.'

"With these convictions, and the consummation of such hopes predestined by an indestructible cause and imperishable national principles, Irish Nationalists can, without fear of compromising such principles, grapple with West-Britonism on its own ground, and strangle its efforts to imperialize Ireland. The popular party in Ireland has a right to participate in everything concerning the social and political condition of the country; to compete with the constitutional and other parties who cater for public support, and stamp in this manner its Nationalist convictions and principles upon everything Irish, from a local board of poor-law guardians to a (by circumstances compulsory) representation in an alien parliament.

"No party has a right to call itself National, which neglects resorting to all and every justifiable means to end the frightful misery under which our land-crushed people groan. It is exhibiting a callous indifference to the state of social degradation to which the power of the landlords of Ireland has sunk our peasantry to ask them to 'plod on in sluggish misery from sire to son, from age to age,' until we, by force of party and party selfishness, shall free the country. It is playing the part of the Levite who passed by the man plundered by thieves. It is seeing a helpless creature struggling against suffocation in a ditch, and making no immediate effort to save him. If we refuse to play the part of the Good Samaritan to those who have fallen among robber landlords, other Irishmen will not. The cry has gone forth, 'Down with the land system that has cursed and depopulated Ireland'; and this slogan cry of war has come from the Constitutionalists.

"In the name of the common good of our country, its honor, interests, social and political, let the two great Irish parties agree to differ on party principles, while emulating each other in service to our impoverished people. Let each endeavor to find points upon which they can agree, instead of trying to discover quibbles whereon to differ. Let a centre-platform be adopted, resting on a broad, generous, and comprehensive Nationalism, which will invite every earnest Irishman upon it. The manhood-strength of Ireland could then become an irresistible power, standing ready at its post, while the whole Irish race, rallying to the support of such a platform, would cry —

"'*We want the land that bore us!*
We'll make that want our chorus;
And we'll have it yet, tho' hard to get,
By the heavens bending o'er us.'"

CHAPTER VII.

WHY THE FARMERS WERE NOT FENIANS.—RADICAL REVOLUTIONISTS AND THE LAND QUESTION.—THE "NEW DEPARTURE" EXPOUNDED AND DEFENDED BY JOHN DEVOY.—THE ABOLITION OF LANDLORDISM.

"Wert thou all that I wish thee,—great, glorious and
free,
First flower of the earth, and first gem of the sea,—
I might hail thee with prouder, with happier brow,
But, oh! could I love thee more deeply than now?"

—MOORE.

IRELAND had long wasted her national strength by division of her people into parties, each striving its own way to do the most good for their common country, but each opposing the policy of the other. In the beginning of Fenianism, James Stephens refused co-operation from leading Irishmen of Constitutional principles, such as George Henry Moore, John Martin and P. J. Smyth; and later, the radical revolutionists refused to co-operate with the Home Rulers. "That there has been," says Mr. Davitt, in his lecture, "an unmethodical application of energies, or rather a reckless waste of Irish national strength in this long contest, is but too patent. We grasped at liberty," he says, "in the intoxication of sincerity, and blindly discarded every practical consideration. We 'resolved,' and 'swore,' and 'determined,' to 'avenge Ireland's wrongs, but took no essential method to win her liberty. . . We refused to shelter ourselves behind the walls of expediency, or to employ any of the justifiable means by which a weak people might utilize their strength, and we therefore marched into the open plain inviting destruction."

The Irish farmers and land-holders, as a class, were not engaged in the Fenian movement, and it is well known that no Irish movement can succeed without the co-operation of this body. Why were not the farmers in the Fenian movement, or in the revolutionary organization continued since that time? Mr. Davitt shows that the Constitutionalists promised more to the farmer than the Revolutionists. The latter told him that when Ireland is free, he would own his land; this appeared rather a far-off benefit and for which he would have to risk life and property. The Constitutionalists said they would compel England to make land laws that would give him a right to his farm, and a means to bring up his children in a better manner; this appeared a more immediate benefit, and there was little risk in supporting an open agitation. A national movement, therefore, that would adopt a platform, broad, liberal, and comprehensive, on which all shades of political opinion could unite, and that would offer redress and security to the farmers, was much needed, and the Irish radical Revolutionists in America were the first to make the overtures which have been since crowned with almost unhoped for success.

In the beginning, much opposition was given to "the New Departure "as it was called. The Dublin *Irishman* condemned the idea that patriots should vote for members of Parliament, and ridiculed the presence of a *Nationalist* in Wesminster. The "Executive of the I. R. B.," or a body calling itself by that name — for most certainly it was *not* the "Supreme Council" of the I. R. B.— issued a manifesto condemning the "New Departure;" and James Stephens, who had recently arrived from Paris, in an interview with a reporter in New York in February, '79, on being asked whether the "New Departure" would not take the place of the Home Rule movement, and keep the Irish people's minds in the groove of constitutional agitation and action, replied: "Not at all; this New Departure has failed. *It never could succeed.* The Home Rule movement sprung up after the defeat of the Fenian physical force movement at that time, and Nationalists joined it because, temporarily dispirited by this failure, they hoped such a movement might accomplish something. In this they have been wofully disappointed, and the fall of the Home Rule party rang the death knell of constitutional agitation among Irish Nationalists." Such has *not* proved to be the case, as subsequent events have shown.

When such men as Davitt, Devoy, and Breslin engage in a project of this kind, they do not do so to fail easily; they promised the co-operation of the revolutionary party on certain conditions. We see how they have verified that promise. While Davitt showed the revolutionists the solid and sensible reasons why they should for *once* join in a constitutional attempt by the whole people, to achieve redress of wrongs which might by this means be attained, that the whole farming class of Ireland could be woke up to a proper patriotic feeling, and won over to the national cause, Devoy ably mapped out the plan of action to be pursued, and defended the policy of the "New Departure" in the following able and comprehensive communication, published in the Dublin *Freeman's Journal*, which circulates all over Ireland. This was the first great impetus given to the new movement. Such an emanation from a man of *proved* patriotism, of sincerity, honor, and ability, had a wonderful effect both in Ireland and in the United States, where it was shortly afterwards re-published. It effected the object for which it was written. We give the letter in full as it appeared in the *Freeman*, as the opening cleared by Mr. Devoy for the great Land League movement, which speedily followed, should never be forgotton by his fellow-countrymen: —

"NEW YORK, Dec. 11, 1878.

"*To the* Editor *of the* Dublin *Freeman.*—Sir: The frequent mention made of my name in the Irish press in connection with the so-called 'New Departure' proposed by a portion of the Irish National party, and the very serious errors which have been committed in interpreting the scope and meaning of that proposition, must be my excuse for obtruding myself on the attention of the Irish public. As the *Freeman* has published so much in connection with thi controversy, I hope you will enable me to state the case from the standpoint of those responsible for the original proposition.

"The question whether the advanced Irish National party—the party of Separation—should continue the policy of isolation from the public life of the country which was inaugurated some twenty years ago by James Stephens and his associates, or return to older methods—methods as old, at least, as the days of the United Irishmen—is agitating the minds of Irish Nationalists on both sides of the Atlantic just now; and certainly no small incident has aroused such wide discussion in Ireland for many a day, as the publication of the views of the exiled Nationalists resident in New York on the subject. This shows conclusively the importance of the action proposed. All intelligent Irishmen feel that the entrance into the every-day political life of the country of a large class of men with strong opinions and habits of organization, but who have hitherto held aloof from it, or only acted on rare occasions when a principle was considered at stake, would be an event that would largely influence the future of Ireland. The eagerness with which the subject has been discussed by all parties would prove this if it were not otherwise sufficiently evident; but, as might be expected, much difference of opinion exists as to the direction that future would take. Almost every newspaper in Ireland which has written on the subject, almost every man who has expressed his opinion, has done so from a purely partisan standpoint. There have, it is true, been notable exceptions, and on the whole, the reception of the proposals has been encouraging to the proposers.

"As it is a question of public policy, to be carried out, if adopted, within the limits of existing law, it can bear the fullest discussion. In fact, the more it is criticised the better, provided the criticisms be based upon actual facts — the propositions made and the views expressed by the proposers — not on data supplied by the fancy of the critics, or phantoms of sinister motives conjured up by diseased imaginations. Fair and free discussion of the public policy proposed for the acceptance of the National party by men who certainly have a right to their opinions and some claim to a voice in the decision, fair and free discussion of their motives in proposing it, as one of those responsible. I am prepared to meet in a frank and friendly way.

"To those who resort to misrepresentation and insinuations of unworthy motives, I will only say that my motives are sufficiently known to my fellow-workers, and I do not propose to defend them. They will bear comparison with those of some who have been rather hasty in resorting to personalities. The policy proposed must stand or fall on its own merits. I would remind some of my 'Nationalist' critics, however, that misrepresentation on the part of men who live by scribbling cheap treason, and who never stir a finger to do any real service to the cause for which they profess such zeal, may, if persevered in, provoke a retaliation that would be somewhat inconvenient to them, and not at all edifying. This is all the notice I propose to take just now of the 'consistent' patriots who pen the twaddle about 'Fenians in Parliament,' and the silly impertinences about 'American babble,'

"That the discussion aroused on both sides of the Atlantic by the proposal of a 'New Departure' has done good, I am prepared to admit; but so many mistakes have been made on your side of the water, and such an amount of misrepresentation indulged in, that a clearer explanation of the objects sought to be attained and the principles professed by the proposers is necessary to enable the Irish people to form a correct judgment on the question. I am convinced that on the judgment formed on this question by the Irish people, and on the action that judgment will dictate, depends Ireland's political future for many years to come. Even at the risk of having merely ambitious motives attributed to me, I am determined that some recent utterances of mine on the subject of Parliamentary and Municipal representation, and on the Land Question, which have been rather freely commented upon, shall be fully understood, at least by those who care to understand them, so that they may not be made the excuse for preventing action approved of in theory by the majority of Irish Nationalists, but not carried into effect through fear of affording help to a certain class of trading politicians. These politicians, it is feared, might succeed in turning the National party into a mere machine for their own advancement if the 'New Departure' were adopted, or if any other public policy were determined upon. I am as much opposed to allowing the National party to be used by worthless aspirants for parliamentary honors as I am to see it made an instrument for the circulation of the nauseating cant about nationality served up by trading speculations calling themselves 'National' newspapers, or that its only public appearances should be when called to applaud the bunkum of 'orators' who keep their tongues and their hands rather quiet when times of danger come. There is intelligence enough in the National party to save it from the parliamentary shams, just as it has intelligence enough to stamp as quacks and charlatans those who talk of fighting and sedulously avoid preparation for it. I am convinced that these fears of the Parliamentarians, where they are honestly entertained, are groundless now, while I fully admit there was ample excuse for them in the past.

"The object aimed at by the advanced National party — the recovery of Ireland's national independence and the severance of all political connection with England — is one that would require the utmost efforts and the greatest sacrifices on the part of the whole Irish people. *Unless the whole Irish people, or the great majority of them, undertake the task, and bend their whole energies to its accomplishment — unless the best intellect, the financial resources, and the physical strength of the nation be enlisted in the effort — it can never be realized.* Even with all these things in our favor the difficulties in our way would be enormous; but if firmly united and ably led, we could overcome them, and the result achieved would be worth the sacrifice. I am not one of those who despair of Ireland's freedom, and am as much in favor of continuing the struggle to-day as some of those who talk loudest against constitutional agitation.

"I am convinced that the whole Irish people can be enlisted in an effort to free their native land, and that they have within themselves the power to overcome all obstacles in their way. I feel satisfied that Ireland could maintain her existence as an independent nation, become a respectable power in Europe, provide comfortably for a large population within her borders, and rival England in commerce and manufactures. I contend she can never attain the development to which her geographical position, her natural resources, and the moral and intellectual gifts of her people entitle her without becoming complete mistress of her own destinies, and severing the connection with England. But I am also convinced that one section of the people alone can never win independence, and no political party, no matter how devoted or determined, can ever win the support of the whole people if they never come before the public and take no part in the everyday life of the country. I have often said it before, and I repeat it now again, that a mere conspiracy will never free Ireland. I am not arguing against conspiracy, but only pointing out the necessity of Irish Nationalists taking whatever public action for the advancement of the national cause they may find within their reach — such action as will place the aims and objects of the National party in a more favorable light before the world, and help to win the support of the whole Irish people. . . . .

"Those who propose the 'New Departure' merely

want to provide good, wholesome work for the National party, which will have the effect of bringing all sections of Nationalists into closer relation by giving them a common ground to work upon, a platform really broad enough for all to stand upon, demanding no sacrifice of principle, no abandonment of Ireland's rights. They have long felt the necessity for some such action, and imagine they can see in the present state of parties in Ireland the best opportunity for proposing it which has yet presented itself.

"Some of the arguments used in favor of the policy of isolation are very plausible, some of them very absurd; but there is not one sufficiently strong to justify a continuance of it, under existing circumstances. When used by men who are, and have been for years, simply doing nothing, they do not deserve to be treated with common respect, as in the case of earnest men who practise what they preach. The proof that these arguments do not convince the people — not even the rank and file of the Nationalists — is to be found in the incontrovertible fact that the great majority of those who believe in independence, and who have the franchise, vote at all elections.

"Even if there were a 'traditional policy,' a 'beaten path,' some of us would take the liberty of going outside of one or the other, if by doing so we thought we could advance the national cause. For myself, I must plead guilty to a strong disinclination to walk in the 'narrows,' 'paths,' or 'tracks,' or 'grooves," marked out for my guidance by people whose ability for leadership, whose earnestness and whose judgment, I have the best reason to doubt. I yield to no man living in the lengths I am prepared to go to get rid of foreign domination in Ireland, but I refuse to be guided by the narrow dogmatism, through the instrumentality of which a few pigmies managed for a sad decade or so, to retain a leadership for which neither nature nor training ever fitted them. I want to see the national will consulted through the only means at present available, and when the country speaks I am not afraid of the result, for I am convinced that Ireland desires independence to-day as ardently as ever, and that nothing less will ever satisfy her. But it is simply absurd to ask the Irish people to follow a dangerous political course with their eyes blindfolded, and trusting implicitly in guides, of whom they know nothing. I am willing to trust the people, and think the issue is safe in their hands. When the country is convinced of the necessity for vigorous and decided action, I am not one of those who think the responsibility will be shirked. It was not the people who failed in recent National movements, but those who, without the capacity, the judgment, or the courage necessary to lead the people in times of trial and danger, assumed the responsibility and broke down when the ordeal came. The Irish people have had more than enough of this kind of thing, and want no more self-appointed leaders or men laboring under a hallucination that they were born with a mission to regenerate them. . .

"The advanced National party in Ireland has never had a clearly-defined policy, further than a declaration in favor of independence, or, sometimes, an independent republic, to be obtained by force of arms. The people have never been told the kind of an Ireland we should have if the making of it depended on the Nationalists, or how the Nationalists proposed to grapple with any of the burning social and political questions which would demand solution if the country were freed to-morrow. The national sentiment of the people alone was appealed to, especially in the Fenian movement, while their judgment as to the capacity of the men who proposed to regenerate them was left entirely out of the question. Of course, the people had many opportunities of forming an opinion on these points through public speeches and writings; but in this respect the constitutional agitators, honest or dishonest, had many advantages over the extreme Nationalists, inasmuch as public profession of their principles or intentions brought the latter into conflict with the law. The lack of political training and of practical acquaintance with public business — such even as could be acquired by membership of a town council — has always told heavily against the Nationalists, while their absence from such bodies left the whole country in the hands of the West Britons, who are only a miserable minority. This enabled the minority not alone to speak and act in the name of the country, but gave its members the means of strengthening and consolidating their party and crushing out their opponents. The more this is examined the more ruinous this policy of isolation will appear, and the more advantages to be derived from an organized, steady, and persistent effort to get possession of those local bodies will be seen. While I admit that Nationalists now vote at these elections, I deny that they act as a body, or with any settled plan or purpose.

"With the majority of these bodies in our possession, even without the parliamentary represention, we should be in a position to do many things we can only dream of now. With the municipal bodies and men of spirit and determination as parliamentary representatives, backed by the country and by millions of the Irish race scattered over the world, there would be no necessity to go to London either to beg or to obstruct, and Irish Nationalists would have no more Tallaghts or 'cabbage-gardens' flung in their faces.

"Can this be accomplished? I claim it can; but only by a combination between all sections of Irish Nationalists — between all those who are dissatisfied with the existing order of things, and desire self-government in any form. The Home Rulers cannot do it, for no one among the people really believes in Mr. Butt's so-called 'Federal' scheme. The Nationalists cannot honestly support the scheme; for it gives to the English Parliament the prerogative, which belongs to the Irish people, of calling the proposed local parliament into existence and defining its powers, therefore having the right to abolish it by a simple act. It is a concession of England's right to rule Ireland.

"The Repealers can never again arouse the enthusiasm of the people; because, though having a strong historical point in their favor, simple Repeal would restore the Irish House of Lords, which few in Ireland would endure now. The Repealers, furthermore, are not organized, and many of them, as well as many weak-kneed Nationalists, support the Home Rulers for want of something better. In fact, the whole rank and file of the Home-Rule party is composed of men who would prefer a larger measure of self-government if it could be obtained.

"The Nationalists could only obtain control of the local bodies and of the parliamentary representation by the adoption of such a broad and comprehensive public policy as would secure the support of that large class of Irishmen who now hold aloof from all parties, but are Nationalists in heart and feeling, and vote for the man or the party that comes nearest to their ideas, and which would further detach from the Home Rule party all who are really in favor of a larger demand than that of Mr. Butt, but who now give the Home Rulers a conditional support.

"The object, however, could be reached much more easily by an honorable compromise. This compromise is only possible by leaving the form of self-government undefined — putting off the definition until a really representative body, with the country at its back, and elected with that mandate, could be assembled and speak in the name of the nation. When the nation speaks, all parties must obey, and a united Irish nation can shape its own destiny. There is no use defining the form of self-government for the mere purpose of bringing forward a motion in Parliament once a year, or once every session, only to be thrown out by a hostile majority; and complete independence cannot be demanded without coming into conflict with the law. As *the battle of Irish freedom must be fought outside Parliament*, and as Home Rulers, Repealers, and Nationalists, all call the form of autonomy they desire 'Self-Government' — as, in addition to this, they agree substantially as to the present needs of Ireland, there should be nothing to prevent them agreeing on a common platform which would bind them together for the common good of the country, till the country itself should speak in such a manner as to command the allegiance of all.

"Such a common platform was suggested in the cable despatch from New York, which has been called the '*New Departure.*' The talk about the 'folly' of publishing the substance of this telegram is almost too silly to waste words upon. It is simply the height of folly to imagine there was anything to be concealed in it. There was nothing proposed which is not strictly within the law, and no man in Ireland would have the slightest reason to fear the consequences of avowing his acceptance of the propositions. They would not bind a member of Parliament to accept the revolutionary policy, nor could he be held responsible for threats or speeches of the proposers in the United States. They simply bind all who accept them to carry them out; and the carrying of them out breaks no British law. It is not an 'alliance' between Home Rulers and Revolutionists which is proposed, but the adoption of a broad and comprehensive public policy, which Nationalists and men of more moderate views could alike support without sacrifice of principle.

"No party, or combination of parties, in Ireland can ever hope to win the support of the majority of the people, except it honestly proposes *a radical reform of the land system.* No matter what may be said in favor of individual landlords, the whole system was founded on robbery and fraud, and has been perpetuated by cruelty, injustice, extortion, and hatred of the people. The men who got small farms in the times of confiscation settled down in the country, and their descendants, no matter what their political party, are now 'bone of our bone'—have become Irish—and perform a useful function in the land. No one thinks of disturbing them. If the landlords had become

Irish, and treated the people with humanity, the original robbery might be forgiven—though a radical change in the tenure of land must come of itself some day; but when, as a class, they have simply done England's work of rooting out the Irish people; when the history of landlordism is simply a dark story of heartless cruelty, of artificial famines, of evictions, of rags and squalid misery, there is no reason why we should forget that the system was forced upon us by England, and that the majority of the present landlords are the inheritors of the robber horde sent over by Elizabeth and James I., by Cromwell and William of Orange, to garrison the country for England. It is the interest of Ireland that *the land should be owned by those who till the soil*, and this could be reached without even inflicting hardship on those who deserve no leniency at the hands of the Irish people. A solution of the Land Question has been reached, to a large extent, in France, in Prussia, and in Belgium, by enabling the occupiers to purchase their holdings. Let the Irish landlords be given a last chance of settling the Irish Land Question amicably in this manner, or wait for a solution in which they shall have no part. Let a beginning be made with the absentees, the English lords, and the London companies who hold stolen land in Ireland, and there will be enough of work for some years to come. *Let evictions be stopped at all hazards*, and the rooting-out process come to an end. But I shall be told the English Parliament will never do any of these things. Then, I say, these things must only wait till an Irish Parliament can do them better; but in the mean time good work will have been done, sound principles inculcated, and the country aroused and organized.

"To those who are alarmed at language like this, in regard to the Land Question, I would say: Look at France, at Prussia, and at Belgium, and you will find that the secret of their prosperity lies in the number of tillers of the soil who own their holdings. Listen to the mutterings of the coming storm *in England*, and ask yourselves what is going to become of the land monopoly after a few more years of commercial and manufacturing depression—a depression sure to continue, because the causes of it are on the increase. The English are a very practical and a very selfish people, and will not let any fine sentiment stand in the way when they think it is their interest to redistribnte the land. What, may I ask, would become of the Irish landlords—especially the rack-renting, evicting ones—in case of a social convulsion in England? It is a question which they themselves must decide within the next few years. With them, or without them, the question will be settled before long, and many who now think the foregoing assertions extravagant will consider them very moderate indeed, by and by. The education question is only approached, at present, from a purely religious stand-point. There is no reason why it should not be treated also from a utilitarian point of view, not to speak of a national one. The curse of Ireland for several centuries past, after foreign rule—indeed, as a direct result of foreign rule—is sectarianism. It is the interest of the Irish people that the rising generation of all creeds should receive a sound, practical training, that will fit them for the battle of life, and enable them to compete with the young men of countries hitherto more favored in that respect. The natural resources of Ireland will never be developed by men trained as the majority of the present generation have been. Why not insist on the history of Ireland being taught in all our schools, and on the nationalization of the schools where the Protestants are trained? It cannot be expected that men trained up in anti-Irish ideas will make good Irishmen; nor can it be expected that any large number of Protestants will join any political party which devotes its principal efforts to a purely Catholic object. It is fear of the Catholic majority more than love of England which makes anti-Irish Irishmen of so many of our Protestant fellow-countrymen; and, if they are ever to be won over to the national side, some sacrifice must be made. He must be a dull Irishman indeed who will assert that their aid is not worth having, and anything that is worth having is worth paying for. The price in this case is the exclusion of all sectarian issues from the national platform. This would not produce any miraculous transformation. We must wait for results, but they are sure to come, for the simple reason that it is for the material interest of the Protestants, as well as the Catholics, that Ireland should govern herself.

"If Ireland were free now, one of the first things, after the Land Question, which would demand solution, would be that of county government, and the principle should be laid down in the national programme. The whole people have an interest in the local as well as the national administration, and should have the selection of a county council or board, having much the same powers as the council-general of a French department. The present abortion of county government, called a grand jury, which enables the foreign garrison to look after its own interests at the expense of the people, will not, of course, be abolished by the English Parliament, though it may be tinkered; but its abolition should be demanded, and the principle of the people's right to do their own business through their elected representatives clearly enunciated. While the right to the franchise of every man born on Irish soil, who has not forfeited his rights of citizenship by conviction of a crime against society, should be affirmed, the very least that should be demanded, at present, is the equalization of the Irish franchise with that of England.

"If a programme, such as I have roughly sketched above, were adopted and vigorously carried out, its acceptance made the test for election to all offices in the gift of the electors, and the people thoroughly organized for its support, the country would soon throb with a vigorous and healthy life from end to end, and we should at last begin to see the dawn of our day of liberation. It would give Ireland the materials out of which a national government could be formed which would command the confidence of the Irish people at home and abroad, and the respect of foreign nations. From the very outset it would seriously embarrass the diplomacy of England abroad; and, if carried out with firmness, resolution, and judgment, it would make Ireland count for something in the world, even before she won self-government.

"It has been objected by some very well meaning people that the publication and explanation of this programme is the avowal of designs that England will take good care to provide against; but a little reflection will convince any intelligent man, that the first public step taken as a result of its adoption would clearly indicate the ultimate object. It would be as clear as the noon-day sun to English statesmen; but England has entered on a career in which she cannot stop, and she can no longer treat us as in the past. That vast agglomeration of hostile races and conflicting interests scattered over the world, called the British Empire, has been held together up to the present by favorable circumstances, which are disappearing day by day. It is filled with inflammable material within, and beset with powerful and watchful enemies without. It was constructed for commercial purposes alone, is conducted on merely commercial principles, and cannot stand a great strain. It cannot last, and the crash will come as sure as fate. It has passed the summit of its glory and its infamy, and is now on the descent which leads inevitably to ruin. It is our turn now. Our watchwords should be: *patience*, *prudence*, *courage*, and *sleepless vigilance*. Great events are coming upon us, and on the way we demean ourselves during the next few years, will depend whether we are to play a considerable part in those events, and build up a nation, or sink in the ruins of one of the broken empires of the world.

"No one who looks at the present condition of the East, who considers the inevitable effects of the policy inaugurated by the present government of England, and the settled policy of Russia — no one who has any knowledge of the immense interests at stake — can seriously think that war on one of the largest scales ever witnessed can much longer be averted. In such a war the blood and treasure of Ireland would be poured out like water for the interests of a power which has robbed us of everything, and rooted out and exterminated our people. Ireland would gain nothing by it. It is time to ask, Shall Ireland have something to say about this expenditure of her vital necessaries, and, if it is inevitable, can she find no better way to apply them? This is a question which Home-Rulers as well as Nationalists will be called upon to answer some of these days, and now is the time to make up their minds.

"It was considerations like these which dictated the proposition of the 'New Departure,' and this explanation is given so that the Nationalists of Ireland may not be misled by the misrepresentations and the mistakes which have appeared in print in reference to it. They have as yet come to no decision; and I hope when they do, it will be a wise one. They must, however, beware of those 'friends' of theirs who raise the cry of 'Dictation from America.' No one in America wants to dictate to them; but these gentlemen must pardon me if I respectfully decline the honor of being classed as an 'American.' Respectfully yours,

"JOHN DEVOY."

Hitherto the demands of the Tenant-Righters were mild and moderate. The Tenant League, in 1852, would have been satisfied with a settlement of the Land Question on a basis of fixity of tenure and fair rents. Now, however, the people were set thinking. The Nationalists, in their "New Departure," advanced a bold demand, embracing the abolition of landlordism, and the establishment of a peasant proprietary system in its place. Mr. Parnell, himself a landlord, publicly expressed his conviction that such was the only possible satisfactory settlement of the Land Question, and Tenants' Defence Associations, Farmers' Clubs, and other bodies came forward with similar pronouncements. The farming classes of Ireland began to awake into new life; they saw something tangible and possible offered in the new programme. The opinions expressed in the "New Departure" movement began to take deep root and develop into a powerful agitation, which was begun under the able management of Michael Davitt in May, 1879, in the counties of Mayo, Galway, and Roscommon.

CHAPTER VIII.

HOW IRISH TENANT-FARMERS ARE GROUND DOWN BY THE LANDLORDS.—WHY THE EXTREMISTS SHOULD AID THE LAND AGITATION.—THE LAW OF PRIMOGENITURE EXPLAINED.—THE ANCIENT IRISH LAW OF GAVEL.—STATISTICS RELATING TO LAND AND LANDLORDS.

"Alas! though feudal terror cease, thy children suffer still,
And keener weapons than the sword are raised to waste and kill;
In vain the care-worn peasant's fate appeals to lordly pride;
The humble hopes that toil inspired are ruthlessly denied!"
—REV. GEO. HILL.

THE fulcrum of Irish liberty is the Land Question. It is the prop on which must rest the lever that is to overturn British dominion in Ireland! Two-thirds of the population live on the land, and have no other means of existence. Ireland is bereft of manufactures and all other sources that might give employment to those who are driven from cultivation of the farms; therefore the people must cling to their holdings, though they may be rack-rented and subjected to a thousand petty tyrannies by their feudal taskmasters, —the landlords. If they throw up their farms, nothing remains but the emigrant ship, the *chance* of a laborer's precarious wages in the towns, or possibly, as frequently happens, the poor-house may be their doom; there is no more land to be hired, unless they happen to have plenty of money, and pay an exorbitant "fine" to a landlord to get it "over other tenants' heads."

The projectors of the Land League acted wisely in selecting this vital question as the issue for a new trial of strength with England. It proved a touchstone that at once called into action the entire nation, and enlisted the sympathies of the people; and the dullest can see—if they want to—that it is or can be made a means towards a great end. The condition of the Irish tenant-farmer since the substitution of an English feudal tenure for the Brehon tribal usages has been one of great suffering. They have been ground down to a serfdom that left them no choice but to bear it or ~ve. The Irish landlord has always exacted the last farthing which the land could yield after giving a miserable sustenance to the tiller, whose sweat brought the acres into fertility. He rarely ever considered or acknowledged that the tenant had rights in the soil,—even when the latter by unceasing and almost superhuman toil cultivated the sterile waste, the mountain slope, or the bog into a garden of productiveness. No! the tenant had no right, but the right to work and improve the land, so that the rent might be raised, and raised, until human or superhuman labor could wring no more from the soil; then, and only then, was the standard rent fixed by the Irish landlord. Was this ghoul-like absorption of the fruits of the toil of sweat and blood of the farmer the only grievance he had to bear from his task-master,—almost owner? By no means: the landlord was the *law*; for whatever there was of it he administered! He was the magistrate, judge, and jury. He controlled the courts, the prisons, the grand jury, the poor-law boards. He was the watchful sentinel of hated British power in a subject country. "His Honor" was "the master," whom it would be a daring risk to displease or offend.

The Irish landlord had less consideration for his tenants than a Virginian planter had for his slaves. If the rent was not forthcoming, no matter if the crop failed or not; if a member of the tenant's family married contrary to the "rules of the estate;" if the tenant dared to vote for a member of Parliament contrary to his landlord's will; if a tenant killed game on the lands "preserved" for the landlord's pleasure, or if another offered over the tenant's head and paid a "fine," or a larger rent, for the lands; if, in fact, he acted in any manner contrary to the pleasure of "His Honor," the landlord,—out on the roadside went he and his family, to starve or die; and, if any other tenant on the property offered shelter to the unfortunates, out he went also. The farmers and their families were reduced to absolute submission to the land-owner's will: if they displeased him, the punishment was a terrible one.

From 1793 to 1829, during the existence of the Forty-shilling Freehold Act, which gave a voting power to tenants of that rating, the landlords granted leases for life of small patches of land to large numbers of the people, in order to create a voting power,—the tenant being expected, of course, to vote at his landlord's beck; but, after the act was abolished, the votes being lost, they swept the people and their families off the land; and from that time to the present the "Crowbar Brigade" has been busy at work depopulating the country. Why have we so many millions of our race scattered through the United States, Canada, the South American republics, Australia, Africa, *in England even*, and over the entire habitable globe? The Irish landlord can best answer the question. He has been a vulture whose talons clutched the throat of Irish industry, progressiveness, and liberty, strangling every attempt to keep pace with the progress of civilization. It is time to shake off the foul parasite, and give humanity a chance to enjoy the fruits of the soil, which are produced by God's sunshine and man's sweat. The Irish tenant-farmer has been blamed for not being as ready as those living in the towns to join revolutionary movements. Who can blame him when the facts we have mentioned are borne in mind? The landlord was watching him, and for his family's sake he kept aloof.

The first real step towards Irish liberty is the destruction of the power that keeps the people bound down, rendering them slaves to a class that really *is* the British garrison of Ireland. Loose the grip of Irish landlordism, destroy the influence it exercises over the masses, give freedom of action to the farming serf, and Britain will the sooner lose her hold on the entire nation.

The promoters of the Land League played for a great stake, and they have won it. They showed the tenants how to right their own wrongs, without begging for legislation from a British Parliament, and, ere the crusade begun by Michael Davitt on the Mayo Hills had had time fully to develop, the British Ministry has been compelled to step in and offer terms of settlement to the tenant farmers. The tillers of the soil were thoroughly aroused: when once shown the way towards emancipation, they sprang into life and action, and they were never so near independence as they are to-day. The words of Thomas Davis in his admirable essay on Irish history, though written thirty-five years ago, are applicable to Ireland's position to-day. He says:—

"She is still a serf-nation; but she is struggling wisely and patiently, and is ready to struggle with all the energy her advisers think politic, for liberty. She has ceased to wail: she is beginning to make up a record of English crime and Irish suffering, in order to explain the past, to justify the present, and caution the future. She begins to study the past,—not to acquire a beggar's eloquence in petition, but a hero's wrath in strife. She no longer tears and parades her wounds, to win her smiter's mercy; and now she should look upon her breast and say, 'That wound makes me distrust, and this makes me guard, and they all will make me steadier to resist, or, if all else fails, fiercer to avenge.' Thus will Ireland do naturally and honorably. Our spirit has increased,—our liberty is not far off."

Charles Gavan Duffy, in his recent admirable book "Young Ireland," which should be read by every man and woman of Irish blood, says of the Irish landlord:—

"The condition of the two classes who live by agriculture furnished a singular contrast. The great proprietors were two or three hundred,—the heirs of the undertakers, for the most part, and absentees; the mass of the country was owned by a couple of thousand others, who lived in splendor, and even profusion; and for these the peasant ploughed, sowed, tended, and reaped a harvest which he never shared. Rent in other countries means the surplus after the farmer has been liberally paid for his skill and labor; in Ireland it meant the whole produce of the soil except a potato-pit. If the farmer strove for more, his master knew how to bring him to speedy submission. He could carry away his implements of trade by the law of distress, or rob him of his sole pursuit in life by the law of eviction. He could, and habitually did, seize the stools and pots in his miserable cabin, the blanket that sheltered his children, the cow that gave them nourishment. . . . There was nowhere in Europe a propertied class who did so little for the people and took so much from them. The productive power of an estate was often doubled and quadrupled by the industry of the farmers; and its rental rose accordingly. . . . Rents impossible to be paid were kept on the books of an estate, and arrears duly recorded to hold the tenant in perpetual subjection. For, in addition to his labor, the landlord required his vote, and various menial services. . . . The food of the peasant was potatoes, with a little milk or salt; flesh-meat he rarely tasted, except when he went as a harvest laborer to England 'to earn the rent.'"

Since the great Emancipation and Repeal agitations carried on under the leadership of O'Connell, the tenant-farmers as a class had taken no active part in national affairs; the memories of the wholesale evictions, famine horrors, and scattering of millions of their race all over the world, seemed to produce a torpor from which it was hard to awake them into national life. Fifty years ago, when Ireland emerged from the dark shadow of the penal laws, four millions of the people could neither read nor write, and a million and a half more who could read a little could not write. England, by her atrociously vindictive and inhuman laws, succeeded in legislating the people into ignorance and wretchedness, the like of which never was known in any civilized country; but she did *not* and she *never will* succeed in breaking the spirit or pride of the race, or in destroying their determination to struggle perpetually until their complete national independence is won. They have never yet cried *peccavi*, or relinquished the fight for freedom. If beaten to-day, they will try again to-morrow, always remembering that

> "Freedom's battle once begun,
> Bequeathed from bleeding sire to son,
> Though baffled oft is ever won."

After the Emancipation Act was passed, the schools were again opened; and since then the youth of Ireland have had some chance of opening and enlightening their minds, through that half-fledged system miscalled "national education." The Irish farmers to-day are intelligent, and quick to see, when pointed out to them, the best means for advancing their own condition, and that of the whole country. It was time, therefore, for Davitt and those who began the land agitation with him, to move. They did move, and soon swept aside those who in the beginning opposed the "New Departure." Yet there are many good and sincere Irishmen who, in their detestation of all parliamentary agitation, refuse to participate in or countenance the Land League movement. Well, we cannot all be of the same mind; we should respect the opinions of others, when honest, as well as our own. Certainly, with the history before them of the failures of so many Constitutional attempts to redress Irish wrongs, and, considering that out of the six hundred and fifty members which compose the House of Commons Ireland has a representation of only one hundred and five members, who can be, and always have been, outvoted on questions relating to Ireland, it is only surprising that the number of prominent Irishmen who refuse aid to the present land movement is so inconsiderable. There is that, however, in the issue raised by the National Land League which appears potent enough to call for the support of all shades of Irish political opinion: and it is, that the question can be forced to a proper settlement *outside the legislature*, if the farmers are true to themselves and to the doctrine preached to them by the leaders of the movement; and, further, the farming classes are being reached and politically educated in a manner that could not be otherwise accomplished than through an open agitation; so that, however the Land Question may result, an immense amount of good will have been done in the destruction of the baleful power hitherto exercised by the landlord oligarchy, and in preparing the great mass of the people for sterner work.

Why should Irish Revolutionists — not prepared themselves to strike, and with their opportunity possibly afar off — be satisfied to stand idly by and witness famines decimating the country; the people leaving the shores in tens of thousands, perhaps never to return; in the year 1880 alone, the official returns say that nearly one hundred thousand persons emigrated,— while those who remain are cowed and bowed down under a weight of misery almost unendurable. Better agitate, or do anything that will keep the people at home, improve their condition, and infuse a healthy national spirit into them, than look idly on, waiting for the hour of "England's Difficulty," while the life-blood of the nation is flowing away. This is practical patriotism of the right sort; the Revolutionary party saw and adopted it.

That the time has come for the settlement of the Irish land problem, we cannot doubt. We have the expression of some of the greatest thinking minds of the age, including political economists and British statesmen, in favor of justice being extended to the tiller of the soil — particularly in Ireland — in a fair and equitable manner. John Stuart Mill, in his "Political Economy," says: "'The surplus is what the farmer *can afford* to pay as rent to the landlord; the rent, therefore, which any land will yield is *the excess* of the produce. This . . . is one of the cardinal doctrines of political economy.'" And the following paragraph in favor of a peasant proprietary occurs in p. 201 of the same work: —

"The land of Ireland — the land of any country — belongs to the people of that country. The individuals called land-owners have no right, in morality and justice, to anything but the rent or compensation for its salable value. When the inhabitants of a country quit the country *en masse*, because its government will not make it a place fit for them to live in, the government is judged and condemned. It is the duty of Parliament to reform the land tenure in Ireland.' There is no necessity for depriving the landlords of one farthing of the pecuniary value of their legal rights; but justice requires that the actual cultivators should be enabled to become in Ireland, what they will become in America, proprietors of the soil which they cultivate."

He further says: —

"What has been epigrammatically said in the discussion on 'peculiar burdens' is literally true when applied to them: that the greatest 'burden on land' is the landlords. Returning nothing to the soil, they consume its whole produce, minus the potatoes, strictly necessary to keep the inhabitants from dying of famine; and, when they have any purpose of improvment, the preparatory step usually consists in not leaving even this pittance, but turning out the people to beggary, if not to starvation. When landed property has placed itself on this footing, it ceases to be defensible; and the time has come for making some new arrangement of the matter. When the 'sacredness of property' is talked of, it should always be remembered that any such sacredness does not belong in the same degree to landed property. NO MAN MADE THE LAND. It is the original inheritance of the whole species. Its appropriation is a question of general expediency. When private property in land is not expedient, it is unjust."

England's greatest statesmen have from time to time condemned the Irish land system, and scholars and writers have a million times cried shame! on the country that alone, of all the European kingdoms, continues to enforce and perpetuate a barbarous feudal land code, in the interest of a small minority that grind and rob the millions of their God-given rights. Let us see what this "insolent prerogative" of primogeniture — as the historian Gibbon calls it — means, and contrast it with the law of *gavel*, which was the original law in vogue amongst the Irish before they fell under the blasting influence of British rule. Prior to the English invasion, the Irish people knew nothing of absolute ownership in land. The lands belonged to the clans: the chief merely held as trustee, or manager, for the sept; and, if by any act of his he became dispossessed, the rights of the people were in no way affected. The law of *gavel*, which emanated from the tribunal of Tara—an assembly of the rulers and learned men of the tribes throughout Ireland, which met triennially in the Parliament of Tara — obliged a rich parent at his death to divide his property, share and share alike, amongst his children. This system was the wisest and best that could be devised; for, as the population increased, each person had an equal share provided for him, which placed him above dependence on others. The subdivision of property among the masses was a security to the entire people. On the other hand, the tendency of the celebrated *baron law* of primogeniture — one of the curses that followed the English invasion into Ireland — is to make beggars and paupers of the masses of the people. This law was instituted in England in the eleventh century by William the Conquerer, and subsequently became the governing law of the landed property in Ireland acquired by the invaders through confiscation and plunder of the natives. The law of primogeniture prohibits the owners of estates from selling any portion of them, dividing them amongst children, or in any way disposing of them, except by the aristocracy-sustaining regulation which it prescribes, of compelling the parent at his death to bequeath the whole to his eldest son, to the exclusion of his other children. The canon of the common law touching descents which pertains to this subject is, that if a man dies seized of real estate of which he had the absolute ownership, without having made any disposition of it by his last will, the whole descends to his heir at law; and this heir at law is that one of his representatives who is the eldest male among those who are in the same degree of kindred. The tendency of primogeniture, therefore, is to keep the land in the possession of a few, who are powerless to dispose of it except as stipulated. They hold the estates for life, and, as too frequently happens, if the inheritor under this system becomes embarrassed through extravagance, dissipation, gambling, or any of the hundred landlord vices, not being able to sell any portion of the estate to satisfy his creditors, he screws the last farthing of rack-rent out of his unfortunate tenants. He will make his life-interest as profitable as he possibly can,— no matter who suffers.

As most of the great Irish estates are inherited under the law of primogeniture and entail, it will be readily seen what misery is produced by that system, when the owners are unscrupulous and unsympathetic with the masses of the people.

The entire of Ireland under land and water contains a total in acres of	20,819,947
Of this there is under water	627,761
Giving a total acreage in land of . . .	20,192,186

This acreage is distributed as follows: —

Under towns, waste, bog, mountain, etc., .	4,153,854
Under plantation.	324,990
Under tillage	5,642,057
Under pasture	10,071,285
	20,192,186

Now let us see how the land of Ireland is divided among the people: —

Proprietors.		Acres.		Acres.
110	holding	20,000 and over,	own	4,151,142
192	"	20,000 to 10,000	"	2,607,719
440	"	10,000 " 5,000	"	3,071,471
1,246	"	5,000 " 2,000	"	3,872,611
1,773	"	2,000 " 1,000	"	2,474,756
2,633	"	1,000 " 500	"	1,871,171
2,271	"	500 " 300	"	884,493
1,916	"	300 " 200	"	471,646
2,788	"	200 " 100	"	408,699
2,082	"	100 " 50	"	152,004
1,460	"	50 " 25	"	52,804
2,377	"	under 25	"	29,056
19,288				20,047,572

The total government yearly valuation of this acreage for taxation purposes is £10,182,681. These 19,288 landed proprietors are classed as follows in the official returns: —

		Acres Represented.
Proprietors resident in Ireland	10,431;	14,095,813
Absentee proprietors . . .	2,973	5,129,169
Public Companies in England, and Proprietary Institutions . .	161	584,327
Proprietors of under 100 acres, not classed	5,982	236,873
	19,547	20,046,182

The Census of 1871, which was the last taken — that of 1881 not being yet published—gives the total population of Ireland at that time as 5,412,377. The *estimated* population for 1879 is 5,299,209; a steady decrease shows itself in the returns each year.

It will be observed from the foregoing figures, that although Ireland is almost exclusively an agricultural country, in which about two-thirds of the population depend on the land for a living, yet only a little over one-fourth of the land is under tillage. The reason for this is the tendency of late by the landlords to create large grazing farms, and their prohibition in leases and agreements against tenants "breaking the land" for agricultural purposes. In carrying out the programme of the amalgamation of small farms into large stock-raising pastures, the landlords have swept away in a wholesale manner tens of thousands of families from the land, and depopulated whole villages, to such an extent that in many parts of the country it is difficult to get sufficient help in the spring and autumn to work the portion of the land which is under cultivation. The object clearly was to get rid of the people, and supply their places with cattle; it being easier to collect the rents from a few large stock-raisers than from numerous tenants with large families depending for support on the wretched pittance left after paying rack-rent and taxes. The extreme poverty and dependence of the masses can be seen at a glance, through the figures giving the number of landed monopolists: 110 persons own one-fifth of the whole country, or over four millions of acres; 192 persons own over two and a half millions of acres; 440 own over three millions of acres; 1,246 own nearly four millions of acres. The total of these few figures shows that nearly fourteen millions of acres are owned absolutely by 1,878 individuals, while nearly four and a half millions more are owned by 4,406 persons; this gives an ownership of over eighteen millions of acres to 6,284 landed proprietors. Of these large land-owners 2,973 are absentees who hold over one-fourth of the entire Island, or five million one hundred and twenty-nine thousand one hundred and sixty-seven acres, and who rarely—if ever—visit their properties. For the millions of pounds in rack-rents which they screw from the farmers, not one cent ever goes back to be expended in Ireland.

From our analysis of these official figures it can be seen that any hope of progress or prosperity in Ireland depends entirely on the destruction of the law of primogeniture and entail; the taking of the lands from the few aristocrats that hold them by law, who have been a curse and a blight for centuries on one of the fairest and most productive countries on the globe; and the creation of a peasant proprietary. "No man made the

LAND." It was made by God for the people, and the people should own the soil they till and enrich by their sweat and labor.

CHAPTER IX.

DAVITT'S RETURN TO IRELAND.—THE AGITATION BEGUN IN MAYO.—DEATH OF ISAAC BUTT.—PRONOUNCEMENTS BY THE CATHOLIC CLERGY.—FAMINE CLOUDS APPEAR ON THE HORIZON.—ARCHBISHOP MACHALE CONDEMNS THE LEADERS OF THE AGITATION.—MICHAEL DAVITT'S REPLY.

"The West's asleep, the West's asleep;
Alas! and well may Erin weep
That Connaught lies in slumber deep.
But hark! some voice like thunder spake:
'*The West's awake! the West's awake!*'"
—THOMAS DAVIS.

MICHAEL DAVITT returned to Ireland from the United States in the latter part of December, 1879, and, ere many months had elapsed, the Land League and anti-rent banner was flung to the breeze in Mayo. He spent the first few months after his arrival in arranging his plans, and organizing for the great meetings which immediately followed. On Sunday, April 20, the first monster meeting of the tenant-farmers of Mayo, Galway, and Roscommon, was held on a plain within a few miles of Claremorris. It numbered from 15,000 to 20,000 people, and was considered the greatest ever held in the province of Connaught. Five hundred horsemen wearing green emblems were present. Mr. James Daly, P.L.G., presided. The land and rent question was ably discussed by J. O'Connor Power, M.P., John Ferguson, of Glasgow, J. J. Louden, of Westport, and other speakers of ability. The grievances under which the tenant-farmers labored were represented, and resolutions pledging those present to the cause of land-law reform were adopted. At this time the distress caused by three years of bad harvests was beginning to make itself felt among the small farmers, and the land-owning cormorants were beginning to swoop down on their prey. At the quarter sessions held in Swineford in April, '79, fifty-four ejectment decrees were granted for non-payment of rent, only one year's rent in each case being due.

The Dublin *Freeman's Journal*, in the beginning of May, alluding to the distress then manifesting itself throughout the country, said: "Scarcely a day passes which does not bring new proof of the magnitude of the distress which has overtaken the agricultural classes throughout the country. At all the recent meetings of the Farmers' Clubs this was the most absorbing topic of conversation, and numerous private letters confirm the melancholy tale. At no period since the famine years has anything like the present collapse been felt. The distress is not confined to a district or a county: it is general and searching. It has already plunged countless families into difficulties little short of ruin,—difficulties which, in many cases, it will cost many years of prosperity to recover. We have it on the most indisputable authority that the farming classes throughout the country have had in numberless cases to plunge heavily into debt to keep themselves afloat, the rent in many cases having been met by the ruinous means of bills and loans."

The agitation, therefore, began just in time to counteract the terrible effects of the famine, which became general throughout the West the following autumn and winter; and also to interpose between the landlords and their intended victims. How well each was done we know to-day.

An event of much importance, although not of any considerable bearing on the future of the new land movement, as the *people* had already decided in its favor, occurred on May 5th. On that day Isaac Butt, the leader of the Home-Rule party, died in Dublin. Mr. Butt—according to his lights—did noble work for his country, and his memory will ever be revered, as it deserves to be, by his fellow-countrymen. From being a stanch supporter of Protestantism and British ascendancy, and a vehement champion of ultra-Orangeism and Kentish fire, he became an earnest pleader of the people's rights, and an exposer of the grievances of his down-trodden country. He subsequently was chosen leader of the popular cause in Parliament, to which he honestly devoted his great talents. Butt's conversion from rabid pro-Britonism was sudden and singular. It came to pass in this wise: At one time when "travelling from Cork to Dublin, he met, at the Limerick Junction, a large band of emigrants, and witnessing, until he was touched to tears, the agony with which their hearts was thrilled at leaving the land they loved so fondly, the thought came to him that there must be something fatally wrong in that Government which would thus compel a people to leave a country rich in resources, lying undeveloped and waste. Out of this thought grew another, until he was covered with them as with so many green boughs, under which sprang up the national faith, and he took up the cause of "Home Rule" and proclaimed it. With what excellent judgment he directed that cause, and with what zeal and sacrifice, and with, considering the circumstances, what success he toiled and worked and spoke for it, history will record."

As the movement in Mayo progressed — meetings being held each Sunday in the various parishes — the Catholic clergy were not long in coming to the aid of the people, as the following declarations will show. In May, at the monthly conference of the clergy of the Deanery of Tralee, County Kerry, the following resolution was adopted: —

"We, the Catholic clergy of the Tralee Deanery, in this trying season of agricultural distress, deem it our duty before we separate to record our solemn and deliberate opinion, that the present year is the most disastrous the tenant-farmers of Kerry have seen since the calamitous famine years of 1847 and 1848. The prevailing distress we believe to be owing principally to the following causes: In the first place, to the excessive rents for the last twenty years. There has been very generally a steady increase of rents, that were already high enough, until they have been advanced to 50 or 100 per cent.; in some cases, even much over the poor-law valuation. These exorbitant rents the tenants have struggled to pay as long as prices kept up and harvests proved favorable. But now that the prices of all kinds of agricultural produce have fallen 20 per cent. they find it utterly impossible to meet the extravagant rents they were heretofore obliged to pay,—rents which we believe to be higher than in any other part of Ireland.

"Again, we have had several bad harvests. The last harvest, particularly, was one of the worst we have had for a long time. The potato crop all but failed, and what remained was not fit for human food; while oats was the worst crop farmers had for years, being as much, or more, chaff than grain. When we add to this that the wages of farm servants and laborers and the expense of their support have trebled for the last few years, we can form a fair idea of the difficulties with which agriculturists have to contend, while the extraordinary severity of the last winter and spring, and which is felt even in this first week of June, has reduced farming stock to a very low condition, and leaves very little hope of the coming season proving a prosperous one. But it may be said that the present depression is only temporary, and that a good harvest or two will restore matters to their former equilibrium. We fear not; because we apprehend that some, at least, of the causes are of a permanent character. We may hope, through God's mercy, for favorable seasons and good harvests; but we cannot hope that the competition of foreign producers on the Continents of both Europe and America will cease or become less active. On the contrary, we regard that competition as only in its commencement. The English markets are as near to French, Belgian, or Dutch products as to us, or nearer; while steam navigation has brought the vast Continent of America, with its free lands and light taxation, within eight days' sail of our shores. We, therefore, ask how it will be possible for our tenant-farmers, overburdened as they are with excessive rents, heavy taxation, and high-farm wages, to compete successfully with their more-favored foreign competitors? Plain common sense will tell us that the thing is impossible, and, therefore, we may not expect to see again the high prices that have been obtained for the last few years. Now, if this state of things continue, the tenant-farmers of Ireland must of necessity go to the wall. Bankruptcy and ruin will speedily overtake them, and the country will be reduced to as bad a condition of things as that of the famine times. The landlords have the salvation of the country in their hands. While times were prosperous, the tenants punctually and satisfactorily paid their rents; and now that the times are adverse, we, the clergy of the people, most respectfully and earnestly implore the landlords to come to the relief of their suffering tenantry, and make such just and reasonable reductions in the rents as will enable the people to hold their ground, notwithstanding bad harvests, heavy taxation, high wages, and foreign competition."

This was followed by like declarations from the Deaneries of Killaloe, Dungarvan, Cahirciveen, Achonry, and Ossory, and later from many others.

During the early stages of the agitation, the British Parliament, as was usual with them, refused to pay any attention to the appeals for justice of the Irish members. So glaring was this, that, on the night of June 26, 1879, John Bright caused quite a scene in the House of Commons by a speech in which he defended the conduct of the Irish members in obstructing the business of the House in order to compel attention to their demands. The Irish members in Parliament, he said, formed only an insignificant numerical minority in the House, and there were only two methods possible for them to obtain what the majority was disposed to refuse. One of these methods was to sell themselves to one of the two English parties, and thus give to the purchaser the balance of power. The other was to exercise their parliamentary rights, and by the obstruction of business under the forms of the House to compel the majority to make concessions to them.

That the land movement, now well under way, never for a moment lost sight of the main question of Irish liberty, will be seen from the following: On Sunday, June 15th, a great land demonstration took place at Milltown, County Galway, at which 14,000 people were present. The first resolution, which was proposed by Mr. Thomas Brennan, was:—

"That, as the people of Ireland have never ceased to demand their right of self-government, we hereby reiterate our resolution to labor for the same until our country has secured its attainment."

In speaking to the resolution, Mr. Brennan said:—

"The speech of the day—the most eloquent and significant speech—was not anything that would be said from that platform; but it was the tramp of the mighty multitude of earnest and determined men whom they saw marching there that day. When he saw that magnificent meeting, and saw their bold brows and hopeful faces, he thanked God that they were no longer slumbering slaves. Their presence there, notwithstanding landlords' frowns and agents' threats, proved that they knew their rights, and were determined to insist upon them. They met that day to declare the rights of their country to national independence, and he believed that it was only in an Irish

Senate their right to the ownership in the land would be recognized."

The farmer's clubs throughout the country also fell into line, and by resolutions supported the movement, until they were finally absorbed in the local branches of the Land League. The farmers of the West were now fairly roused to a sense of their condition; and their determination to resist rack-rents and eviction was decided. At a meeting of tenant-farmers held at Carnacon, Mayo, June 29th, to consider their condition, and take action against threatened evictions at Clougherlinch, the meeting adopted these resolutions:—

"We, the tenant farmers of the Clougherlinch estates, respectfully request that his Excellency the Duke of Marlborough, Lord Lieutenant of Ireland, and his Secretary, Mr. James Lowther, do appoint a commission, who will visit and investigate our deplorable condition, now ejected for non-payment of rent by far in excess of the actual value of our holdings. We are determined to pay fair rent in proportion to the present decreased value of agricultural produce; but will hold out, constitutionally and legally, against the exaction of the rack-rents that have already reduced us to actual starvation, thereby leaving us unfit to emigrate, and only fit subjects for the workhouse, after the threatened evictions, which we are determined to resist at the sacrifice of our lives.

"That we, the tenant farmers of the parishes of Carnacon, Ballintubber, and surrounding parishes, assembled, do indorse the resolutions in favor of fair rents passed at the Irishtown, Westport, Milltown, Crossboyne, and Mayo Abbey meetings. We are furthermore resolved to keep up this agitation, despite of any opposition by Church or State, until the tenantry of this island are rooted in the soil by fair and constitutional laws, which will protect them from capricious eviction or from rack-rents."

The language used in these resolutions is moderate, yet at the same time bold and determined. Six months previously they would not have dared to use it. The land movement was only a few months begun, and this was the sort of fruit it was already bearing. The dark clouds of famine were beginning to be seen on the horizon in the summer of 1879. The condition of the farming districts was fast becoming alarming. A correspondent of a leading American newspaper, who had been through the country, raised the following note of alarm in a communication from Ireland to his paper, written in July. He said:—

"Those who can recall the fearful scenes of misery and destitution which prevailed in this country during the years 1847–48, rendered remarkable by the failure of the potato crop, are not unlikely to witness a period almost as trying. A succession of bad seasons, extravagant rents, which are not only demanded, but wrenched from the unfortunate tenantry at the point of the bayonet, and lowering prices on account of the vast increase in the importation of all edible commodities, have reduced the condition of the farming classes to a state bordering on bankruptcy, while the depression felt by the agricultural community has spread and continues to expand over all grades among the industrial classes.

"Dark clouds, indeed, hover over the land; and in many places they have descended, bringing starvation and positive ruin wherever they have fallen. Factories are closing *in toto*, the banks refuse to advance money except when unexceptionable security is forthcoming, and, although some landlords are returning from ten to twenty-five per cent. of the rents, the vast majority must have their 'pound of flesh;' and thus there is every prospect of the country drifting into a state worse than what decimated it in the famine years already alluded to. Misery in its chrysalis condition only has as yet made its hideous appearance in Ulster and Leinster; but the western portion of Munster, and the entire province of Connaught, have already bowed down under the awful visitation.

"From inquiries which I have personally instituted in Mayo and Sligo, I can assert that in these counties the farming classes are on the threshold of the workhouse. Unprofitable seasons have, as I have said, led to this; but there is a contributary cause, and this is the system of credit which traders allowed, and which made the population anything but thrifty; and now, that dark days have arrived, their energies are paralyzed and efforts in any direction appear unavailing. That districts not as yet included in the scope on which desolation has come, must, in a short time, feel the terrible depression, is certain, unless Providence interposes. Within twelve months Leinster farmers have had their rents increased by more than twenty per cent., and with fully thirty per cent. of a decrease in the value of all produce their position can be easily understood. Ireland's oldest duke, the head of the Geraldines, has led the way: and, just as the prospect of bad times had become assured, his representatives set to work to increase his rent-roll, the process being, in many cases, repeated in the short space of a dozen years. Agreements, commonly called leases, were issued, only to make the heel of oppression the more keenly felt, as clauses, rendered legal by an abortive Land Act, were introduced to cripple the tenantry, and oust them from any claims which the most stupid enactment in the British statute-book contains. Rents are still forthcoming on some places; but in the counties which I have named above, Sligo and Mayo, the landlords have, in many instances, not a penny to receive. Their own cruel misrule has turned on themselves, and, by impoverishing those by whom they had to live, they at last feel the biting of want.

"Not a week ago an agent informed me that on the day he appointed for collection of rents he had not received a cent, nor does he see any prospect of payment. Monster meetings occur weekly, at which the people declare that they are willing and would have no difficulty to pay fair terms for their holdings. Of course, the landocracy hold aloof; but how long they can afford to do so remains to be seen. In the course of one year eight hundred ejectments have been served in Mayo alone; so that, taking the small average of six to each family, we would have 4,800 persons in this county, alone, houseless,—cast on the wide world, with no other shelter in their own land save that afforded by the unions. On Sunday, the 29th of June, I attended a public meeting at Castlebar, which was promoted for the purpose of calling attention to the threatened evictions on the estate of Miss Crean Lynch; and on that occasion, a Mr. Daly, in speaking of the state of the district, said he challenged any commissioner from Dublin Castle, or elsewhere, to find within the walls of many of the people who are to be evicted 'a second animal,' barring a cat, and in some cases he was aware that there was not sufficient food for the rat-watcher without pinching the supply of some member of the family.

"But it is useless to pursue this strain. It is patent to every one that the owners of property must either reduce their rents or take the land on their own hands. They are not likely to adopt the latter course, and may err in postponing the former until it becomes too late. The importation of cattle and sheep weighs heavily on prices of beef and mutton; but at the same time, if it were not for the supplies from America and Spain, meat would be a luxury only within the reach of the moneyed classes."

In addition to the foregoing communication, the following spirited address, signed by the priests and people of Connemara, and issued at Clifden, County Galway, July 2, will give an insight into the state of public feeling then existing:—

"No place has felt more than Clifden the neglect of successive governments, and in general the rigorous treatment by the landlords, of the poor, industrious tenants. We are bound to explain to the public how it has happened that a monster meeting of the entire population of Connemara has been deferred to another day. The accident of the parade of military suggested the prudence of contenting ourselves at present with a smaller medium of proclaiming to the world and to the empire at large the wrongs and the wants of as pious, as patriotic, and as peaceable a population as can be found anywhere. A public meeting was fixed for this day, and the streams of people entering by all the approaches to town gave abundant evidence that the meeting would be a monster one; but the Government poured into our neighborhood and the town a *posse* of police, who, it appears, were sent to fight a foe that proved imaginary.

"We, the clergy and the people of Connemara, proclaim to the world, that, as long as landlord injustice and ill-treatment from one class and utter neglect by the governing classes shall continue, there will not and ought not to be any chance of popular contentment nor of permanent peace. To heighten the bitter results arising from the manifold sources of misery here in Connemara, a new phase of anti-Catholic and anti-Irish ascendancy is evidenced in the unquestionable partiality of what are called the upper classes and their leaning to as vile and as detestable a system as curses any district under the sun. We allude to the troops of proselytizing vagabonds, who forfeit by their blasphemies and misconduct anything like good neighborhood from the inhabitants of any district cursed by their presence. We do hereby in conclusion, and without the parade of braggadocio, proclaim to all whom it may concern, we shall continue to agitate until the order of death by starvation and the slow process of hunger shall have vanished, and until death by eviction and extermination shall be drawn from within the right which landlords enjoy; that is, of perpetuating the hideous crime of murder by rack-rent and extermination.

"The Rev. Dean McManus, P. P., V. G., Clifden; the Rev. B. McAndrew, P. P., Ballinakill; the Rev. Joseph J. R. Moloney, P. P., Roundstone; the Rev. Patrick Grealy, P. P., Carna; the Rev. Michael O'Connell, C. C., Ballinakill; the Rev. W. Rhatigan, C. C. Clifden; the Rev. John J. Healy, C. A., Boffin; the Rev. J. Connolly, C. C., Roundstone; the Rev. T. Flannery, C. C., Clifden; the Rev. P. Colgan, C. C., Carna; Messrs. Peter John King (Honorable Secretary), John P. Darcy, Cornelius King, Joseph Gorham, Kennedy O'Brien, John M. Lyden, John J. Lyden, Michael Lyden, William Casey, James Casey, Fenton Kavanagh."

The Tory Government, up to this, affected to ignore the reports of distress and impending famine, and sought, as pointed out in the address from the Connemara clergy, to intimidate the land meetings.

In the House of Commons, on the 26th of June, Mr. O'Connor Power asked the Chief Secretary for Ireland if he would inform the House on what authority he had formed his belief that the persons who took part in a recent tenant-right meeting, at Milltown, in the County of Galway, "were not tenant-farmers, and were unconnected with the neighborhood;" and whether he would lay upon the table of the House copies of the instructions given to Colonel Bruce, Deputy Inspector-General of Constabulary, and the constabulary authorities in the West of Ireland, in reference to the land agitation going on in that part of the country, so as to enable the House to express an opinion on the subject. Mr. Power said that "The agitation in Ireland was a grave one, which the Government were bound to notice; but when the people asked for bread, and the Government answered their appeal with bullets, they would be held responsible for the peace of the country. The Government were willing to be guided by the opinions of the clergy in reference to the maintenance of order, but not with respect to the grievances of Ireland. He hoped the Chief Secretary would be warned to be more careful in the future as to the sources of his information. If the instructions asked for had reference to something being done in Zululand, the refusal to produce them would have been regarded as an arbitrary proceeding, which the House would not have tolerated. The people of Ireland had never had to deal with a more hateful power than that of the Conservative party and Government. They proposed to deal with the land question by shooting the people down. An extra police force, the cost of which was levied on the district, was the remedy of the Conservative party for the redress of Irish grievances. He moved the adjournment of the House."

Mr. Parnell rose and seconded the motion, and said "The circumstances of the people of Ireland were so desperate that matters could not be allowed to go further without the subject being brought before the House. The Government had quartered a large force of constabulary on a people so distressed that they could not pay their rents."

Mr. Mitchell Henry said "He could bear his own testimony to the wretched condition of the people in the West of Ireland, and the Minister should think less of winning the cheers of his followers, and more of the extreme misery existing in the country with which he was officially connected."

During the early part of the agitation, Davitt had many obstacles to contend against and overcome; this he was enabled to do from the absolute confidence which the masses of the people had in his honor and tried patriotism. In July, '79, he found it necessary to defend himself against an aspersion from the great and good "Lion of the Fold," the Archbishop of Tuam. The Archbishop was suspicious of the leaders of the new movement, and no wonder, having so often seen the people and their cause betrayed by blatant politicians, who crept into government positions on the shoulders of popular agitations. But the noble sentinel of Irish honor and freedom did not then know the men who were leading the new land movement. We believe no person would be readier now to do them justice than John of Tuam—if occasion demanded it. On June the 5th, the following letter from the Archbishop appeared in the *Freeman's Journal*:—

"DEAR SIR,—In a telegraphic message, exhibited towards the end of last week in a public room of this town, an Irish member of Parliament has unwittingly expressed his readiness to attend a meeting convened in a mysterious and disorderly manner, which is to be held, it seems, in Westport, on Sunday next. Of the sympathy of the Catholic clergy for the rack-rented tenantry of Ireland, and of their willingness to coöperate earnestly in redressing their grievances, abundant evidence exists in historic Mayo, as elsewhere. But night patrolling, acts and words of menace, with arms in hand, the profanation of what is most sacred in religion,—all the result of lawless and occult association,—eminently merit the solemn condemnation of the ministers of religion, as directly tending to impiety and disorder in church and in society. Against such combinations in this diocese, organized by a few designing men, who, instead of the well-being of the community, seek only to promote their personal interests, the faithful clergy will not fail to raise their warning voices, and to point out to the people that unhallowed combinations lead invariably to disaster and to the firmer riveting of the chains by which we are unhappily bound as a subordinate people to a dominant race. I remain, dear sir, faithfully yours,

JOHN, *Archbishop of Tuam.*

Again, in July 7, another letter, addressed to Michael O'Donohue, C.C., M. J. Fitzgerald, P. Flanagan, Martin Curran, and Thomas Kelly, honorary secretaries of a large meeting of tenant-farmers, held in Ballyhaunis, was printed in the same newspaper; it was as follows:—

"ST. JARLATH'S, Tuam, July 7, 1879.

"GENTLEMEN,—I beg leave to return my warmest acknowledgment to your committee for their kind invitation to attend the great meeting to be held in Ballyhaunis on the 10th of August.

"The rooting of the people in the soil of their own country, on equitable terms, is a question that must engage the earliest and earnest attention of the legislature, as a measure essential to the peace and happiness of Ireland. Next to a repeal of the disastrous Union between Great Britain and Ireland, without which the condition of this country will ever be that of a nation trampled under foot for the welfare of a people of another land, beneficent legislation, defining the just rights of the landlords and tenants, is the measure dearest to the hearts of the people, the solution of which cannot be much longer deferred.

"Let the tenant-farmers of Mayo, as of all Ireland, act judiciously: let them be guided, as of old, by their faithful allies, the priests; who, as a body, in good report and in evil report, stood in the front ranks of the combat, sacrificing time and personal interests to the public welfare, with no other object in view but that of shielding the weaker members of society against the violence of their inveterate foes.

"The patriotic spirit that at all times animated the

breasts of both priests and people in Mayo is as vigorous to-day, and as free from baneful elements, as when they fought constitutionally against the insignificant *shooneens* and the powerful oligarchy of the country.

"Let no attempt at dissevering so sacred a union, fraught with blessings to the people, be tolerated.

"In some parts of the country the people, in calmer moments, will not fail to be astonished at the circumstance of finding themselves at the tail of a few unknown, strolling men, who, with affected grief, deploring the condition of the tenantry, seek only to mount to place and preferment on the shoulders of the people; and, should they succeed in their ambitious designs, they would not hesitate to shake aside at once the instrument of their advancement as an unprofitable incumbrance.

"I am glad to find, among the gentlemen invited to the meeting, the names of the patriotic proprietor of the *Freeman's Journal*, of the two universally respected members of the County Galway, and of the faithful Mr. Biggar. I miss one name from the list—a name that sheds lustre on a country no less famed for the oratory than for the seasonable courage of her sons—namely, Mr. A. M. Sullivan, M.P.

"I remain, gentlemen, faithfully yours,

JOHN, *Archbishop of Tuam.*

To this letter Mr. Davitt found it necessary to reply; and published the following respectful but manly answer:—

"DUBLIN, July 10, 1879.

"*To the Editor of the Dublin Freeman*,—There are few men to be found among our seemingly destiny-divided people who would not prefer to lie under an unmerited rebuke, or remain silent to even uncalled-for aspersions upon their motives or actions, rather than utter a single word in defence, which might irritate or offend the venerated Archbishop of Tuam. But censure from one who is looked upon as the patriarch of his race is the more heavy from the certainty of its acceptance from the millions who love to call him such, as being deserved, and unbearable from a consciousness of its not being earned, in face of assertions, which, if left uncontradicted, would carry conviction to the contrary to almost every Irishman's mind. Under these circumstances, and with nothing but respect for his personal worth and veneration for his years, I feel compelled to defend myself against the (to me) serious imputations contained in the following portion of his Grace's letter in this day's *Freeman*:—

"'In some parts of the country the people, in calmer moments, will not fail to be astonished at the circumstance of finding themselves at the tail of a few unknown, strolling men, who, with affected grief, deploring the condition of the tenantry, seek only to mount to place and preferment on the shoulders of the people; and, should they succeed in their ambitious designs, they would not hesitate to shake aside at once the instrument of their advancement as an unprofitable incumbrance.'

"As one who has taken part in the meetings to which his Grace refers, I beg respectfully to say that I am neither a strolling nor an unknown man in the West, but one who works for his daily bread, and who is known in Mayo, my native county, where my relatives are now, in common with others, experiencing the severity of the times, and a want of that assistance in the struggle of life which a beneficial change in the land-laws of Ireland would afford them. Some twenty-five years ago my father was ejected from a small holding near the parish of Straed, in Mayo, because unable to pay a rent which the crippled state of his resources, after struggling through the famine years, rendered impossible. Trials and sufferings in exile for a quarter of a century, in which I became physically disabled for life, a father's grave dug beneath American soil, myself the only member of my family ever destined to live or die in Ireland, and this privilege existing only by virtue of 'ticket of leave,' are the consequence which followed that eviction. If all this but entitles me to an imputation of affected grief at the condition of the families of my kindred and others who are threatened with a fate similar to mine, I can only regret that fortune has not placed me in such a position in life where the mere knowledge of the miserable condition of the tenantry of Ireland, without undergoing its bitter, heart-crushing experiences, would entitle me to the credit of unaffected grief at the mendicant existence which an inhuman government and heartless land system inflicts upon our people. Men who merit the additional imputations of seeking only to mount to place or preferment upon the shoulders of the people, invariably ambition either to enter Parliament by their aid, or patriotically dispose of themselves to the Government for anti-national services.

"So far as the first of these ambitious designs is concerned, I am not qualified for its perpetration, for two reasons: one being that, as I have been a 'treason felon,' I could not, on that account, sit in the 'first assembly of gentlemen in Europe;' and the second, but most particular one, is that, even if the foregoing disqualification were removed, I would never consent to misrepresent the aspirations of the Irish people in an English Parliament after representing my country's right to independence in England's prisons. As for any other advancement on the people's shoulders, the only one I am likely to obtain by their patronage will be in the direction of oakum-picking in Millbank, or stone-breaking in Dartmoor convict prison; preferments which, with their indignities and suffering, I am in a fair way of being convinced, are more easily borne than the imputations, insults, and injuries which the participant in Irish politics receives for his endeavors. Yours, etc., "MICHAEL DAVITT."

CHAPTER X.

THE LANDLORDS REFUSE TO LOWER THE RENTS.—THE AGITATORS DEMAND THE ABOLITION OF LANDLORDISM.—REPEAL OF THE IRISH CONVENTION ACT.—THE FIRST NATIONAL CONVENTION HELD IN MAYO TO FORM A LAND LEAGUE.—APPEAL TO IRISH-AMERICANS.—MANIFESTO OF THE TRUSTEES OF THE IRISH NATIONAL FUND.

"Abject tears, and prayers submissive,—
Have they eyes and cannot see?
Never country gained her freedom
When she sued on bended knee."
—LADY WILDE.

NOTWITHSTANDING the public and private appeals made to the landlords for reductions of the rack-rents exacted from the people, very few of them responded; instead of doing so, they cried out for coercion and their full "pound of flesh." Numbers of English and Scotch land-owners had reduced their rents, owing to the low prices received by the farmers for home produce, in consequence of the great quantities of provisions daily imported from America. Not so with the Irish landlords: they met the popular cry for low rents in a different manner. At the Summer Assizes in Mayo, held about the end of July, the grand jury — all of whom are landlords — passed the following resolution: —

"*Resolved*, That the judge of the assize having, in his charge to us, spoken in the strongest terms of the state of this county, we feel it our duty before separating to call the attention of the Government to the unsettled state of the county, and to the serious agitation against the payment of rents without regard to the rate or time at which the lands were let, or to the other circumstances connected therewith. This illegal design is pursued by a system of wholesale intimidation by words and acts of menace, and by violent speeches, exciting the people to outrages against both landlords and tenants. We think these evils cannot be effectually removed without additional powers being conferred on the executive by Parliament. Our foreman is requested to forward copies of this resolution to the Chief Secretary for Ireland, and to the Lieutenant for the county, the Earl of Lucan. Passed unanimously.— (Signed), J. T. BROWNE, *Foreman*."

Such a response as this, and others like it, acted as a spur to the agitation; so that the demands made from the public platforms at the great meetings became sterner and more exacting. At a meeting of the priests and people, held in Claremorris on July 13th, in response to a resolution demanding that the weight of the agricultural depression should be borne equally by the landlords and the tenants, Mr. Davitt said: —

"They were assembled to advocate every plank of the platform laid down at the Irishtown, Westport, and Milltown meetings. Canon Bourke had given them very excellent advice when he told them to deport themselves as men who were entitled to their freedom. He [the speaker], though he went further in Irish politics than Canon Bourke, did not wish to add a word to that. They had been told that inflammatory language had been used at previous meetings; but he asked the Government to point to any outrages that had resulted from it. They had been called 'Communists' and 'Fenians' because they asked the right to live in Ireland; but they might retaliate, and ask what right landlords have to the soil, and they would find it very difficult to get convincing proofs from Lord Sligo, Lord Lucan, Sir Roger Palmer, or Lord Oranmore. They had been up to this too moderate. They had simply asked for a reduction of rents which was utterly impossible for them to pay. John Stuart Mill said rent was the surplus of the profits that came from the tenant's industry and outlay in tilling the soil. Where was this surplus of profits in Ireland to-day?

In face of the depreciation of produce and large importations from America, he did not say they were justified in paying no rent at all; but he did not say that a time might not come when they would have to make a protest as a nation against paying salary to a caste in Ireland that were fulfilling the duties of a landlord garrison. The old cry of 'Fixity of tenure at fair rents' would do no longer. They must tell the English Legislature that the concession they gave would be taken as instalments only of their just demands, and they must not be satisfied with their representatives unless they supported the full demand, that the soil of Ireland should be returned to the people of Ireland. Mr. Lowther had tried to cast a stigma on his character by describing him as a 'ticket-of-leave man;' but as long as chief secretaries had only insults to offer to Irish demands, and as long as the juggling legislation of Lord Beaconsfield could even make a subject of play of the hierarchy of Ireland a great question, so long would 'ticket-of-leave men' for political offences be cherished in Irish hearts. They must organize their strength openly and above-board. There was no necessity for occult meetings; but there was a necessity for determined organizations, and a double necessity that organization should be utilized judiciously and effectually in order to break down the structure of landlordism which had cursed and depopulated Ireland, until they bequeathed an emancipated soil to their children and a regenerated Ireland to posterity."

And again, at a great land meeting held in Shrule, Sunday, July 27, Mr. Davitt proposed the following resolution:—

"That, as our country has never forfeited the right to be mistress of her own destinies, nor abandoned her resolve to struggle for the recovery of the proud prerogative of a nation, we hereby declare self-government to be the inalienable right and the chief want of Ireland."

In speaking in its support, he delivered a spirited address, in which he said,—

"This successful *exposé* of the inhuman land system, by which Ireland is cursed and her people impoverished, is both encouraging and hopeful, and must be persevered in until the public opinion of the civilized world shall seize landlordism by the throat and compel it to disgorge the plundered heritage of a suffering people. A reduction of rents may tide you over the present crisis, and procure you a little relief from an epidemic form of the land evil; but what the prosperity of your country and the social amelioration of yourselves and children demand is a remedy for the evil itself, a total eradication of a chronic malady which has eaten to the very vitals of Ireland, paralyzed her energies, and condemned her people to almost perpetual destitution. The principle of sacrificing private interests to the good of the masses, and establishing government on the basis of the people, is that which enlightened statesmanship has always propounded as a preventive to revolution, or even acted upon in obedience to the growing necessities of an awakening civilization. Such a principle has been acted upon in Ireland, to some extent at least. Such a change as making the tiller of the soil the proprietor has been effected in most continental countries, with results so satisfactory to the people and government that there never will be a feudal system again tolerated by or forced upon those who have been freed from its accursed tyranny. Name the institution which the lords of the soil have raised in this country for the moral and intellectual elevation of the people. What encouragement is given to the social progress of Ireland in return for the twenty millions annual rental which landlordism extracts from its soil? Landlords' mansions, prisons, workhouses, and constabulary barracks occupy the place where laborers' institutes, agricultural societies, hospitals, and gymnasiums should stand, if landlordism were not robbing the Irish nation of twenty million pounds every year. These are some of the answers which apologists for that system would have received if they ventured to plead for its continued toleration. Your fight is against a system which will be held to by the landlords like grim death. Organize, unite, and sap its foundation by intelligent and persevering operation. Expose its inhuman structure to the world. In the words of the illustrious Mitchel, 'Act as if every tillage farm in Ireland was a fortress to be held, not for the occupant and the landlord only, but for the country.' Whether Ireland is to become a free nation or not, or her land emancipated, depends upon the way in which the garrison of farmers acquit themselves, and stand upon their right to the soil of the fatherland, and to the fruits of the labor by which they cultivated it."

The agitation now rapidly spread through the whole south of Ireland, causing alarm to the landlords and the British Government, and people began to inquire to what the national movement would tend. At the great monster meetings held each Sunday in the various counties, the reformers demanded the abolition of the existing land code, and the substitution in its place of such a system as would establish the cultivator of the soil as its proprietor; they demanded the total abolition of the landlord system. These demands were re-echoed and indorsed by the priests and the press. Amongst the resolutions passed at a meeting held in Balla, Mayo, on Lady Day (August 15), was one which reads thus:—

"That as the land laws of this country were conceived in a spirit of hostility to the well-being of its people, and are enforced with a total disregard to the social right and necessities of the tiller of the soil, we demand their abolition as an act of justice, as well as an indispensable requisite to the contentment and prosperity of Ireland, and the substitution of a small proprietary system, which will protect the fruits of the farmer's industry by placing him in the undisputed possession of the land he cultivates."

This is a sample of those adopted at the other meetings.

A most important event occurred in the session of Parliament just closed; namely, the repeal of the Convention Act. It was eighty-six years since the people of Ireland held a convention for the discussion of their national affairs; in 1793 the Irish Convention Act was passed for the purpose of preventing them from deliberating upon their political affairs. This incident was speedily taken advantage of by Michael Davitt to start the National Land League in Mayo; and also at a meeting of the Home Rule League in Dublin, September 11, it was decided to hold a National Convention the following February, before the meeting of Parliament. Mr. Parnell, in his speech at the meeting, said,—

"Unless we unite to a great extent all shades of political opinion in the country, I fail to see how we can expect ever to attain to national independence; and I think now, when we are considering what we are to do for the future, when we are taking this very important step, we should endeavor to bring along with us as many men as possible of all shades of opinion, — we should endeavor to close up our ranks, and not create unnecessary stumbling-blocks in the way of men joining the national movement, who otherwise might be disposed to join it, but who are prevented by one cause or another from taking part in the work."

The first Irish convention since the repeal of the act was held on August 16 by the farmers of Mayo. Over fifty delegates attended, representing twenty-four districts in the county, the object being to establish a *National Land League.* Mr. Louden, barrister, of Westport, who presided, said the object of their present movement was the abolition of landlordism and the substitution for it of a peasant proprietary. At the approaching election they would vote for no candidate whose cry would not be "the land for the people." The rules for the proposed club, drawn up by Mr. Michael Davitt, were adopted by the meeting. In the manifesto, also adopted, it was stated that the object of the club would be to expose landlord injustice wherever it existed, and to act as a vigilance committee on the Members of Parliament, Grand Jurors, and representative bodies of the County Mayo. It was decided to print and circulate returns of the number of landlords in the county, the acreage each possessed, and how the land was acquired by them; the excess of rent paid by the tenants over the government valuation; to publish, by placard, notices of contemplated evictions, and convene public meetings at the scene and time of these evictions; to publish full particulars of all cases of eviction and rack-rent, with the name of the landlord and agent; to publish the names of all persons who took land, or bid for land, from which the tenants had been evicted; and, finally, to publish particulars of all acts of kindness or justice on the part of landlords.

Mr. Davitt said that the soil by right and justice belonged to the people of Ireland who tilled it; yet twelve Irish landlords owned between them one million three hundred acres, and five millions of Irish tillers of the soil did not own a single acre. The farmers of Ireland did not ask that the landlords' interest in the land should be confiscated, but simply asked that compensation should be given the landlords for those rights when the state, for the peace, benefit, and happiness of the people, should decree the abolition of the present landlords. The establishment of a peasant proprietary was the only thing that would satisfy the people of Ireland.

This was Davitt's first start of the Irish National Land League in Ireland, in a concrete form; and the occasion was a fitting one, being the first convention held in Ireland for nearly ninety years! It augured well for the future success of the movement.

The agitation in September and October, 1879, became intense; it had spread through the entire South, and the North was beginning to wake up, and demand low rents. The distress, now becoming prevalent throughout the West, was attracting great attention and sympathy from other countries; and the Government, true to its routine record in such emergencies, was pouring thousands of troops into the country. The monster land meetings were attended by vast multitudes, numbering from ten to forty thousand people at each meeting. Davitt all the while was working unceasingly, attending and speaking at all the meetings he could reach, everywhere infusing vigor and determination into the people. On October 5, at a meeting in Ballinrobe, Mayo, addressing twenty thousand people, defending himself against landlord slanders, he said:—

"That magnificent gathering was the answer which the manhood of Mayo returned to the slanders heaped on that county. He had the honor of attending most of the meetings held in Mayo since the inauguration of that movement; and he hurled back with scorn and contempt the charge that he had used words which had, directly or indirectly, encouraged the commission of acts of violence. He had always insisted that the man who would commit offence in connection with that movement would injure the cause he thought of advocating. He deliberately charged the landlord system with the murder of two millions of Irish people, with the forced exile of two millions more, and with the impoverishment and misery of two-thirds of the people whom it had left alive; and he declared that such a system stood convicted before high heaven as infamous and inhuman, and that it was a duty incumbent on every one of its living victims to work and labor unceasingly until that system was abolished in Ireland."

Mr. Parnell and his associate Home Rulers issued the following appeal for aid to the Irish in America and elsewhere, October 8: —

"The land and rent agitation which has originated in the West of Ireland, and is rapidly spreading throughout the country, has now assumed such national proportions that it becomes a question of first importance, to all who sympathize with its legitimate objects, how best to guide the popular movement to the attainment of those ends. Temporary abatements of excessive rents are being, and may continue to be, obtained through the various agencies of a sympathetic but unorganized advocacy, which the existing widespread and alarming distress elicits from the press and bodies of the community; but, without the creation of some constituted guide or directing influence, the primary if not the sole cause of the existing poverty of the agricultural classes will not be removed. Independent of the effect which the products of the vast free lands of America and other favored countries must have in competition with the produce created under rent-tied and paralyzing conditions in Ireland, almost all the evils under which her people suffer are referable to a land system glaringly antagonistic to the first principles of justice and fair government, which place the good of the greatest number above the privileged gratification of the few. Landlordism, founded as an institution of systematic partiality, has proved itself but too true to the spirit of its origin, by reducing all who are dependent on, but unprotected by ownership of, the soil to a degraded, semi-mendicant existence, and in addition induces the loss of that independent character which arises from an independence of position. The duties which feudal laws and customs exacted, in return from those in whom they recognized certain arbitrary rights, have been ignored by Irish landlordism in its relations to the soil and those dependent upon the fruits of its cultivation, thus adding to the other indictments against the system a non-fulfilment of essential obligations. Any land system which does not tend to improve the value of land, and enable cultivation to meet the exigencies of those dependent upon its produce, stands self-condemned as barbarous, unjust, and reprehensible.

"The diminished population of our country, the

millions of our race who perished in, or fled from, a land in which God intended they should not die by hunger; the continued struggle with poverty which those have to maintain who yet cling to their native soil; and the periodic climaxation of the impoverishing influences which landlordism exercises upon the social life of Ireland,—demand at last, in face of yet another impending national calamity, the application of a remedy which can no longer be denied the salvation of a people. In contrast to the social wretchedness to which a barbarous land system has reduced our country is the rapidly progressing prosperity of those people at whose demand, or for whose benefit, such a system has been swept away, and the cultivator of the soil has replaced the landlord as its proprietor. The surplus produce of lands thus freed, with agricultural industry thus relieved from its rent taxation, is now placed, by easy transit over sea and land, in competition with what is produced under conditions of land tenure the most unfavorable, and incentives to toil the least encouraging that ever regulated the chief industry of any civilized country. When to this is added the adverse influences of successive bad seasons, on the point of culminating in what threatens to be the worst yet experienced since famine years, the position of the Irish farmer and those depending upon the fruits of his enterprise and labor assumes an aspect of menacing ruin, which to consider as transient or accidental would be a criminal disregard of the vital existence of a people. Impelled by the desperate circumstances of their situation, the farming and other classes concerned have proclaimed their grievances in public meetings and by the press, demanding the remedies which alone can redress them. A *consensus* of opinion, apart from immediate interestedness, has declared that the remedy put forward by the present agitation is founded on justice, reason, and expediency, and that its application is absolutely essential to meet the evils complained of and insure the prosperity and contentment of Ireland. In formulating a demand for ownership of the soil by the occupiers in substitution for that of the landlords, the people of Ireland neither contemplate nor ask for the confiscation of those proprietorial rights which existing laws must necessarily recognize and protect, but that, for the transfer of those rights to an industrial ownership, a fair compensation may be given to those who shall be called upon to agree to such transfer for the settlement of the agrarian strife of the country and the supreme good of its people. To carry out a project as vast as that which we contemplate must require means in proportion to the difficulties that must be encountered in the undertaking. Tenants' defence associations must be organized in every county, and assistance be rendered to farmers who may be called upon to defend themselves against an unjust or capricious exercise of landlord power. The wealth of Ireland is almost entirely in the hands of that class which we propose, for the good of the country, to deprive of the absolute possession of the soil; and it is but natural to expect that strong and influential opposition will be offered by those who will be called upon to surrender the privileges they have so long enjoyed, — even in virtue of compensation and expediency. To meet this opposition, and guide the national movement for freeing the land of Ireland, assistance of two kinds must be forthcoming; the one, and most essential kind, is an organized development of earnestness, and a resolute attitude on the part of the 600,000 landless farmers of Ireland, as well as those whose daily bread depends upon the prosperity of their fatherland, in demanding their just rights as guaranteed in the settlement we propose. The second aid required is money. Neither has ever been wanting when the national spirit of our country and the patriotism of her exiled sons have been appealed to in a patriotic cause; and we are confident they will not be withheld now when the very soil of Ireland is the object we desire to free, and the land slavery of our people the thing we are resolved shall be abolished forever. None of our race have had such bitter experience of the wrongs of landlordism as those who have been compelled to seek abroad the food denied at home, and none should more readily and generously sympathize with those who are resolved to retain a firm grip of their Irish homesteads than the exiled who were forced by iniquitous laws to leave them.

"In the great Shelter Land of Peoples 10,000,000 of the Irish race have found a home. The system we aspire to abolish has banished them from Ireland. Benefiting by laws which afford equal protection and encouragement to all citizens of the great Republic of America, they can appreciate the efforts which aim at affording equal incentives to progress to their crushed and persecuted kindred here. Not alone to our fellow-countrymen in America, but to all whom evil laws have scattered the world over, as well as to all other nationalities who sympathize with a wronged and impoverished people who at last are resolved upon a remedy for the evils afflicting them, do we call for an advocacy of our cause, and support in our efforts to achieve success. In constituting ourselves a committee for the purpose of carrying out this work, we are animated with but one desire, — to aid the tenant-farmers, and those depending upon the soil of Ireland, to lift themselves from the misery and social degradation in which they are plunged, into a position where the notice to quit and the rack-rent will not operate against their industry, security, and contentment. We are influenced by no party-spirit in making this appeal, nor do we in any way purpose to place this committee in antagonism with existing bodies or organizations employed in other departments of national labor. To free the land of Ireland from the unwise and unjust restrictions which militate against its proper cultivation and prevent the development of its full resources should be a labor above the customary influences of party or sectional strife, and be guided alone by motives of disinterested effort for the benefit of our common country, and the improvement, contentment, and prosperity of the greatest number of our fellow-countrymen. The grounds upon which we feel authorized to issue this appeal are the fact of our being either directly or indirectly connected with the agitation which has sprung from the distress that has evoked a national condemnation of the present land system. As this land movement has won an indorsement from public opinion of an occupier proprietary settlement of the land question, those who have advocated such a remedy prior to and in conjunction with the national demand now made for it, feel themselves justified in taking such steps as may be best calculated to insure its application to the existing land evils of our country. In pursuance of this intention, we issue this appeal to Irishmen the world over, and to those who sympathize with the object in view, to aid us in our efforts to obtain for our people the possession of an unfettered soil, and for Ireland the benefits which must result from an unrestricted development of its products and resources."

The appeal was signed by Messrs. Parnell, O'Connor Power, Finnegan, Biggar, and others. It evoked much sympathy. New York at once responded by guaranteeing $250,000 if an Irish Member of Parliament of the advanced party would visit the United States. Two days before the appeal was issued in Ireland, a great meeting of Irish-Americans was held in Faneuil Hall, Boston, to express sympathy and tender aid to the struggling tenant-farmers in Ireland, at which the following resolution was adopted :—

"WHEREAS, News has reached us across the Atlantic that the people of Ireland are working with unexampled unanimity to obtain local self-government and the abolishment of feudal landlordism,

"*Resolved*, That we, the citizens of Boston, native and foreign-born, who enjoy these inestimable blessings in this land, in Faneuil Hall assembled, send back our sympathies and pledge ourselves to a substantial support of the tenant-farmers of Ireland in their noble and patriotic efforts."

The Chairman of the meeting read a letter from Mr. Davitt, which said,—

"This land agitation is destined to do more for Ireland than all the movements since '98. The entire country has accepted the proposal for abolishing landlordism. All the known and active Nationals will combine. A convention is shortly to be summoned, which will endeavor to weld the two sections of National politicians into one."

It was decided in October that Mr. Parnell should visit the United States, and personally state the case of his countrymen then in the midst of a gigantic struggle for bread, and freedom from landlord tyranny. The famine cloud was beginning to cast its dark shadow on the land, and there was no hope of saving the lives of thousands of the small farmers and laborers, except by outside aid,—nothing was expected from the British Government, and next to nothing was got.

The trustees of the "skirmishing" or Irish National Fund issued an important manifesto on the Irish question, in October, which did a great deal towards arousing the Irish-American people into active sympathy with the Irish struggle. The document deserves to be remembered, as it is but rarely we have an emanation of the kind from such names as are appended to it The manifesto is as follows:—

"NEW YORK, Oct. 11th, 1879.

"TO THE IRISH PEOPLE OF THE UNITED STATES.

"*Fellow-Countrymen*,—The threatening aspect of affairs in Ireland calls for prompt and vigorous action on the part of Nationalists in this country. It is no time for idle talk, but for serious preparation for the stern work that is before us. The National movement is fast approaching a crisis when its members must be prepared to make larger sacrifices, and work with redoubled zeal, so that the hour of trial may not find them unprepared.

"In view of the change in the situation, it has been decided, with the concurrence of several trusted friends in the National party, to enlarge the Board of Trustees of the National Fund, and to appeal once more to the Irish people here for their support.

"The National Fund was started with a view to providing means to strike a telling blow against England whenever an opportunity should present itself. Its object was at first distinct from the general movement for Irish independence, and not influenced by any particular crisis in Ireland calling for immediate action. Its originators never calculated that it should perform more than a small portion of the work of driving the foreigner from the soil of Ireland. It was intended, in short, to hasten, if possible, the advent of Ireland's opportunity, by inflicting injury on England at vital points and at critical moments, while showing the Irish people the immense power lying unappreciated in their hands for the destruction of that empire which has robbed them of land and liberty, and driven them homeless over the earth.

"The call was responded to chiefly by that class of

the Irish people in America who can least afford pecuniary sacrifices, and under the pressure of unprecedentedly hard times. There was no apparent prospect, except for a very brief period, of England becoming involved in foreign war; no evidence of vigorous political life in Ireland; no unusual danger menacing our countrymen at home; nothing, in short, to stimulate Irish-Americans to unusual activity: and yet, taking all the circumstances into account, the amount subscribed was very creditable. It was enough to show that, under more favorable conditions, and with an object the proximate realization of which could be made clear to the majority of our people,—with, above all, the evidence of vigor, determination, and steadiness of purpose in the political life of Ireland—Irish-America would be prepared to do its whole duty, and would sustain the struggle for the regeneration of the old land with its last dollar and its last man.

"The amount contributed, however, though larger than was anticipated, and sufficient to carry out some of the minor things indicated by its founders, would not warrant the undertaking of such enterprises as would inflict real and lasting injury on our enemies or be of real benefit to Ireland. It was determined that when operations of this nature were commenced we should be able to deliver blow after blow with crushing effect; and that, once begun, the work should go on till the power of England should be so crippled that our countrymen at home would not have the same odds against them as at present. It was seen, also, that the commencement of such work would force on a crisis in Irish national affairs, and that the

National party would be compelled by the circumstances thus created to take action for which they were not prepared. After earnest consultation with the trusted men of the National party, it was decided that preparatory steps only should be taken, and that all action likely to precipitate a crisis in Ireland should be postponed to a more fitting opportunity. It is only by the closest union and the most complete concert of action that the Irish people can hope to succeed in overthrowing English domination; and all the branches of the National party must act as the divisions of an army, animated by a common purpose, and guided by an authority whom all must recognize, towards the point where the enemy is to be met.

"Such was the position of the National Fund from its foundation to a few short weeks ago. Since then the whole situation of affairs has changed. New duties are imposed on us, new sacrifices demanded. Ireland is face to face with one of the greatest crises in her history. Her people are menaced with extermination, and appeal to their expatriated kindred for help in this, their hour of sorest need.

"The foreign landlord system, which has cursed the country since the final triumph of English rule, and dwarfed the energies of a people endowed with natural gifts fitting them for one of the highest places among the races of the world, has at length reached the climax of its infamous history, and reduced the people to the verge of beggary.

"Bad seasons and the competition of American produce perform but a minor part in the desolation which now overspreads Ireland. It is the foreign landlords, the inheritors of the successive robberies of

Tudors, Stuarts, Cromwellians, and Williamites,— an idle horde who perform no useful function in the land,— who drain the life-blood of the nation, and render it incapable of resisting even the most transient depression of trade or the effects of one bad season. Remove the blight of landlordism, make the tiller of the soil independent of the caprices of a petty autocrat, with no one to stand between him and a government which shall be the expression of the will of the whole people, and his quick intelligence and strong arm will provide from the teeming soil of his native land ample remedies against bad seasons and foreign competition.

"Such a revolution the English Government and the English landlords of Ireland will never consent to. It can only be accomplished by the complete overthrow of British power in Ireland. But it must be plain to every thinking Irishman that the day of our final deliverance from English rule and from English landlordism has not yet come. Our enemy must be more beset by difficulties than at present, and the whole Irish race the world over must be aroused and thoroughly organized for the effort. Without being too sanguine, we are satisfied that our opportunity is fast approaching, and that our duty is to wait for its certain advent. The duty of preparing for that event devolves on the organized Nationalists; but the danger which menaces a large section of our countrymen at home imposes a duty on us that it would be cowardly to shirk.

"Troops are being hurried to Ireland, and a reign of terror is about to be inaugurated. The impoverished people have no money to pay the exorbitant rent demanded of them, and preparations are being made to drive them off the land at the point of the bayonet. Day after day brings news of fresh bodies of infantry and cavalry being drafted into the rural districts. There has been no disorder among the people, nothing to justify the resort to coercive measures; but the Government expects that, driven to extremity, the afflicted people may refuse to leave their homes. A mere refusal to leave their homes may be the signal for the slaughter of the people, and the English Government expects thus to stifle the voice of the country and crush for a generation the spirit of resistance to wrong.

"Irishmen of America, will you stand tamely by while your countrymen at home are being butchered, or will you come to their assistance and enable them to stand by their households?

"Victims of landlord tyranny! look back to your shattered roof-trees and desolated hearths; remember the horrors of the eviction which scattered your kindred through foreign lands, and resolve to save those you have left behind you from a similar fate. You can at least supply them with the means of avenging the murder of their friends and neighbors, and of beginning a movement that will end in the destruction of that landlord system which has blighted one of the fairest lands on this earth, and inflicted centuries of misery on your race.

"Survivors of '47, have you forgotten the countless horrors of the famine, and the weary years of suffering and sorrow that followed it? Can you think of your murdered kindred without a burning desire to avenge them? Does the memory of the hunger pang, the pestilence, the reeking emigrant ship, and the ghastly fever-shed arouse no righteous indignation in your souls; and can you calmly contemplate a repetition of these horrible scenes in the persons of the generation which has grown to manhood since then? Remember that English landlordism in Ireland was the chief cause of that famine, and that to-day it is as cruel and relentless a monster as ever. It menaces the very existence of our people, and must be destroyed. You who have suffered most from its blighting influence should make yourselves missionaries of retribution, and arouse your countrymen to the necessity of its final extirpation.

"Irishmen of all creeds, this is no sectarian strife, but a struggle for human rights, in which all have equal interests to maintain, common dangers to face, and common enemies to overcome. Those whose fathers settled among us in the times of confiscation have acquired a title to the land they till by their labor, have mixed with the people, and become as Irish as we. To-day we recognize no distinction of religion, and hope to see the feuds of the past forever buried.

"We do not wish to provoke a hopeless resistance; but wholesale evictions at the bayonet's point are sure to end in bloodshed, and many will prefer to die like men, defending their homes from the foreign robber, than to live paupers in the workhouse, or starve by the roadside. The action evidently contemplated by the English Government may provoke such a conflict between the people and the foreign soldiery as will precipitate a general movement. This is a danger which must be foreseen and provided for.

"In the event of such a conflict, the funds at our

disposal shall be used to enable the people to stand by their homes, to strike down the robber rule of the landlord, and to inflict speedy punishment for acts of cruelty or murder. We know the consequences of the steps it may be necessary to take, and do not hesitate to assume the responsibility. Will you share that responsibility with us, and enable us to take really effective measures by sustaining the fund?

"WILLIAM CARROLL,
"THOMAS CLARKE LUBY,
"JOHN J. BRESLIN,
"THOMAS F. BOURKE,
"JAMES REYNOLDS,
"JOHN DEVOY.

"AUGUSTINE FORD, *Secretary.*"

CHAPTER XI.

THE IRISH NATIONAL LAND LEAGUE FORMED IN DUBLIN. — THE DISTRESS INCREASING.—IRISH MEMBERS INVOKE GOVERNMENT AID.—DAVITT ARRESTED.—LODGED IN SLIGO JAIL.—"ON TO BALLA."—COMMITTED FOR TRIAL.—PARNELL TO CHICAGO.—DAVITT'S LECTURE IN ENGLAND.

"Pass the word that bands together,—
Word of mystic conjuration,—
And as fire consumes the heather,
So the young hearts of the nation
Fierce will blaze up, quick and scathing 'gainst the stranger and the foe."
— LADY WILDE.

THE agitation having now assumed gigantic proportions, the need of a central directing power became apparent; a thorough cohesion of the various political sections that had embraced the new platform was indispensable. While the new doctrine, so ably and unceasingly preached by Davitt and his co-workers, was received and adopted by the masses, embracing Home Rulers, Revolutionists, Repealers, and Conservatives, it was necessary to weld the entire into a concrete organization, in order that the agitation might be properly sustained, and that its rapidly increasing power might be judiciously exercised and directed. Davitt, by his unceasing labors and logical eloquence, with the assistance of Brennan, Killen, Loudon, Kettle, Daly, and the others who early espoused the land programme, including the patriotic clergy of Ireland, had educated the farmers on the Land Question, and showed them where lay their remedy against landlord exactions and oppression. He had already won over to the new project Mr. Parnell, who, up to this was recognized merely as the leader of the active section of the Home Rulers in Parliament. The time had arrived, therefore, for the establishment of an executive body with its local branches to represent the country on the questions at issue. Davitt accordingly had a meeting of the leading agitators convened at the Imperial Hotel, Dublin, on Tuesday, October 21, 1879, to establish the Irish National Land League. The meeting was harmonious and unanimous in its proceedings, and adopted the following set of resolutions, which created THE IRISH NATIONAL LAND LEAGUE: —

"That an association be hereby formed to be named the 'Irish National Land League.'

"That the objects of the League are — first, to bring out a reduction of rack-rents; second, to facilitate the obtaining of the ownership of the soil by the occupiers.

"That the objects of the League can be best attained by promoting organization among the tenant-farmers; by defending those who may be threatened with eviction for refusing to pay unjust rents; by facilitating the working of the Bright clauses of the Land Act during the winter; and by obtaining such reform in the laws relating to land as will enable every tenant to become the owner of his holding by paying a fair rent for a limited number of years.

"That Mr. Charles S. Parnell, M.P., be elected President of this League.

"That Mr. A. J. Kettle, Mr. Michael Davitt, and Mr. Thomas Brennan be appointed honorary secretaries of the League.

"That Mr. J. G. Biggar, M.P., Mr. W. H. O'Sullivan, M.P., and Mr. Patrick Egan, be appointed treasurers.

"That the President of this League, Mr. Parnell, be requested to proceed to America for the purpose of obtaining assistance from our exiled countrymen, and other sympathizers, for the objects for which this appeal is issued.

"That none of the funds of this League shall be used for the purchase of any landlord's interest in the land, or for furthering the interests of any parliamentary candidate."

The Land League barque, built by Michael Davitt and other Revolutionists, was now fairly launched, with Charles Stewart Parnell for captain, John Dillon, first officer; J. G. Biggar, boatswain, and Davitt as pilot, and with a loyal and experienced crew, competent to bring her safely through all the storms that John Bull and the Irish landlords might raise.

Davitt had now mustered his forces, and there was no mistaking the directness of his frequent assaults on the stronghold of landlordism. At a land meeting held at Aughmore, County Mayo, October 26, he delivered a speech replying to a resolution in which were embodied two demands, of which he said,—

"The first was an instant and adequate reduction of rents; and the second was the sweeping away, once and forever, of the accursed system of landlordism. He did not mince matters about landlordism. He did not believe any phase of landlordism should be tolerated in Ireland. He was not there to pronounce a laudation of good landlords, who might be giving reductions now, for they were only giving back the money they had robbed the people of; at the same time he could discriminate between a rack-renting landlord and a just one: but he was there as the uncompromising enemy of landlordism in any shape or form; and until the whole system was abolished, and the soil of Ireland given to the people who tilled it, there never would be peace or contentment. They were not there to talk about fixity of tenure at fair rents, which meant fixity of landlordism; for that they were resolved never should be fixed on Irish soil. When forty or fifty meetings throughout Ireland had issued a demand for a peasant proprietary, were they there, in the barony of Costelloe, to talk about fixity of tenure? These meetings were not organized with the expectation that the English Government would concede all their demands, but with the intention of having a great truth circulated, and that was, that God intended the land to be for the people, and not for the landlords."

And again, at a meeting in Killala, October 31, he said: —

"They were not there to confiscate, but to reform, and the reform they demanded was abolition of landlordism and the substitution in its place of such a system of laws as would establish the tillers of the soil as the owners of the soil they tilled. If paying the hanging gale, which would be due in November, entailed hardships upon their wives or children or sisters; if it caused them to be pinched during the coming winter, and threatened their family with destitution and starvation in March, — they had no right to pay that rent: not only that, they committed crime if they made their children suffer in order that the territorial avarice of the landlords should be satisfied at their expense. They must not imagine that they would be turned out by the roadside to die as in 1847. There was a spirit abroad in Ireland that would not stand that a second time in a century."

The distress throughout the West was now making rapid strides, famine was staring tens of thousands of people in the face. The Government, though frequently appealed to, had affected to ignore the seriousness of the situation: instead of devising means of relief, it was sending spies and special reporters to the public meetings to collect evidence against the agitators; and preparing to make a swoop on the leaders, and endeavor to break up the agitation. This policy turned out a miserable failure.

On November 5, a declaration, signed by seventy Irish Members of Parliament, was addressed to Lord Beaconsfield, the head of the Tory Government, then in power. It pointed out the serious necessity of taking immediate steps to avert the consequences which must result from several successive bad harvests, and the widespread distress already prevailing, and which was likely to result in famine.

The Archbishops and Bishops of Ireland, assembled in Dublin, October 24, the Primate of all Ireland in the chair, and made a similar appeal to the British Government, to prevent the people from dying of hunger. The appeals proved of little avail. Repression of the agitators, who were pleading for the lives of the people, was all that the Government thought Ireland needed; and they speedily put their project into execution, by arresting Michael Davitt, James Daly, and James Bryce Killen.

This was the first direct blow dealt by the Government at a peaceful and constitutional agitation; but it hurt the giver more than those it was intended for.

On November 19, 1879, Michael Davitt and James Bryce Killen were arrested in Dublin, and James Daly, editor of the *Connaught Telegraph*, was arrested in Castlebar, charged with having used language in public speeches calculated to incite a breach of the peace. The three prisoners were conveyed to Sligo and lodged in jail there, bail being refused. The speeches for which the arrests were alleged to have been made were delivered at a monster land meeting held at Gurteen, County Sligo, on Sunday, November 2; Rev. Roger Breman, P. P., of Gurteen, being in the chair. The following are the portions of the speech of each on which the law officers of Dublin Castle depended for convictions. Mr. Davitt, in his address, said: —

"The papers stated that the Right Hon. James Lowther (the Irish Chief Secretary) was now the guest of their highly consistent and patriotic (?) Home Rule member, Colonel King-Harman. The papers also credited Mr. Lowther with an original discovery, that the tenant-farmers of Ireland had £30,000,000 in the Irish banks to their credit, and that money formed a good security to the landlords to obtain their rent during the winter. Supposing the discovery was a true one, it only represented £16 or £18 to each of the 600,000 farmers of Ireland, and they were not, after their years of toil, going to hand that over to the landlords. They must first attend to the wants of their homes and families; and if after that they had a charitable disposition towards meeting the wants of the landlords, they might give what they could spare. He believed that rent for land under any circumstances, in prosperous times or in bad times, was an unjust and immoral tax upon the industry of the people. Landlordism was an open conspiracy against the well-being, prosperity, and happiness of the people, which ought to be crushed by those who suffered in consequence of it. The three thousand Irish landlords received twenty millions annually, or half the net earnings of the six hundred thousand tenants, without putting hand to work. That was not all: they spent nearly all that money in licentious and voluptuous living in London, Paris, and elsewhere, thus draining the country of her resources. They were not there to listen to any schemes of fixity of tenure at fair rents, with periodical valuations. That was fixity of landlordism, of poverty, and degradation. They must have the land owned by the tillers. It had been hinted that the Government would endeavor to send them out to colonize Zululand. He did not believe that; because England had been taught that the Zulus could use the assegai about as well as the men of '98 used the pikes, and the amalgamation would be dangerous. He called on the people to hold by their land, to pay rent only when they had a surplus after everything else, and could afford it, and to labor on unceasingly for free land and liberty. Fixity of tenure was simply fixity of landlordism, fixity of poverty and degradation. Abolition of landlordism was the only certain remedy. The time had come when the manhood of Ireland must spring up to its feet, and say it would tolerate this system no longer."

Mr. James Daly, in replying to a resolution pledging the meeting not to take a farm from which a tenant had been unjustly evicted, said, —

"That was the 26th meeting of the kind he had had the honor of addressing. He had been described as an agitator. There were landlords and agents in his own county who said they would prefer to be hanged, drawn, and quartered, rather than yield to the demands made at these assemblages. But he had compiled a list of twenty such landlords in his county who, since the first meeting (held at Irishtown), had made abatements of 25 per cent. on their rents. Canon John McDermott, who is an enthusiastic, a good, and pious priest, had stated last Sunday in Aughamore that the people would not be satisfied with a peasant proprietary, and he [the speaker] was delighted to see by his words to-day that he had changed that opinion. He advised the farmers not to allow themselves to be evicted. If the sheriff came to any of them, it was their duty to assemble in their thousands, and reinstate the evicted person the next day. Above all, said he, let there be no coward found to take his lands."

Mr. J. B. Killen said, —

"Since the time when the cursed feudal laws were introduced by Norman savages the land of Ireland had been three times confiscated, but always in favor of the aristocracy. They wanted a fourth confiscation, or rather restitution, now in favor of the people. He left it to them to say whether that was to be done by the pen, the pencil, or the sword. In the North of Ireland, where he came from, there was an old legend that there were a thousand warriors resting on their swords who would spring into existence when the spell of their enchantment was broken; and when he saw this large meeting before him he felt that the hour had arrived when Ireland's liberty would be consummated. There were amongst them reporters from London, who were noting every single word said, for the purpose of, by a little legal frippery, putting them in dungeons. As in other countries, they should obtain their rights by using the voice, the pen, — he was going to say the sword, — but swords were not used in this country."

Very Rev. Canon McDermott here said Mr. Killen should not be advocating the use of physical force.

Mr. Killen denied that he did so; but he "would like to see every one there armed with a rifle, and knowing how to use it. The days of namby-pamby speaking were over."

A further incentive for Davitt's arrest was his baffling of the Government spies and reporters by making a speech in Irish, which they were unable to report, at a meeting held at Corofin, County Galway, on Sunday, November 9, at which thirteen thousand people were present. In his Irish speech Mr. Davitt alluded to the presence of Government reporters, and urged the people not to be intimidated, but to organize their strength for the overthrow of landlord power. Davitt's example was followed by other speakers. Father "Tom" McDonough, the patriotic parish priest of Corofin, also addressed the people in the mother tongue, and said that every one of his auditors understood him. One of the tenant-farmer speakers, who failed in the English, then delivered in Irish a most impassioned speech on the wrongs of his class, and a fierce invective against persons who encouraged the landlords in rack-renting by coveting their neighbors' land. Indignation meetings denouncing the arrests were held all over Ireland and in England.

The day after the arrests the following placard was extensively posted throughout Mayo: —

"To the People of Mayo: Fellow-Countrymen,—
"The hour of trial has come. Your leaders are arrested. Davitt and Daly are in prison. You know your duty. Will you do it? Yes, you will. Balla is the place of meeting, and Saturday is the day. Come in your thousands, and show the Government and the world that your rights you will maintain. To the rescue, in the mightiness of your numbers, of the land and liberty. God save the people. Balla, Balla, Saturday next."

On the day announced, November 22d, a most remarkable and critical scene in the land movement in Mayo was enacted close to Balla. A small farmer, named Anthony Dempsey, holding under Sir Robert Lynch Blosse, was under sentence of eviction for non-payment of a year's rent. The land was taken possession of a week previously. The man's father was lying on a bed of fever, and his children were stricken with measles. The sheriff did not, under the circumstances, insist on completing the eviction at that time, and Saturday, November 22, was fixed for the final expulsion of the family from their home. It was the first eviction in Mayo since the beginning of the land movement, and the placards summoned the people to assemble at the scene of the eviction. The summons had hardly been issued, when the arrests were made, and the men lodged in prison. Thereupon the proclamation, printed above, urged the people to make a double protest against the eviction and the arrests. It was felt to be a crisis. All sorts of rumors began to circulate: that the meeting had been abandoned, — that it would be suppressed by force, — that the eviction would take place, — that the eviction would not take place, — that anything or everything might happen. The leading London newspapers and news agencies despatched special correspondents to the spot as to a seat of war. A military officer boasted in Castlebar that the military would disperse any assemblage with bullets, and that the leaders would be specially picked off. On the other hand, it began to leak out towards the end of the week that certain communications to the Castle had ended by the determination to defer or abandon the eviction; but to the last all remained in a state of painful uncertainty. On the morning of the day of meeting the following placard was extensively circulated:—

"PARNELL AND DAVITT TO THE PEOPLE OF MAYO,—*Men of Mayo*: We earnestly counsel such of you as intend to be witnesses of the eviction scene, to be dignified, orderly, and peaceful, in your conduct. The future of our movement depends upon your attitude this day. Give no excuse for violence on the part of the Government, and our great cause is won."

Thousands assembled to take part in the meeting, which passed off quietly, as the sheriff agreed to give Dempsey more time, so that the eviction did not take place. An eye-witness gave the following description of a remarkable scene observed from the place of meeting: "A 'Rath' within fifty yards of Dempsey's house on the brow of the hill was fixed as the place of meeting. The whole road below for more than a mile was covered by this huge peasant procession. As the head of the column reached the foot of the hill it parted, two to either side, and climbed the hill in an immense semicircle extending over the whole face of the hill. The two horns of this vast crescent advanced quickly and simultaneously, as if with the intention of surrounding the house, and with it a large body of the police. The police immediately prepared to retire; but Mr. Parnell exerted himself to stop the movement, and both sides of the advancing procession, having halted, came quietly together around the speakers. There must have been quite eight thousand men in that extraordinary array, and their self-possession, orderliness, and enthusiasm were even more remarkable than their numbers."

Messrs. Parnell, Louden, Dillon, Brennan, and others delivered speeches. Mr. Brennan made an ardent appeal to the patriotism of the policemen, who were within hearing, not to join in the inhuman work of the destroyers of their own race, against the people. For this he was subsequently arrested.

On November 25, Davitt and Killen were brought up in the police court for examination. The court was crowded with spectators. Messrs. Killen and Davitt appeared perfectly cheerful and fearless. Mr. Monroe, Queen's counsel, said if he could prove the utterances of Mr. Davitt's alleged words, that the manhood of Ireland should spring to its feet and say it would tolerate landlords and landlordism no longer, the magistrates would be bound to commit him. Police evidence was called to prove their utterance. Davitt, who had been occupied all the morning preparing a written defence, before commencing to deliver it protested against Mr. Monroe's remark that he had already experienced the clemency of the Crown, and declared that he was innocent of the charges on which he was convicted in 1870. Mr. Monroe, in his remarks, said that Davitt was probably the most dangerous of the Irish agitators, and specially pointed to his language comparing the Zulu assegai to the Irish pike. Davitt was committed for trial; but, bail being accepted, he was discharged from custody. The town of Sligo was on the verge of a riot that night; the police were stoned, and had to charge the people and clear the streets. Mr. Davitt was serenaded by two bands.

The attempt of the Government to intimidate and put down the agitation by making the arrests proved a signal failure. It was condemned by the press and the people everywhere, and gave renewed energy and strength to the agitation.

The agitation continued to gain strength under the management of the Land League. The tenants in several districts had now taken a positive stand, and refused to pay any more rent unless suitable reductions were made. The Government had refused to take any adequate measures for the relief of the distress, so that the people were compelled to look to outside quarters for aid. Parnell sent the following message to Chicago, December 12th: —

"DUBLIN, December 12, 1879.

"*To the Editor of the Chicago Daily News*,—

"The arrest of Davitt was prompted by the desire of the Government to get rid of him as the chief organizer of the land agitation, and also in hopes that the people would be intimidated by this step of prosecution, or driven to illegal and violent action. The result, instead of arresting the movement, has powerfully assisted it. Land clubs are being organized in every part of the kingdom, and subscriptions pour in. The Nationalists, Repealers, and Home Rulers are united, and have found a common platform and watchword, "The Land for the People." In its attempt to crush the movement, it may resolve upon future illegal and unconstitutional action, and the arrest of other leaders; but the landlords are cowed, and the Castle is intimidated by the determined action of the people. The threatened evictions are abandoned, as the result of the success of Balla's anti-eviction; there is no bidding for estates at the sales; in landed estates, the *courant* tenants are allowed to become owners on easy terms; the leading English reformers are in strong sympathy with our movement. The French press at last is showing its appreciation of the true position of affairs, and send special correspondents to watch the progress of the campaign. The cause of the people is maintained with redoubled vigor, notwithstanding the snow on the ground, and that famine and cold already pinch many. Great suffering is anticipated after Christmas, and the Government trusts that in this way the courage of the masses may be broken. Swarms of paid spies are infesting the country; additional troops are despatched to stations in the South and West, and large levies of constabulary recruits are just ordered; all indicating the determination of the Government to take advantage of the sufferings of the people, and drive them to deeds of violence. No relief works have yet been undertaken, nor is there any prospect of State assistance; but orders have been issued to prepare additional workhouse accommodations. The attitude of our people up to the present time is magnificent: they are self-restrained and reliant, and resolved not to be betrayed into any precipitate or illegal action.

"An important meeting of the executive committee of the National Land League was held to-day, when, among other important business, it was decided that I should leave for New York with John Dillon, son of the late John B. Dillon, as soon as possible.

(Signed) "CHARLES STEWART PARNELL."

Great meetings were now organized throughout England to protest against the arbitrary action of the Government, and aid the Irish Land League movement. On November 30th, one hundred thousand people assembled in Hyde Park, London, to sympathize with the agitation in Ireland. Messrs. Parnell, Davitt, and Finigan delivered addresses at meetings in various English towns.

On Sunday, November 30th, Mr. Davitt addressed a crowded meeting of the Irishmen of the Tyneside, in the Music Hall, Gateshead. A tremendous crowd assembled in front of the Central Station, Newcastle, and, preceded by a banner and band, accompanied Mr. Davitt in procession across the Tyne to the meeting-place in Gateshead. The streets of the latter place were lined with spectators, and the large Music Hall was crowded to the doors. Mr. Councillor McAnulty occupied the chair.

In his address Mr. Davitt said,—

"The definition of rent given by John Stuart Mill was the surplus profit left to the tenant-farmer after he had paid the wages of his laborers and provided for his own and his children's wants. Now, in Ireland this year there was not only no surplus profit, but there was not a sufficiency to keep the people alive. Therefore, according to John Stuart Mill's definition of rent, there was no rent in the country, and therefore there was no rent to pay. But, although he had adduced that argument on many platforms, he had not told the people to act up to its logical conclusion, and to pay no rent. He had told them to see to their own and their children's wants, and then to go to the landlord and offer him what they had left; and surely, under the circumstances, no people could be asked to do more. Regarding this solemn contract that they heard so much about between the tenant-farmer and his landlord, he held that a compulsory contract was not as binding as if it was a voluntary one; and he said that the contract between landlords and tenants in Ireland was compulsory,—and why? Ireland was essentially an agricultural country. They had no factories; they had no industries, such as were in England; they had no Manchesters, Liverpools, Tynesides, or Gatesheads.

If the tenant-farmer in England found he had to pay what he considered was a rack-rent, he could throw up his farm and go into the next manufacturing town and get employment for himself and his children. But in Ireland he could not do that: if he gave up his farm, he had only one of two courses to take,—either to walk into the workhouse, or to leave Ireland forever and seek his bread in exile. Hence when a landlord went to a tenant and said he would raise his rent from £10 to £12, or from £12 to £15 a year, what alternative had he? Would they ask him to go to the workhouse, would they ask him to take his family to England or to America, while he had that love for his fatherland which characterized all the Irish people, and which he hoped would always characterize them? Certainly not. And that was the compulsion, and a contract entered into under those circumstances was not a fair contract, was not a just contract; and was not as binding as a contract would be here in England, where the tenant had the alternative either of paying his rent, or throwing up his farm and seeking employment in his own country, which employment the Irishman could not find in Ireland.

"Having said so much upon this question of rent, he came to another demand that they had made in Ireland, and that demand was that the four or five millions of acres of waste land to be found in Ireland should be reclaimed. Now, surely if there was anything wicked in his having asked for assistance to prevent the people from starvation, there was nothing malicious, to quote the words of the warrant for his arrest, in asking that the waste land of Ireland should be reclaimed, in order to find employment for the people, and in order to benefit the country. Surely there was nothing revolutionary in that. There was nothing to alarm even the Government of England, or to frighten the landlords with the ghost of Communism or Socialism. Travelling throughout Ireland, they would see in all parts, in every county, splendid land running to waste; and the explanation they would get from the car-driver, or from those with whom they came in contact, was that those lands had been quitted in the famine years. The people were driven from them, and sent to the workhouse to die, and some across to England. Since then this land had lain fallow. Well, when that land was created by Almighty God, it was not intended to lie fallow, it was not intended to run waste: it was intended to produce food to support the people whom God intended to be the inhabitants of Ireland; and if they now asked that that land should be put to the use for which it was created,—namely, that it should be reclaimed in order to give employment to willing people, to keep capital in the country, and to increase the value of cereal produce,—surely there was nothing wicked or revolutionary in that. That was one of the demands that they had made from those 'violent and inflammatory' platforms in Ireland during the last twelve months.

"They had asked that some of the church surplus should be employed in reclaiming this waste land.

"Landlordism was a system which was responsible for the deaths, he might almost say to the number of two millions of their people, during the famine years of 1847–48; and when he saw the hovels their people were compelled to live in now on account of that system,—when he saw the poverty and degradation which prevailed on a land made fruitful by the bounty of God, — it was impossible for him to restrain his indignation. This system was responsible for the misery of the Irish people; and when he saw their forced exile to England, often to spend a life of toil and misery, and yet was asked to speak of it in buttered phrases, he answered 'No.' He held that he had a double duty to perform in denouncing it; and so long as he had brain to plan, hand to dare, or heart to feel for Ireland, so long would he stand an uncompromising enemy to landlordism.

"He had taken part in this agitation from a sense of duty. He had felt that a crisis was coming to his country, and that it was necessary to rouse the people of Ireland in order that they should not be guilty of the suicidal act, the guilty act, of lying down to die as their kindred did in '48. That was a blot upon their country. Although he could lay the blame on alien misgovernment, still it did not redound to the credit of the people of 1847–48 that they lay down on the roadside and died. Mr. Parnell and others were determined that such a state of things would not be allowed to come without the Government being forewarned of it. In conclusion, he asked the support of the Irishmen of Tyneside in behalf of the Irish National Land League, of which Mr. Parnell was the head. This league made war against no political party in Ireland; it was a neutral platform, upon which the Nationalist, Home Ruler, Repealer, and Non-participant could stand together,— upon which every Irishman worthy of the name could join without compromising his particular principles on these heads; and its object was to root the people on the soil, and make them prosperous, contented, and happy. Surely there was no man who would stand on a quibble of principle, and refuse to co-operate in this great labor. He was a Nationalist, and not a Home Ruler; but still on this platform he recognized no difference, for he believed that Home Ruler and Repealer were anxious to have their people comfortable and happy. In this league they sunk political differences, and grasped hands in order to rescue a starving people, and to raise Ireland from that social degradation in which landlordism had sunk it."

After speaking at some of the great English meetings, Mr. Parnell, accompanied by Mr. Dillon, sailed for America, where they arrived by the steamer *Scythia*, on Friday, January 2. Receptions for the Land League delegates had meanwhile been arranged in many of the American cities.

CHAPTER XII.

PARNELL AND DILLON IN NEW YORK.—GREAT MEETING IN MADISON SQUARE GARDEN.—PARNELL ADDRESSES CONGRESS.—THE FAMINE IN IRELAND.—HOW THE LANDLORDS ACTED.—THE RELIEF BILL.—LAND MEETING ON THE SPOT WHERE DAVITT WAS BORN.

"A million a decade! What does it mean?
A nation dying of inner decay;
A churchyard's silence where life has been;
The base of the pyramid crumbling away;
A drift of men gone over the sea,
A drift of the deȧd where men should be."
—SPERANZA.

The critical condition of affairs in Ireland, coupled with the recent appeals for aid made to the Irish race in America, produced great sympathy in favor of the agitation, and a desire on the part of Irish-Americans to render all the aid possible, both for the people who were on the verge of starvation, and for the prosecution of the agitation. Meetings were held in various cities throughout the States to devise the best means of meeting the emergency. From many of those meetings delegates were sent to New York with offers of aid, and invitations to Messrs. Parnell and Dillon, who had just arrived, to visit the several towns represented and address the people.

The first great meeting at which the Land

League delegates — Messrs. Parnell and Dillon — spoke, was held in Madison Square Garden, New York, on Sunday evening, January 4th, 1880, nine thousand persons being present. The reception given the delegates by the vast multitude was intensely enthusiastic. Mrs. Parnell and her three daughters were present. Judge Alker, Chairman of the Reception Committee, introduced the Hon. Henry E. Gildersleeve — the rifleman — as chairman of the meeting, who introduced Mr. Parnell. After Messrs. Parnell and Dillon had delivered speeches, the following resolutions were adopted : —

"*Resolved*, — 1. That Mr. Charles Stewart Parnell and Mr. John Dillon are deserving of our earnest gratitude and most unqualified confidence; that the sacrifices they have made and the perils they have encountered in coming to this prosperous land to plead the cause of a suffering nation are entitled to a generous and practical recognition and response; and that the promises made by us in our welcoming address it should be our pride as well as our duty to redeem.

"2. That we give our suffering brothers in Ireland our heart-whole sympathies in these the days of their deep distress; and, while giving sympathy, we would counsel hope for the better day which, in God's good time, will assuredly come.

"3. That while the relief of the immediate suffering has a claim upon our immediate action, we cannot overlook the fact that the system which produces this suffering needs change; that money for the purchase of food, fuel, and raiment for the afflicted poor is needed at once, and that, beyond and besides this primary call, funds are needed to strengthen the hands of the Irish Land League in their struggle against landlord monopoly; and that, therefore, we suggest to the generous public that, while remembering the pressing claims now presented for relief, there is an obligation to aid in the prevention of the recurrence of such claims; and this latter can only be effected by that readjustment of the land tenure of Ireland contemplated by the Irish Land League.

"4. That subscription lists be at once opened, a finance committee, secretaries, and treasurers appointed, and that a formal and earnest appeal be made to aid in the grand achievement of giving an ancient people a living in their own land; realizing the idea given utterance to by Mr. Parnell, on arrival, of giving Ireland a place among the nations of the earth, — in other words, 'Ireland for the Irish and the Irish for Ireland.'"

The visiting delegates were now fairly before the American people. They travelled continuously, and spoke at meetings all over the United States during January, February, and March. Mr. Parnell said, before his departure, they had travelled 10,000 miles and spoken in 62 cities. They were everywhere accorded enthusiastic receptions by the American people, as well as by the Irish-Americans. The object of their visit proved eminently successful, both as regards sympathy and material aid, $200,000 having been subscribed, according to Mr. Parnell's own words.

On Monday, the 2d of February, by vote of Congress, Mr. Parnell addressed the House on the state of Ireland. The action of Congress on the matter was as follows: On the 29th January, Mr. Young, of Ohio, submitted the following resolution, which was read, considered, and agreed to:—

"*Resolved by the House of Representatives*, That the invitation extended to this body to hear the address of Hon. Mr. Parnell, a member of Parliament, to be delivered in this city on the evening of February 2, on the distressed condition of Ireland, be accepted."

Mr. Cox, of New York, proposed the following resolution, to follow that of Mr. Young:—

"In response to the invitation just presented and accepted, requesting the House to agree to take part in the ceremonies to be observed in the reception of Mr. Charles Stewart Parnell, a representative of the Irish people, for the delivery of an address on Irish affairs, and because of the great interest which the people of the United States take in the condition of Ireland, with which this country is so closely allied by many historic and kindred ties: Therefore,—

"*Be it resolved*, That the Hall of this House be granted for the above purpose, on the 2d day of February next, and that the House meet on that day and time to take part in the ceremonies."

On the evening of the day named the House was packed with Congressmen, Senators, ladies, and visitors. At 7.30 o'clock, Speaker Randall entered the Hall, accompanied by Parnell. The Speaker read the resolution under which the session of the evening was held. He then said, that, in conformity with that resolution, he had the honor and pleasure to introduce Charles Stewart Parnell, M. P., who had come among them to speak of the distress of his country.

Mr. Parnell was received with applause from the floor and galleries. He commenced his speech by thanking the House for the honor conferred upon him, and entered at once upon an explanation of the wrongs of the Irish people and the causes of it, which he ascribed to the system of land tenure. Every allusion that was made to the help that America was giving to Ireland was received with demonstrations of approval. In the course of his speech, Mr. Parnell said it would be a proud boast for America if it should aid in reforming the land tenure of Ireland and solving the question without the shedding of one drop of blood, as it could do. He alluded to the fact that he had American blood in his veins, and this elicited a perfect storm of applause. He thanked Americans for the generosity of their contributions, and hoped this would be the last Irish famine they would have to aid. He concluded his speech at 8.22 o'clock, and the House immediately adjourned. At the close of the meeting Mr. Parnell held a levee in the hall, and was introduced to members and others by Speaker Randall.

Parnell's speech was cabled to London by the British minister at Washington, as soon as it was delivered: it was a bitter pill for John Bull to swallow; but he had to swallow it, all the same.

While Messrs. Parnell and Dillon were pursuing their patriotic mission in the United States, most appalling accounts of the dreadful suffering caused by the famine in Ireland were being published daily in the press. In the beginning of January, 1880, Mr. Davitt visited Connemara to see for himself the state of affairs in that wild region. On his return to Dublin he reported at a meeting of the Irish National Land League, January 13, that both priests and people with whom he had conversed expressed the belief that private charity would be insufficient to cope with the distress between March and June, and that Government aid would alone prevent starvation. The people along the sea-coast from Spiddal to Clifden were, he said, eating the potatoes that should be kept for seed. He suggested that relief committees should not overlook the necessity of providing seed for districts where people had been compelled to use as food what should be reserved for the coming seed-time. No out-door relief was given by unions along the Connemara sea-coast.

A few of the particular cases of distress reported in January and February will give a fair idea of what the general suffering must have been in those months. On January 14, sixty able-bodied men with their families were admitted to the Killarney workhouse. On the same day, a woman with three children, one of whom was dead in her arms from hunger and exposure, applied for admission; she had walked from Cahirciveen, forty miles, seeking food for her children.

On January 23, a letter from Clifden, County Galway, was published in Dublin, which said,—

"Last evening Clifden presented an appalling picture. Crowds of ragged, famished men and women thronged around the doors of the meal-shops, clamoring for food. Many had waited up all through the night in the bitter frost, besieging the houses of the relief committee. Several thousands flocked into town during the day, demanding relief. Several men seized members of the committee, crying, 'We are starving; we must have food!' The police had to be called in to clear the meal-shops of the mob. They gathered threateningly around the house where the relief committee were sitting. Knots of men and women, who could not be reached that day by the relief committee remained in the street until midnight, although the air was intensely cold. Fever has broken out at Carna; four families are stricken down in one village."

On February 13, a poor woman, named Mary Hurley, whose sense of shame put begging and the workhouse out of the question, died of absolute want in Fermoy, County Cork. Many others in the same town were reported to be approaching the last stage of misery. On February 21, a case of insanity, resulting from destitution, was reported from Straloffath, near Letterkenny, County Donegal. A man named Denis Martin lived with his sister and a brother's child on a high mountain farm of twenty-six acres, the rent of which was £4 3s. 8d.,—an increase, it was stated, of 50 per cent. over the rent paid some years ago. Three months previously his cows were seized for arrears of rent, and his horse, by which he was able to eke out a living by carting turf to Letterkenny, died. Their extreme poverty was concealed until the day named, when Martin's sister made an attempt on the life of the child, whose screams attracted the neighbors, and it was discovered that they had had no food for four days. The sister was put into an asylum, and Martin, who had likewise exhibited symptoms of lunacy, was taken care of by his brother, who was also in distress.

At a meeting of the Mansion House Committee on January 31, Lord Mayor Gray referred to the reports that three inquests had been held in the neighborhood of Parsonstown, wherein verdicts were rendered of death from destitution.

The Registrar General for Ireland stated, at a

meeting of the Marlborough Relief Committee, that according to the best information in his possession two-thirds of the potato crop, representing five and three-quarter million of pounds sterling, failed in 1879. This, coupled with the bad harvests the two previous years, brought the people to the verge of the famine-graves from which they were rescued by the Land League; for, had it not been for the timely and energetic action of that body, thousands of trenches would have been filled with famine-corpses, as in 1846–47.

The landlords were by no means idle spectators of what was transpiring around them. They thought it high time to go for their "pound of flesh," while a little yet remained on the bones of their gaunt victims. Ejectments and processes were being showered in on the famine districts, so that the price of the last loaf which was to save the life of a hungry child might be captured before it was devoured. The people resisted the writs which would deprive them of their last hope, and police bayonets were frequently reddened in the blood of the starving peasants. Here are a few instances worthy of being remembered and placed to the debit side of the landlord account.

In the beginning of January a process-server, named Langley, surrounded with police, went to serve ejectments at Knockrickard, six miles from Claremorris, County Mayo; their way was barred by about five hundred women and girls, who precipitated themselves on the constabulary to get at Langley and take the writs from him. The report of the affair says: "A scene of terrible confusion and dread ensued. The officers drew their swords and rushed among the women, most of whom were bareheaded and barefooted. One young woman had her scalp cut by a sword; another had a bayonet thrust in her arm; several were knocked down, trampled on, and had their dresses torn."

Again, in the same month, the Irish correspondent of the *New York Herald*, who at that time would not err in favor of the peasantry, writing to his paper in reference to a similar incident, said,—

"The actual scene of this business was the village of Carraroe, which is on the coast, about twenty miles from the town of Galway. The local police anticipating a popular movement, occupied the house before the arrival of the crowd, and thus frustrated their intentions. Messengers were dispatched to the station at Spiddal, five miles distant, asking for re-enforcements. These arrived during the evening, and the police remained on the premises all night. Meanwhile the telegraph wires had been in operation, and the next morning an additional detachment of fifty constables arrived on the scene. In the midst of this little army, Fenton, the process-server, issued from the house to execute his legal mission. The first house visited was that of William Faherty. Women surrounded the door, and, as Fenton advanced to effect service, they clutched the process and tore it to shreds. The police then charged all round with their sword bayonets, wounding several severely. The women were bayoneted right and left; and one of them, Mrs. Conneally, sustained such injuries that the last rites of the Church had to be administered to her by the Rev. P. J. Newell, the Catholic priest of the place, who was an eye-witness of the scene.

"The police then proceeded to the cabin of a man named Connéally, about three hundred yards distant. They smashed open the door, which was closed, and service was effected. James Mackle's house was next visited. The women again surrounded the door, and endeavored to wrest the process from Fenton. The police charged a second time indiscriminately, knocked some of the people down, and, it is stated, bayoneted one man while on the ground, unmercifully. Up to this the men had not interfered beyond crowding round, and no missiles were thrown at the constabulary; but now sticks and stones were freely used, and a terrible *melée* ensued. The police became much excited, and at last fired some shots over the heads of their assailants. Then the process-server attempted to deliver the document. The women, as before, snatched it out of his hand and destroyed it. Sub-Inspector Gibbons rushed into the house, and, as he advanced to the hearth, Mrs. Mackle lifted a blazing turf, and smashed it on his neck. Smarting from the burning, the officer rushed back to the door, and in the struggle his sword was knocked out of his hand. The commanding officer considered that the situation was now too critical to act without the presence of a magistrate, whose orders would relieve the constables of the legal responsibility of a conflict with the peasantry. Accordingly the whole force was withdrawn, and concentrated at the police barrack in the village, where the process-server remained for protection."

On January 17, the police, escorting a party of process-servers, at Kilmina, County of Mayo, were severely maltreated, and obliged to retreat, though they had their rifles loaded and bayonets fixed. Several of the police were cut about the head and face. The process-servers had their clothing torn, and the processes were captured by the mob.

Such was the state of Ireland when the Irish National Land League, through its delegates, was appealing to the American people to save the lives of the Irish peasantry.

On January 23, Messrs. Davitt, Brennan, Daly, and Killen were served with writs calling on them, in answer to their recognizances, to appear before the Court of Queen's Bench, failing in which they were to be again arrested. When they appeared in court, further time to plead was granted. The Government, however, saw they had bungled in making the arrests, and allowed the case to drop.

At a meeting of the Irish National Land League on January 26, it was resolved "that Mr. Michael Davitt should be deputed to wait upon the editors of the French and other continental newspapers, to enlist their support in efforts for the relief of distress in Ireland." Accordingly Mr. Davitt, accompanied by Mr. Killen, shortly afterwards visited France and Belgium to collect information regarding the land system in those countries, and to carry out the mission delegated to them.

Parliament was opened on February 5, and a relief bill was introduced shortly afterwards, which disqualified from voting those who received aid through its provisions, and which was afterwards so tied up with red tape that it proved of little value. The whole country might have starved while the Board of Works were getting ready to administer it.

Meanwhile the agitation was continued with unabated energy. On February 1, 1880, over 15,000 people assembled on the spot where Mr. Michael Davitt was born. The platform was erected over the very ruins of the old homestead from which the family had been evicted. It was at this meeting Mr. Davitt delivered the speech, a portion of which we quoted in our second chapter. His vigorous denunciation of landlordism was as follows: —

"The public mind of Ireland is at present occupied with two absorbing questions, each of which has succeeded in obtaining prominence; namely, through the instrumentality of this agitation. The distress is, unfortunately, the agony cry of the hour, and must, therefore, be considered by all Irishmen as constituting the one supreme object round which the sympathy and assistance of all parties must rally in vigorous efforts to raise our people from starvation, and to minimize the miseries which dog the footsteps of famine. While every nerve must be strained to stave off, if possible, the horrible fate which befell our famine-slaughtered kindred in 1847 and 1848, the attention of our people must not for a moment be withdrawn from the primary cause of these periodical calamities, nor their exertions be relaxed in this great social struggle for the overthrow of the odious system responsible for them.

"Let landlordism be removed from our country, and labor be allowed the wealth which it creates, instead of being given to legalized idlers, and no more famine will darken our land or hold Ireland up to the gaze of the civilized world as a nation of paupers. England deprives us annually of some seven millions of money for Imperial taxation, and she allows an infamous land system to rob our country of fifteen or twenty millions more each year to support some nine or twelve thousand lazy landlords; and then, when famine extends its destroying wings over the land, and the dread spectre of Death stands sentinel at our thresholds, an appeal to English charity — a begging-box outside the London Mansion House — is paraded before the world, and expected to atone for every wrong inflicted upon Ireland by a heartless and hated Government, and to blot out the records of the most monstrous land code that ever cursed a country or robbed humanity of its birthright. It is humiliating to the last degree that a few thousand land-sharks should have so long and so successfully trod upon the necks of millions of Irishmen, and defrauded them of the fruits of their land, while at the same time robbing, insulting, and dragooning our country with an inhumanity unsurpassed by the titled plunderers of the Middle Ages. An average landlord may be likened to a social vulture hovering over the heads of the people, and swooping down upon the earnings and the food which that industry produces, whenever his appetite or his avarice prompts him. The tenantry in the past have stood by like a flock of frightened sheep, timid and terrified, unable to prevent this human bird of prey from devouring their own and their children's substance. While rack-rents were paid by the farmer, his family must live in semi-starvation, in wretched hovels, amid squalor and privations, barbed by the thought that the money earned by labor and sweat from day to day was being spent by his own and his children's deadly enemy, in another land, in voluptuous ease and sensual gratification. If the rack-rent was not paid, and this black mail levied upon labor in the shape of rent was not forthcoming, to be squandered by one who never earned a penny of it, out upon the roadside the earners would be cast, to take their choice of death by exposure, workhouse degradation, or banishment from home and Ireland for ever."

CHAPTER XIII.

THE NATIONAL LAND LEAGUE STARTED IN AMERICA.—DAVITT AGAIN VISITS THE UNITED STATES.—FIRST LAND LEAGUE CONVENTION IN NEW YORK.—AMERICA'S AID DURING THE FAMINE.—THE COMPENSATION FOR DISTURBANCE BILL REJECTED.—EVICTIONS.—DAVITT IN SAN FRANCISCO.—THE LADIES' LAND LEAGUE BEGUN.—DAVITT LEAVES FOR IRELAND.—BOYCOTTING BOYCOTT.—THE STATE TRIALS.—THE COERCION ACT IN FORCE.

"Beautiful Ireland! who will preach to thee?
Souls are waiting for lips to vow;
And outstretched hands, that fain would reach thee,
Yearn to help, if they knew but how,
To lift the thorn-wreath off thy brow."
—SPERANZA.

BEFORE his return to Ireland, Mr. Parnell announced that it was his intention to call a convention in Boston for the purpose of effecting a permanent organization of Irish-Americans; and, in anticipation of that event, meetings were held in a number of cities, so that delegates might be chosen. This project was frustrated by the early recall to Ireland of Mr. Parnell, in consequence of the dissolution of Parliament. He sailed from New York on the *Baltic*, on Thursday, March 11. New York had previous to this taken the initiative to form an organization in connection with the Irish National Land League. On Sunday, March

7, two important meetings were held in that city, —one at the Astor House, the other at Military Hall, 193 Bowery.

The Astor House meeting was composed principally of gentlemen who had taken an active part in the reception of Mr. Parnell; and among them were prominent Nationalists, members of the Ancient Order of Hibernians, the St. Patrick's Mutual Alliance, the 'Longshoremen's Union, the Temperance Societies, and the Catholic Young Men's Society. Mr. John C. Hennessy presided, and Mr. Wm. B. Clarke acted as Secretary. Among those present were Walter M. O'Dwyer, J. J. W. O'Donoghue, Dr. Wallace, Dr. Charles S. Smith, Stephen J. Meany, T. R. Bannerman, Dennis A. Spellissy, John J. Breslin, Charles A. O'Rourke, John Henry McCarthy, James J. Treacy, John Devoy, and Roger Burke. After a very harmonious discussion, a resolution was passed forming the meeting into the "Irish National Land League and Relief Association of New York." Sixteen sub-committees, appointed at a meeting the previous Sunday, reported having succeeded in establishing a nucleus of an organization in their respective wards, and gave encouraging assurances of the good-will manifested towards the movement. A committee consisting of John Devoy, Thomas R. Bannerman, Dr. C. J. Smith, John J. Breslin, Walter M. O'Dwyer, Wm. Connolly, and John C. Hennessy, was appointed to draw up a constitution and by-laws, and report at the next meeting, and these, with Mr. O'Dwyer as chairman, Drs. Donlin, Wallace, and McGuire, and Colonel Michael Kirwin added, were appointed as a temporary Executive Committee.

At the Military Hall meeting, five delegates each from twenty Irish National organizations were present. Mr. Cornelius Roche was elected chairman. After some discussion, it was unanimously resolved to organize an association to aid the Irish National Land League, to be called the Irish National Land League of New York. A committee to draw up an address to the Irish people of New York and a constitution and by-laws was appointed.

In the evening an informal conference took place between some of the officers elected at each of those meetings, and arrangements were made for a formal conference at the Astor House, with a view to having a joint meeting on the following Sunday, merging the two bodies, and uniting their efforts to thoroughly organize New York City.

On the day of Mr. Parnell's departure for Ireland, in response to an invitation issued by him to the representatives of various Irish societies and prominent Irishmen, a conference was held in the New York Hotel. There were twenty-eight Irish organizations represented; after some discussion, it was decided to form a National Irish Land League in the United States, to be auxiliary to the

Irish National Land League in Dublin. Mr. Parnell, in addressing the conference, said that in his absence Mr. Dillon would fill his place. He asked that the conference sustain him, and spread the Land League organization all over the continent. The meeting adopted the following resolutions:—

"1. That in the opinion of this meeting it is expedient that an auxiliary organization of the Irish Land League be formed in America, in harmony with the organization in Ireland, and to assist its objects.

"2. That the Irish Land League in America be organized by States, Territories (and District of Columbia), with an Executive Council for each, the members of which are to be elected by the several local branches in the State; each being entitled to a representation in the council, in proportion to membership. The President, Secretary, and Treasurer shall reside in the same city.

"3. That there shall be a Central Council in the Union, consisting of representatives from the several State Councils, through whom official communications and funds may be forwarded to the Dublin Executive of the Irish National Land League. The Secretary, Treasurer, and President to reside in the same city.

"4. That a convention of local associations to elect their State Council for the transaction of business meet within their State at least once a year.

"5. That a convention of representatives of State Councils be held yearly to elect the Central Council in the same way.

"6. That a Committee on Rules be hereby appointed

to draw up suggestions for the guidance of the councils and the local associations, such rules being held to be the rules of the councils and associations, unless objected to by a majority of the branches and councils after the lapse of one month after the notification thereof.

"7. That an Executive Committee of this meeting, consisting of one from each organization represented, be appointed to select said committee."

Mr. Parnell deputed to the Committee itself the work of appointing the Committee on Rules; and he suggested the adoption of the following resolution as defining said duty:—

"*Resolved,*—That a committee be appointed, with power to add to its number gentlemen from all parts of the Union, to carry out the resolution adopted at the full meeting; this committee to have power to consult with leading gentlemen in various parts of the country, and to extend and promote the organization."

In accordance with the last resolution, the committee appointed issued the following circular, on March 30, to one hundred and eight gentlemen in all parts of the United States, whose names had been approved of for a provisional Central Council. Mr. Parnell had himself selected many of the names before his departure:—

"*Dear Sir,*—A Conference of representatives of Irish societies, and gentlemen friendly to the Irish Land movement, was held, on Mr. Parnell's invitation, at the

New York Hotel in this city, on Thursday, the 11th March, inst., for the purpose of taking counsel as to the best means of furthering the cause of land reform in Ireland. After a thorough discussion of the subject, it was decided that an Irish Land League should be formed in the United States, for the purpose of rendering moral and financial aid to the Irish National Land League of Ireland. The resolutions herewith enclosed, and the statements of the objects of the Irish Land League, will explain the action already taken.

"Pending the complete organization of the American branch of the League, and the election of a representative Central Council, the Conference decided that the supervision and direction of the movement should be intrusted to a Provisional Central Council, to be appointed by Mr. Parnell, aided in his choice by the advice of a committee appointed by the Conference. On account of Mr. Parnell's hasty departure for Ireland, he found it necessary to depute the selection of this Provisional Central Council to the committee appointed by the Conference. That committee held several meetings, and at its final gathering at Mott Memorial Hall, in New York, on Sunday the 21st of March, the names of the following gentlemen, many of whom were suggested by Mr. Parnell, were unanimously selected as the Provisional Central Council of the Irish Land League of the United States. [Here occur the names selected.]

"After the appointment of a sub-committee of seven for the purpose of notifying the gentlemen elected, and arranging for a meeting of the Provisional Central Council, the committee adjourned *sine die*.

"We, the undersigned members of the sub-committee, have, therefore, the honor to inform you that you have been duly elected a member of the Provisional Central Council of the Irish Land League of America, and to request the favor, at your earliest convenience, of a reply, stating your acceptance or declination of the position, and the time and the place which you would find most convenient for a meeting of the Council. We enclose blank for that purpose. Very respectfully,

"T. J. KEARNEY, M. D., Chairman.
"DAVID T. LYNCH, Secretary.
"THOMAS J. BYRNE, Treasurer.
"JAMES W. O'BRIEN.
"STEPHEN J. MEANY.
"JOHN DEVOY.
"J. C. McGUIRE.
"*Committee.*"

The other great cities were not far behind New York. Meetings were held, and organizations on the basis of the rules of the New York central body were formed. In Boston, on April 15, a great meeting was held in Faneuil Hall, at which Mr. John Dillon spoke. After the meeting, some hundreds of those present handed in their names as Land Leaguers, and subsequently held a meeting and appointed Hon. P. A. Collins, Chairman, with P. J. Flatley and P. J. O'Daly as Secretaries, and the following committee to perfect plans for a permanent organization of the League: Messrs. Patrick Donahoe, M. F. Lynch, Thos. O'Flynn, John Tighe, Thos. E. Lambert, John J.

Hayes, and D. B. Cashman. The organization was perfected at a meeting in John A. Andrew Hall, April 23.

Michael Davitt left Ireland on Sunday, May 10, for the United States, as the representative of the Irish National Land League, to assist, with Mr. John Dillon, in the organization of the League throughout the States. He arrived just in time to attend the first National Convention of the Central Provisional Council, which was held in Trenor Hall, New York, on May 18, pursuant to a call issued by the sub-committee of seven. The Convention was opened by Mr. John C. McGuire, of Brooklyn, N. Y., when Mr. John Boyle O'Reilly, of Boston, was elected temporary chairman. On taking the chair, Mr. O'Reilly delivered the following address: —

"He who should strike the true tone for the Land League of America must be one who looked over the whole field of Irish political, social, and industrial interests, and who should speak a word to linger in the mind and smelt into harmony every healthy element of the race. This convention was essentially one of unification. To-day, with millions in America, Irish nationality was only a sentiment. To-morrow it should be a system. The duty of the Convention was to reduce into operative form the best aspirations and principles of the people. When this is done, a danger is averted. It is wiser to follow organized principles than to follow men, however excellent they be. When the masses follow men, they may be dangerous to their enemy; when they follow principles, they become terrible. Impotent action breeds contempt and pity. Too much of Ireland's national action has been futile and impotent. It is time to reduce the fight to reason and science, and take advantage of every opportunity. Ireland must plead her case and make her charges against her powerful enemy,—not in the dark, where she may be strangled and gagged, as heretofore,—but in the market-place, before the world."

The Hon. P. A. Collins, of Boston, was subsequently elected permanent President of the Convention; Rev. S. Cronin, Buffalo, first Vice-President; Patrick Madden, of Peoria, Treasurer; and Dr. R. Shields, Westchester, N. Y., Secretary. The Convention adopted the following resolutions:—

"Whereas, A famine has been raging in Ireland for the past six months, and at the present moment hundreds of thousands of the people are being fed by the charity of foreign nations; and whereas, the terrible national affliction is of periodical recurrence, we deem it our duty to declare our conviction that these famines do not arise from natural causes, but are the results of bad laws enacted by the English Government and maintained despite the Irish people. Therefore, be it

"*Resolved*, That it is the duty of every Irishman to aid to the utmost of his ability all honorable effort made by the Irish people to free themselves from these ruinous laws.

Resolved, That we regard the present system of land tenure in Ireland as one of the chief causes of famine, and of the chronic poverty and oppression which prevails in that country.

Resolved, That the National Land League of Ireland, having appealed to the Irish of America to assist them in removing the cause of poverty, we hereby pledge the earnest co-operation of this organization to the Irish Land League, in the work of abolishing the present English land system, and establishing a peasant proprietary in Ireland.

Resolved, That, while prepared to aid the Irish Land League to the utmost of our ability, we desire to place on record our conviction that the kindred interests of manufacturing, mining, fisheries, and commerce are also being protracted by deliberate and wickedly selfish restrictive legislation, and that poverty must remain the normal condition of the Irish people until they recognize the power to regulate and protect these interests."

The board of officers elected by the Convention for the National Organization were: President, James J. McCafferty, Lowell, Mass.; Vice-President, William Purcell, Rochester, N. Y.; Treasurer, Rev. Lawrence Walsh, Waterbury, Conn.; Recording Secretary, Michael Davitt; Council,—Thaddeus Flanagan, San Francisco; Lawrence Harmon, Peoria, Ill.; Wm. Carroll, Philadelphia; Jas. Gibson, Paterson, N. J.; J. O. Reddy, Richmond, Va.; P. K. Walsh, Cincinnati, and M. E. Welsh, Providence, R. I.

The Central Council was instructed to meet regularly once in three months to pass on all questions of discipline and adjust disturbances in the branches of the League, and to fix the time for general conventions. A general convention was directed to be held once a year. To it each branch having 300 members or under was entitled to send a delegate, and each branch having over 300 delegates to send an additional delegate. The initiation fee was fixed at $1, and the annual fees not more than $1.

After Mr. John Dillon had delivered a speech, in which he gave an account of his three months' labors in America, Mr. Davitt was called for by the Convention. In response, he delivered the following address: —

"My first duty is to thank this Convention for the privilege of being present. I feel proud to find so many able and intelligent men earnestly working to help us in destroying landlordism. This movement extends from Dublin to San Francisco. It is a good omen that it will succeed when it reaches out so far and interests so many, and a sign that it will not fail like other movements. I am happy to say that the Land League movement in Ireland is in capital hands and trim, after a series of successes during the past six months. But these successes are only indicative of what is to come. While satisfied with them, we cannot still be content. We have succeeded all along the line, and what we have already done is a guarantee of what the future has in store. By your action to-day you have widened the programme outlined by the Land League in Ireland; but, although we omitted the Industrial question from the movement, it was not because we were unaware of its importance, or of the evils which Ireland's commerce suffers through unjust laws.

"I can assure you now that the addition which you have made to the platform to-day will be accepted by the Irish people on the other side. *As the movement for the abolition of the Irish landlord system was first started here*, I am glad that this later addition to it is made here also. I thank you warmly on behalf of the Irish people and the Land League for the magnificent support you have given them in the past, and for your generous preparations for the future. With such aid we will soon dispose of the greatest enemy to Ireland's welfare and progress. The organization of land leagues is now going on rapidly in the four provinces; and I am happy to say that the farmers in Ulster are following the example of those of Leinster, Connaught, and Munster in the grand work. The plan we work on is simple. We resort to every fair means to pull down and destroy the tyrant landlordism, and to trample it in the dust of its own rottenness. We cannot do it by parliamentary action alone, and we don't propose to confine ourselves to that means. What we propose is that the action of our men in Parliament shall be the reflex of the work going on in Ireland. It is an action of no compromise, and no man going to the House of Commons can say that our people will be satisfied with fixity of tenure or other mild reforms.

"There are two means which we pursue to accomplish our end. The first is a policy of destruction by hammering against the landlords and landlordism,—rack-rents. We are satisfied with nothing but their total abolition. In the House of Commons we pursue a constructive policy, so that you will be able to reconcile the speeches in Ireland against landlordism and in favor of the abolition of rents, and the speeches in the House which might not seem to be in keeping with those delivered by members of the same party in Ireland. If a landlord evicts a tenant, then the Land League takes action in the courts against him; and in every case, so far, we have won a victory. I don't think, in the face of the feeling prevailing at present in Ireland, that many wholesale evictions will take place, and I don't think a Liberal Government could afford to permit them. We aim to impress the farmers with the necessity of refusing to take any farm from which another tenant has been evicted, nor to bid for any cattle sold for rent. As an instance, a farmer named Reddington had his cattle seized for rent; but previous to the seizure he branded their horns with the words, 'rack-rent.' When the sale took place there were few bidders, although many persons attended, and the cattle were sold for one-third of their value.

"In conclusion, let me say, gentlemen, that the people of Ireland are full of confidence in you, and I think from what I have seen here to-day that they will not be mistaken. I can pledge to you their warmest gratitude for the sinews of war which you have furnished them to fight their great battle."

The Convention adjourned after having placed the national movement in America on a solid foundation, on which has since been built throughout the Union over eleven hundred branches, that are weekly sending to Ireland large amounts of money for the prosecution of the crusade against landlordism.

On Sunday, May 23, a reception was given to Mr. Davitt, in Jones' Wood, New York, at which Mrs. Parnell, the honored and patriotic mother of Charles Stewart Parnell, and her daughter, Miss Fanny Parnell, were present. The following is an extract from the speech delivered on that occasion by Mr. Davitt: —

"I speak to-day in the hearing of an illustrious Irishwoman, the mother of an illustrious Irishman, and cannot allow myself to be placed before him, the leader and the guiding spirit to whom is due the series of successes scored during the past year. The problem before us when we organized was simple, and our platform contains this single plank, — the destruction of landlordism and the winning of the land for the people, to whom it belongs. The Irish League includes all parties, — Nationalists, Moderates, Home Rulers, Repealers, and all sects,— Catholics and Protestants meeting in council to work until Ireland's social rights are won and her enemy struck down forever. We work by teaching peasants and all people that the land was made for them, and not for 10,000 lazy Englishmen; that, if they allow themselves to be trampled upon, they are worthy of oppression, and that they are to rely on themselves alone and not upon foreign or hostile legislators. Together with this system of instruction, we warn them not to despise the honest efforts in their behalf of Irishmen in Parliament, and that no principle is sacrificed by recognizing the courageous fight of

Parnell. When the people of Ireland find that united they can strike down rack-rents and prevent evictions while their friends labor in legislation, they can herald the day when these abuses will be swept away forever.

"We ask your aid, moral and material. We mean to attack this system openly and fairly, unscrupulous though our enemy be. We want you, too, to be united, —you who hope to see Ireland a nation; and you who think she is too weak for that, but still desire her independence."

Davitt now went to work to build up the League throughout the States. His first official act as Secretary of the Irish National Land and Industrial League was to have issued to "the Irish race in America" an address from the Council of the League, which bore his signature as Central Secretary, with those of the other officers. In this address occurred the following paragraphs, showing how the Land League expected its supporters in America to aid the objects of the home organization:—

"*First.*—By enlightening American public opinion as to the working of the Landlord System, and by exposing through the columns of the American press the oppressions and outrages which are practised on the tenant-farmers of Ireland.

"*Second.*—By the immense moral influence which their support exerts on the people at home, encouraging them to be steadfast in the struggle, and not to give way to despair.

"*Third.*—By contributing sufficient means to enable

the League to carry on the movement in Ireland on such a scale as is necessary to insure success."

And also the following purposes for which assistance was asked in America: —

"Up to the present," said the document, "through want of money, the League has been obliged to confine its operations chiefly to a few counties. The purposes for which funds are needed are: —

"*First.*— To enable the League to spread its organization throughout the thirty-two counties of Ireland.

"*Second.*— Pending the abolition of landlordism, to aid local branches of the Land League to defend in the courts such farmers as may be served with processes of ejectment, and thus enable them to obstruct such landlords as avail themselves of the poverty of the tenantry and the machinery of the law to exterminate the victims of the existing system.

"*Third.*— To enable the League to afford protection to those who are unjustly evicted. Already the League has been obliged to undertake the support of the families of the men who were recently sentenced to imprisonment for resisting eviction in one of the famine districts, and it is now supporting evicted families.

"*Fourth.*—To oppose the supporters of landlordism whenever and wherever they endeavor to obtain any representative position in Ireland which would be the means of aiding them in prolonging the existence of the present land laws and perpetuating the social degradation and misery of our people."

Mr. Davitt was now unceasing in his exertions in establishing branches. He visited a great many cities all through the country, leaving perfected organizations after him wherever he went, and arousing the people to greater exertions; so that, along with the large sums weekly sent from America to aid the starving people, very considerable amounts began also to be sent for League purposes; the Irish National Land League being particular to expend for the relief of distress the money sent for that purpose, not touching a cent for League objects, except what was specifically mentioned as being intended for such.

The noble conduct of America during this terrible famine crisis in Ireland will ever be written on the memory of the Irish race in letters of gold, and in significant contrast to the callous and mean conduct of the British Government in treating the distress. The *Constellation*, which sailed on March 28, laden with America's practical bounty for the starving people, was met on her arrival in Queenstown, April 20, by a Royal Duke, and a British Admiral with his war ship. They became so officious in *helping* the mode of distribution of the cargo as to almost give the impression that the relief ship and the food had come from England, instead of from the United States; and they certainly *did* filch a great share of the credit of that transaction. England is mean enough to rob a beggarman, and refuse him an alms out of the plunder.

An important event occurred some time after

Mr. Parnell's return to Ireland. The elections had resulted favorably to the supporters of the Land League, and the active section in Parliament was considerably increased. At a conference of the Irish parliamentary party, held in May, Mr. Parnell was elected leader, instead of Mr. Shaw. This position of prominence to Mr. Parnell was of the utmost importance to the furtherance of the objects of the League, which were placed in the fore-front of all questions emanating from the party. It also guaranteed that the people's fight against the landlords would be vigorously prosecuted in the House, until suitable legislation on the subject would have been obtained.

In the beginning of July, Mr. Forster, Chief Secretary for Ireland, introduced a relief bill into Parliament, entitled, "The Compensation for Disturbance (Ireland) Bill." The bill met with great opposition, even from some members of Gladstone's Cabinet,— one of whom, the Marquis of Lansdowne, the owner of 135,500 acres in Ireland, resigned his position as under-secretary for India, in consequence. In the debate on the bill, July 5, Mr. Gladstone said,—

"The greater part of the opposition to the bill was a revival of smouldering hostility to the Land Act. The bill must be judged from the standpoint of the Land Act, which created for the tenant an interest in the land, and improved the value, though it interfered with, property. Evictions, he said, were lamentably increasing; and it was necessary to employ a large number of police to enforce processes. Such a state of things nearly approached danger of civil war, and it was therefore necessary to take measures to prevent a serious crisis. The best means to combat anti-rent agitation was to remove justification for agitation."

The bill finally passed the Commons, but was killed in the House of Lords by a vote of 282 to 51. The landlord influence was at work in the aristocratic "Upper House," and succeeded in inducing the "titled idlers" to strangle the bill.

For the portion of the year up to July 1, 1880, 1696 evictions were reported in Ireland, distributed as follows: In Ulster, 552; in Munster, 495; in Leinster, 417; and in Connaught, 232. This would represent about 8,000 people who were thrown on the roadside by the landlords. After that date, owing to the thoroughness of the Land League organization, the ejectments considerably decreased.

Davitt travelled much, and worked hard through the summer months, in organizing branches throughout the West; and in the early part of September he was attacked with nervous fever, in Omaha, Nebraska, brought on by overtaxing his brain and physical powers. The gigantic work which he accomplished within a year was sufficient to break down a much stronger man. He soon rallied, however, and continued his tour to the Pacific coast, where he lectured in the chief towns. On September 21, an address from "the reformers of the West to Michael Davitt, the persecuted agitator and heroic apostle of the new civilization," was presented to him, in San Francisco, by Denis Kearney. The address abounded in the peculiar figures of speech for which Kearney was celebrated. Davitt's satirical reply was a hit which Denis should remember and profit by. He said, —

"To 'agitator' I make no objection, as every reformer must stir up and agitate the mass of his people if they are to achieve the object for which they struggle; but as to the title of 'heroic apostle of the new civilization' I can lay no particle of claim, as I am *too* irreverent for the dignity of an apostle, and too ignorant of what is to constitute the new civilization you credit me with propagating. I am fond of old names, about the meaning of which there can be no mistake, and I am of opinion that there is no advantage gained for the cause of reform by enveloping ideas or clothing principles in ambiguous or new-fangled language."

A new and novel feature in the agitation occurred in October. On the 15th of that month, Miss Fanny Parnell, assisted by other patriotic ladies, called a meeting in the New York Hotel, at which about fifty ladies were present. The meeting organized the "Ladies' Land League of New York," and appointed the following officers: — President, Mrs. D. T. Stewart Parnell; Vice-President, Miss Ellen Ford; Financial Secretary,

Miss Fanny Parnell; Treasurer, Mrs. Andrew Maguire; Recording Secretary, Miss Mary E. Maguire; Corresponding Secretary, Miss Jane Byrne. The Ladies' League has since been wonderfully developed by the untiring energy of Mrs. Parnell and Miss Ellen Ford. Its branches are spreading out in all directions where exists the National Land League, and Miss Anna Parnell has established a large number of branches in several counties in Ireland.

The news from Ireland that the Government was to indict Mr. Parnell and the other Land League leaders brought Mr. Davitt again to the East, determined to start at once for Ireland. Mr. Parnell and the Executive of the League requested Mr. Davitt to remain in the States, where his services would have been invaluable; but this he positively refused to do, saying that where there was danger there his post should be. Just before his departure for Ireland an immense meeting, organized by the Ladies' Land League, was held in New York, and presided over by the president, Mrs. Parnell. At this meeting Mr. Davitt delivered his last address in America.

He arrived in Queenstown on Saturday, November 20, and two days afterwards spoke at a Land League demonstration held at Mallow. In his speech he gave the following temperate advice: He said he understood the temper of the American people pretty well, and he believed that the late acts of agrarian violence in Ireland had done the Land League cause much harm in the United States. While he knew that the Land League was not, and could not be, held responsible in any way for those outrages, he would urge upon its members to use every effort to prevent a recurrence of them, if they wished to retain American sympathy. Such an organization as the Land League was the only one that could remove the terrible incubus of landlordism. The League, like the Government, desired the security of life and property; but, unlike the Government, it desired it for millions instead of for a few.

A great deal of excitement was caused all through Ireland, early in November, by the war on "Captain" Boycott,—an Englishman, agent for Lord Erne. Boycott's residence was at Lough Mask House, near Ballinrobe, County Mayo. He was an agent of the worst type, and had had difficulties with his workpeople, which showed him to be a paltry, mean-souled fellow. The culmination of the trouble arose out of his having ejectment notices served on Lord Erne's tenants. A body of police were protecting the process-server when serving the writs. The people attacked the party, who retreated and found refuge in Lough Mask House. Next day the whole side of the country struck against Boycott, and reduced him and his family to a state of siege. His servants were ordered to leave him, and they did so. No person could be hired to do a hand's-turn for the Englishman. A party of Orangemen were then organized, which, protected by a large force of military, proceeded to Lough Mask to save the agent's crops, that were rotting in the ground for want of harvesting. When the crops were gathered, the Orangemen, with Boycott and his family, surrounded by the small army of horse, foot, and artillery sent to protect them, left that part of the country, amid the groans and hootings of the people. The "Captain" left Lough Mask with a whole skin, owing to the advice of the Land League to the people. It is not likely that he will soon again visit that section. This was a caution to other land agents in the West. Shortly afterwards thirteen landlords, agents, and others were "Boycotted" at Knockamore, a village near Walshtown, and from that time "Boycotting" has become a wonderful power in the hands of the people. It completely ostracizes a man from communication with his neighbors. No one will buy or sell to him, or perform his work. It was just the weapon needed to scourge the enemies of the people "inside the law," and it has proved more effective than bullets.

The Gladstone Government had now determined on a vigorous crusade against the Land League, which had become powerful enough to shake the foundations of Irish landlordism. Its commands and decrees were religiously obeyed by the people. When Mr. Parnell was in America there were only thirty branches of the League in Ireland, and they were very weak. There were, in December, 1880, fully five hundred, and in each branch about two hundred paying members were enrolled, making altogether one hundred thousand paying recruits under its flag.

The Government began its skirmishing against the League by arresting Messrs. Healy and Walsh, who were tried for sedition at the Cork assizes, December 15, and acquitted by the jury after one hour's deliberation. More troops were being daily drafted into Ireland, with immense quantities of war material, including 20,000 rounds of buckshot from Woolwich, as landlord pills, to be given the people with the ejectment writs; in case the latter was refused, the former were to be administered.

On Tuesday evening, November 2, indictments were lodged by the Government against Messrs. Parnell, Dillon, Biggar, Timothy O'Sullivan, Sexton, Egan, Brennan, Malachy O'Sullivan, Boyton, Gordon Harris, Nally, Welsh, and Sheridan, for conspiracy. They comprised nineteen counts, including preventing payment of rent, defeating legal process, and obstructing the letting of farms and exciting hatred.

The trials began in Dublin on December 28. The line of defence, which was sketched by

Michael Davitt, was to deny the League's responsibility for agrarian outrages, and to fortify the denial by quoting press statements; also, to show that, notwithstanding the sufferings and distress through which the country had passed, the percentage of attacks on individuals was unusually small. The state trials lasted twenty-eight days; and on January 25, 1881, when the jury came into court, the foreman stated that it was impossible for them to agree, whereupon they were discharged; a juror previously stated that ten stood for acquittal, against two for conviction.

The Government, anticipating the failure to suppress the agitation through the law courts, determined to suspend the Constitution and strangle the agitation by the brute force of coercion. Accordingly, the day before the acquittal of the traversers,—on January 24, 1881,—the Coercion Bill now in force, entitled a "Bill for the protection of life and property in Ireland," was introduced in the House of Commons. Under its provisions any person may be arrested and thrown into prison, to remain there until the 30th of September, 1882, without trial or appeal, on the mere suspicion of a policeman or magistrate. Under this infamous Act a large number of the principal organizers of the Land League have since been arrested and consigned to Kilmainham and Galway prisons. The active section of the Irish party in Parliament gallantly fought the Coercion Bill, step by step, through all its stages, and were so successful in obstructing its passage through the House that the Government had to resort to the *clôture* gag, and expel them from the House of Commons before it was possible for it to pass. The British Parliament destroyed, by this act, its boasted independence, a member being at present completely at the mercy of the Speaker, who at any time may "name him," and have him suspended during the sitting.

After Mr. Davitt's departure for Ireland, the National Land League in America was left without an executive head, by the disappearance, rather suddenly and unexpectedly, of its President, James J. McCafferty, of Lowell. A convention was therefore convened at Buffalo, N. Y., on January 13, and the following Board of Officers elected: President, P. A. Collins, of Boston: Vice-presidents, Rev. P. Cronin, of Buffalo; Major T. P. Powdery, of Scranton, Penn.; Treasurer, Rev. Lawrence Walsh, of Waterbury, Conn.; Secretary, Thomas Flatley, of Boston.

CHAPTER XIV.

Davitt Arrested.— Again in a Convict's Garb.— Portland Prison described.— The Ticket-of-Leave. —The News in the House of Commons. — Expulsion of Thirty-four Members.— The National Land League Convention.— No Peace in Ireland while Davitt is in a Convict's Cell.

"Though the Saxon snake unfold
At thy feet his scales of gold,
And vow thee love untold,
Trust him not, Green Land!
Touch not with gloveless clasp
A coiled and deadly asp,
But with strong and guarded grasp
In your steel-clad hand!"
—R. D. Williams.

Michael Davitt arrested! was flashed through the Atlantic wires, February 3, 1881. The mean and vindictive *Liberal* (!) Government, foiled by Parnell and his colleagues in its purpose of rushing through Parliament the Coercion Bill, had pounced on the leader of a people struggling to free themselves from an oppression condemned by the same Government, and flung him back into a convict cell, into the company of the scum of British crime. Gladstone and Forster, while pretending sympathy to the wronged and suffering millions in Ireland, were tying up their victim with coercion cords, that they might the more easily vent their brutal malice on the agitators. The Irish law courts refused to convict the Land League leaders: therefore, the British Government suspended the law, to punish the people who were bold enough to demand their God-given rights. Davitt, the noble-hearted, gifted, and honored champion of his country's cause against oppression, who had already suffered long years of torture, dragged back to a British dungeon on a contemptible pretext of having violated the terms of his ticket-of-leave,—the civilized world cried shame! on the miserable tyrants who could stoop to so paltry a trick of *state policy* to serve an ignoble purpose. Mr. Davitt's arrest was effected in the following manner: On Thursday, February 3, Mr. Davitt had been working at the League offices with the Ladies' Relief Committee, who were busy getting out their addresses to the Irish people. Between two and three o'clock he left the offices to dine. With him were Mr. Brennan, the Secretary of the League, and Mr. Matthew Harris, of Ballinasloe,—both of them defendants in the recent State trial. They walked down Sackville Street, and were crossing O'Connell Bridge, when a detective officer named Sherridan approached Mr. Davitt and said, "Mr. Davitt, you are wanted at the Castle." Mr. Davitt said good-by to his friends, and walked to the Castle with the officer. There he was taken in charge by two English detectives, who told him that they had orders for his arrest on the ground of breach of the conditions of his ticket-of-leave. He at once yielded to circumstance, and handed over his revolver, requesting the chief detective to give it to Mr. Brennan. About half an hour afterward, Mr. Brennan went to the detective office at the Castle, and asked Superintendent Mallon, chief of the detective force, what had become of Davitt. Mallon refused to give information, and simply stated that English detectives had taken him away in a cab a few minutes previously.

The detectives — Chief Superintendent Williamson and detective officer Swanston — drove with their prisoner in a cab to Kingstown, where they went on board the mail steamer *Connaught*, and sailed for England that evening. To Dr. Kenny, who obtained an interview with him before the boat sailed, Mr. Davitt said that the Government had done a cowardly act and committed a gross blunder. Mr. Michael Davitt arrived in London on Friday morning, February 4, when passage was taken from Kingstown to Euston. There was a considerable assembly on the arrival platform at Euston; but, to avoid any demonstration, Superintendent Williamson, who had eight or nine officers with him, alighted at Willesden Junction with Mr. Davitt, and proceeded to Broad Street, whence they drove to Bow Street, where the prisoner was lodged until his appearance before the sitting magistrate. A pilot engine preceded the train which brought Mr. Davitt to London. Upon reaching Bow Street, arrangements were made that Mr. Davitt should be immediately taken before the sitting magistrate. Sir James Ingham was in attendance, and at once proceeded to hear the case. The evidence consisted simply of the production, by Superintendent Williamson, of the warrant, and the evidence of that officer that the prisoner was the same Michael Davitt who was convicted at the Central Criminal Court on July 11, 1870. The prisoner wished to put some questions regarding the reason of the revoking of the license; but he was informed that that was no question for the magistrate, who had simply to ascertain that he was the convict whose license had been revoked. Sir J. Ingham thereupon signed a warrant for the committal of the prisoner to Millbank, to which prison he was at once conveyed, escorted in a similar way to that on his arrival at the court.

Michael Davitt, in charge of a party of detectives, left Millbank Prison on Saturday morning, February 5, and proceeded by the quarter to six train from Waterloo, which arrived at Weymouth just before noon. They travelled in a special first-class carriage, scarcely any one appearing to know, at either the departure or arrival station, who the occupants were. When the train arrived at Weymouth, one of the platform porters, as usual, was about to open the door, not knowing who was in the carriage, when one of the officers requested him to wait a few minutes, and then, when most of the passengers had left, the party emerged and proceeded to a carriage. Davitt was not dressed in convict uniform, and walked with a bold, defiant air to the carriage, which immediately drove off; and before two o'clock he was lodged in Portland Prison, not a dozen individuals being aware of it. A report said he looked haggard and pale. The authorities at the prison have received orders to use the greatest vigilance and care, the sentries and guards being considerably increased; whilst the police and military had full instructions how to act, should any emergency arise. Strangers were closely scrutinized, and no one was allowed to loiter near the prison without being challenged.

"Mr. Davitt's transfer to Portland," said a correspondent, writing to an Irish newspaper, "removes him to the spot as 'far from the busy haunts of men' as any which can possibly be conceived within the limits of the British islands. It is not so inaccessible as Dartmoor, where the convicts are lodged upon the highest of the bleak tablelands of humid Devon; but the solitude is equally depressing, and to a man of active temperament must be terrible in its intensity. Upon a map of the British Isles, you may see," he says, "off the county of Dorset, a place not much bigger than a pin's head, which, if marked at all, is described as the Isle of Portland. This, however, is not correct; it is not an island, but a peninsula, joined to the mainland by an extraordinary formation known as the Chisel Beach,—an enormous ridge of pebbles which in the course of thousands of years has been thrown up by the sea. Along the base of this natural breakwater runs the railway connecting Portland with Weymouth. It is a single narrow-gauge line; the accomplishment of the journey takes twenty minutes, and there is a little station named Rodwell half-way between the twain. Standing upon the parade at Weymouth on a summer evening, and listening to the music of the bands which never fail to enliven life at a fashionable watering-place, it is difficult to believe that, in yonder rocky islet, hundreds of desperadoes are confined in what to them must be a living tomb; for upon the portals of that grim prison might appropriately enough be inscribed the words of Dante, '*Abandon hope, all ye who enter here!*' Leaving Weymouth by the little railway, after passing Rodwell, you seem suddenly to have lost sight of civilization; for scarcely a sound is to be heard beyond the deep diapason of the sea. Landing at Portland, at a primitive village called Castletown, you find yourself at the base of a precipitous hill, at the top of which stands the convict prison. On a hot day Bunyan's Hill of Difficulty is nothing to this toilsome ascent. There is not a tree or a shrub in the whole of the peninsula; so that shade amid the noontide heat is impossible. Standing upon the summit of that acclivity on a hot day, and looking down upon the West Bay, solitary amid the activity which marks the great highway of the Channel, one is irresistibly reminded of

Tennyson's description of Enoch Arden's place of exile —

"'The blaze upon the waters to the east,
The blaze upon the island overhead,
The blaze upon the waters to the west,
Then the great stars that globed themselves in heaven,
The hollow-bellowing ocean, and again
The scarlet shafts of sunlight — but no sail"

Portland is one vast mass of stone, where the quarries have been worked for centuries; and, so far as convict labor is applied to them, very hard work it is. Wherever the eye turns, there is no relief from the white, blinding aspect which meets the view. Houses, hedges, garden walls, roads, hills, valleys,— all are of stone. The free population of the peninsula subsists in seven isolated and scattered villages, each lonely in its desolation; and close outside the prison walls is the loneliest of these — the village of Reform. Previously to my day of toil over Portland, I had always thought the Island of Sark was about the quietest place in the creation; but Sark possesses the advantage of luxuriant vegetation, while Portland is a mere arid rock. Even a free man gets away from it with a feeling of relief, and with an idea that he would rather dwell in the midst of alarms than live in that horrible place."

Such is the present abode of Michael Davitt, the life and soul of the Irish National Land League, and the organizer of the greatest agitation ever witnessed in Ireland.

The following is a copy of the ticket-of-leave

that furnished the pretext for the arrest. *Apropos* of this ticket-of-leave, the following were the reasons why Mr. Davitt did not report monthly at the nearest police-station, which was the regulation not complied with: When Mr. Davitt, and Messrs. Chambers, McCarthy, and O'Brien were released, a compact was entered into between them that they should observe the regulations so long as any of the political prisoners were kept in custody; but, when the remaining prisoners were amnestied, they did not feel themselves longer obliged to comply with the rules, and they acted accordingly.

MICHAEL DAVITT'S "TICKET-OF-LEAVE."

ORDER OF LICENCE TO A CONVICT MADE UNDER THE STATUTES 16 AND 17 VICT., C. 99, S. 9, AND 27 AND 28 VICT., C. 47, S. 4.

WHITEHALL,

19th day of *December*, *1878*.

HER MAJESTY is graciously pleased to grant to *Michael Davitt*, who was convicted of *Treason-Felony* at the *Central Criminal Court*, *holden in the City of London* on the *20th* day of *July*, *1870*, and was then and there sentenced to be kept in Penal Servitude for the term of *fifteen years*, and is now confined in *Dartmoor* Prison,

Her Royal Licence to be at large from the day of his liberation under this order, during the remaining portion of his said term of Penal Servitude, unless the said *Michael Davitt* shall, before the expiration of the said term, be convicted of some indictable offence within the United Kingdom, in which case such Licence will be immediately forfeited by law, or unless it shall please her Majesty sooner to revoke or alter such Licence.

This Licence is given subject to the conditions endorsed upon the same, upon the breach of any of which it shall be liable to be revoked, whether such breach is followed by a conviction or not.

And her Majesty hereby orders that the said *Michael Davitt* be set at liberty within Thirty Days from the date of this Order.

Given under my hand and seal.

Signed, *R. A. Cross.*

TRUE COPY.
LICENCE TO BE AT LARGE.

E. F. DuCane,
Chairman of the Directors of Convict Prisons.

THIS LICENCE WILL BE FORFEITED IF THE HOLDER DOES NOT OBSERVE THE FOLLOWING CONDITIONS.

The Holder shall preserve his Licence, and produce it when called upon to do so by a Magistrate or Police Officer.

He shall abstain from any violation of the law.

He shall not habitually associate with notoriously bad characters, such as reputed thieves and prostitutes.

He shall not lead an idle and dissolute life, without visible means of obtaining an honest livelihood.

If his Licence is forfeited or revoked in consequence of a conviction for any offence, he will be liable to undergo a Term of Penal Servitude equal to the portion of his term of fifteen years which remained unexpired when his licence was granted.

The attention of the Licence-holder is directed to the following provisions of "The Prevention of Crimes Act, 1871."

If it appear from the facts proved before a court of summary jurisdiction that there are reasonable grounds for believing that the convict so brought before it is getting his livelihood by dishonest means, such convict shall be deemed to be guilty of an offence against the Prevention of Crimes Act, and his licence shall be forfeited.

Every holder of a licence granted under the Penal Servitude Acts who is at large in Great Britain or Ireland, shall notify the place of his residence to the chief officer of police of the district in which his residence is situated, and shall, whenever he changes such residence within the same police district, notify such change to the chief officer of police of that district, and whenever he changes his residence from one police district to another, shall notify such change of residence to the chief officer of police of the police district which he is leaving, and to the chief officer of police of the police district into which he goes to reside; moreover, every male holder of such a licence as aforesaid shall, once in each month, report himself at such time as may be prescribed by the chief officer of police of the district in which such holder may be, either to such chief officer himself or to such other person as that officer may direct, and such report may, according as such chief officer directs, be required to be made personally or by letter.

If any holder of a licence who is at large in Great Britain or Ireland, remains in any place for forty-eight hours without notifying the place of his residence to the chief officer of police of the district in which such place is situated, or fails to comply with the requisitions of this section on the occasion of any change of residence, or with the requisitions of this section as to reporting himself once in each month, he shall in every such case, unless he proves to the satisfaction of the Court before whom he is tried that he did his best to act in conformity with the law, be guilty of an offence against the Prevention of Crimes Act, and, upon conviction thereof, his licence may in the discretion of the Court be forfeited; or if the term of Penal Servitude in respect of which his licence was granted has expired, at the date of his conviction, it shall be lawful for the court to sentence him to imprisonment, with or without Hard Labor, for a term not exceeding one year; or if the said term of Penal Servitude has not expired but the remainder unexpired thereof is a lesser period than one year, then to sentence him to imprisonment, with or without Hard Labor, to commence at the expiration of the said term of Penal Servitude, for such a term as, together with the remainder unexpired of his said term of Penal Servitude, will not exceed one year.

Where any person is convicted on indictment of a crime, and a previous conviction of a crime is proved against him, he shall, at any time within seven years, immediately after the expiration of the sentence passed on him for the last of such crimes, be guilty of an offence against the Prevention of Crimes Act, and be liable to imprisonment with or without hard labor, for a term not exceeding one year, under the following circumstances or any of them: —

FIRST. If, on his being charged by a constable with getting his livelihood by dishonest means, and being brought before a court of summary jurisdiction, it appears to such court that there are reasonable grounds for believing that the person so charged is getting his livelihood by dishonest means; or,

SECONDLY. If on being charged with any offence punishable on indictment or summary conviction, and on being required by a court of summary jurisdiction to give his name and address he refuses to do so, or gives a false name or a false address; or,

THIRDLY. If he is found in any place, whether public or private, under such circumstances as to satisfy the court before whom he is brought, that he was about to commit or to aid in the commission of any offence punishable on indictment or summary conviction, or was waiting for an opportunity to commit or aid in the commission of any offence punishable on indictment or summary conviction; or,

FOURTHLY. If he is found in or upon any dwelling-house, or any building, yard, or premises, being parcel of or attached to such dwelling-house, or in or upon any shop, warehouse, counting-house, or other place of business, or in any garden, orchard, pleasure-ground, or nursery-ground, or in any building or erection in any garden, orchard, pleasure-ground, or nursery-ground, without being able to account to the satisfaction of the Court before whom he is brought for his being found on such premises.

Mr. Davitt's arrest caused intense excitement and indignation in Ireland, England, and America. When the news of the arrest was announced in the House of Commons, it was received with "howls, cheering, and signs of uproarious joy" by "the first assembly of gentlemen in the world." Then occurred, on February 3, the memorable scene of the expulsion of thirty-four Irish members for denouncing this infamous act of tyranny.

In reply to Mr. Parnell, Sir William Vernon Harcourt, who signed the warrant of arrest, said that Mr. Davitt had been arrested in consequence of having violated one of the conditions of his ticket-of-leave.

Mr. Parnell.—What conditions?

No reply being made, angry cries of "Answer, answer, answer!" came from the Irish benches. Mr. Gladstone then rose, and Mr. Dillon also stood up simultaneously, amid the most terrible din and cries of "Shame, shame!"

Mr. Gladstone said, "I rise, sir, in conformity with the notice I gave yesterday."

Mr. Dillon.—Mr. Speaker! Mr. Speaker!

The Speaker.—The right honorable gentleman is in possession of the House.

Mr. Dillon continued to stand with his arms folded.

The Speaker.—I call upon the honorable member to resume his seat.

Cries of "Name, name!"

Mr. Dillon continued to stand, the Irish members crying, "Point of order!" Mr. Gladstone then moved that the honorable member be suspended during the remainder of this day's sitting. The Speaker then put the motion from the chair, amidst cries of "Privilege!" and "Order!"

Mr. A. M. Sullivan.—Mr. Dillon rose to a point of order. I object to the division.

The House then divided. For the suspension there were 395; against there were 33. Majority, 362.

The Speaker.—Mr. Dillon will withdraw.

Mr. Dillon.—I beg—

The Speaker.—The honorable member must withdraw.

Mr. Dillon.—I decline to withdraw.

The Speaker directed the Sergeant-at-Arms to remove Mr. Dillon.

Mr. A. M. Sullivan rose to a point of order, amid the greatest confusion, during which the Sergeant-at-Arms approached Mr. Dillon, accompanied by five officers.

Mr. Dillon.—You are not going to use force, I hope.

The honorable member then rose, and, amid cries of "Shame," left the house.

And so the scene went on until the thirty-four were expelled.

Great meetings were subsequently held all over Ireland, in England, and the United States, at which the arrest of Mr. Davitt was condemned as arbitrary and tyrannical; and on Thursday, April 21, the voice of all Ireland declared, through eleven hundred delegates, assembled at the National Land League Convention held in the Round Room of the Rotunda, Dublin, that there could be no peace in Ireland while Mr. Davitt was a prisoner.

This great assembly of the Irish Nation, comprising delegates from all sections of the country, including Catholics, Protestants, and Orangemen, of all shades, was convened by the Irish national Land League, to express the opinion of the country on the Land Bill introduced by Gladstone into the House of Commons, and to decide whether the bill should be opposed by the Irish members or allowed to go to a second reading. It was decided, after a two days' debate, to let it go to a reading, the parliamentary party endeavoring to eliminate the objectionable clauses and introduce beneficial ones. The first act of the convention after organizing, however, was to pass the following resolution: —

"WHEREAS, The recommittal to a British prison of Michael Davitt has been caused by his heroic defence, in a time of distress, of the landlord-persecuted tenant-farmers of Ireland, We, the delegates of those tenant-farmers, in convention assembled, do hereby declare it to be the duty of the Government to restore him to freedom, and thus remove from the breasts of Irishmen the irritation which his continued incarceration will perpetuate and intensify."

Mr. Thomas Brennan, in replying to the resolution, said:—

"It is an act of public duty upon our part to show our deep sympathy with the suffering and our admiration of the brave soldier of liberty, the patriot of humanity, who inhabits a cell in Portland Prison to-day. It is well, too, I think, that from this convention there should go forth the declaration that there can be no peace in Ireland as long as Michael Davitt shall remain in prison; and no matter what may be the merit of the bill which we are now about to consider, or any other bill which we may be called upon hereafter to consider, there can be no message of peace as long as the man who was mainly instrumental in forcing such measures remains in the convict's cell."

Mr. Brennan echoed the voice of Ireland,—ay, and of America, too. THERE CAN BE NO PEACE WITH ENGLAND WHILE MICHAEL DAVITT REMAINS IN A CONVICT'S CELL.

www.ingramcontent.com/pod-product-compliance
Lightning Source LLC
Chambersburg PA
CBHW020340030726
47496CB00007B/1954
* 9 7 8 3 7 4 4 7 1 9 6 3 6 *